GAIJIN

SARAH Z. SLEEPER

Published in North America and Europe by Running Wild Press. Visit Running Wild Press at www.runningwildpress.com Educators, librarians, book clubs (as well as the eternally curious), go to www.runningwildpress.com for teaching tools.

ISBN (pbk) 978-1-947041-67-7
ISBN (ebook) 978-1-947041-68-4

For Jimmy, Vivian, Dixie, Max and Mini.

Susan

PROLOGUE

MONO NO AWARE

Awareness of Impermanence

> *Love, tea and flowers.*
> *Impermanent, transcendent.*
> *Are you aware of beauty that flames up and out*
> *before it can root itself in the earth of truth?*
> *Memory is truth, like brown dirt*
> *smeared on a cherry-blossom pink canvas*

> — INSPIRED BY ANTIQUE
> JAPANESE PORCELAIN GILDED
> WITH *MAKIE*

A person or a memory can sit inside you and you might have no choice about it. You don't have to *think* about a person for him to be part of you. That's what my best friend Rose told me years ago, in a moment when she saw me more clearly than I saw myself, a moment when I was restless and heartsick and about to board a plane to Japan.

"I can't believe it," she said. "You're going to hunt down Owen."

I scoffed and lied, said I never thought of him.

Now years later, I know Rose was right, that you don't get to decide what sticks and what doesn't, who gets in and who gets blocked. You like to think you control your destiny and choose your path, but that's not always the case. Sometimes you're propelled forward in the most unexpected way when something or someone takes hold of you and doesn't let go.

That's how it happened to me. My college love, Owen Ota, burrowed his way into me one tantalizing moment at a time, over the course of a sweltering Indian summer at Northwestern University. He etched himself into the side of my neck and he took root in the pit of my stomach. He changed the trajectory of my life, set me in motion, and then he disappeared, like a puff of smoke or a phantom I'd hallucinated. He gave no feasible explanation, stopped all communication, and fled back to Tokyo in the same startling way he'd arrived. He was gone but I couldn't let go. I needed to find Owen, and to experience the Japan he described. I clung to the notion that my dreams of the person and the place would match the reality.

Nothing, not Rose, not the application of common sense, could have dissuaded me from leaving Chicago on that over-heated afternoon at O'Hare, when car horns, screeching voices and jet engines drowned out our goodbyes. A jumble of images jostled around in my brain, crowding out logical thoughts. Delicate pink cherry blossoms on porcelain teacups, a thin ivory book of *haiku*, a red silk blouse on polished glass skin, steaming spicy cuttlefish served on a black lacquer tray; a dazzling collage of the things Owen had shown me.

I was naïve and grief hollowed out my heart; I was determined to solve the mystery of his disappearance, as if finding him could erase the pain I'd felt when he abandoned me. I didn't put it together then, the folly of searching for someone who didn't want to be found, moving to a country I didn't understand. And so, I went, flying into the unknown with a single suitcase of clothes, clutching my computer and cell phone as if they were life preservers.

On the plane I read the latest news from Japan. There were stories about the failed economic policies of the prime minister, the scandal of the royal princess who wanted to marry a commoner, the looming threat of North Korean missiles. Of course, I'd studied Japan in college, but looking back on that day, I knew nothing of the true character of the country.

The flight took an eternity and I immersed myself in a book of Japanese art filled with photos of ancient pottery and porcelain, chipped and faded, but glowing and glorious at the same time. I was striving to be a poet back then, a person who dealt in beauty and art, not only a journalist who worked with black ink and cold data. The art book held a luminous photo of a powder blue teacup swirled with feathery gold patterns, captioned, *"Makie."* I Googled and learned that it meant "sprinkled picture." *Makie* was an art object sprinkled with gold or silver powder, so that it gleamed with warmth. Inspired, I wrote a little poem on the plane, which I still have today. I titled it *"Mono No Aware,"* Awareness of Impermanence, a Japanese term I would come to understand deeply over time.

On my way to my new life in Japan, memories of my moments with Owen colored my mind with a *makie* haze. The landing of the plane brought the crash of reality. I was confronted by a gritty, dangerous nation, so unlike the exotic islands he'd described to me. A place where coworkers gave me gifts wrapped in gold foil while darting disdainful glances at me. I found few of the glamorous, mannered people I'd expected, and instead found an angry schizophrenic culture, alluring and hostile by turns, that kept me constantly at bay and confounded. And as I ventured further, in my quest to discover Owen's fate, I realized I might not be able to find him before Japan chased me out, like the *gaijin* I was, a foreigner, unwelcomed by my adopted country.

CHAPTER ONE
JAPAN, 2016

At Okinawa's Naha International Airport men and women stole glances at me. In the dank baggage claim, a boy grabbed my hair and refused to let go. His mother stood beside me holding him on her hip as he leaned over and clutched my curly ponytail. The father scolded, and the kid yanked harder. After a few uncomfortable moments, the mother muttered "sorry," over and over. When the child finally let go his father said, "Not seeing yellow," which confused me. Then I realized his meaning; the kid hadn't seen blonde hair before. The family bowed and fled. The boy never took his eyes off me, leaning back over his mother's shoulder to watch me as they exited. I slumped on a concrete bench and shivered with a rush of nervous energy.

I dragged my bags into the closest bathroom and splashed water on my cheeks. My eyes looked swollen and droopy in the mirror. My skinny arms had become even thinner because I had eaten little in the past week. Walking through the terminal, shadowy angles from Owen's face were all around me in other

Japanese faces. I'd always been overly serious, but in the past two years, I'd become close to haunted.

I had flown twenty hours, Chicago to L.A., L.A. to Osaka, Osaka to Okinawa, and when I walked outside the sudden smack of heat nauseated me. Amista Noga, a colleague at my new workplace, *Okinawa Week*, had offered to pick me up at the airport. Car exhaust curled into my nose and I coughed as I scanned the curbside for the beat-up white Nissan she'd described.

When Amista said hello, she studied me intently, as if perceiving my heavy heart. I bucked up and offered my friend-liest smile, trying to hide my unease and sadness. Probably I'd made a huge mistake by coming here and the hair-pulling inci-dent was a sign I wasn't welcome. I got in the car anyway.

Amista was about twenty years older than me, tall and tawny, long legs bent up under the steering wheel. Her hair shone like black vinyl and her black shirtdress was unwrinkled. I was struck by her appearance as my precise opposite. She was fleshy and full, not fat, but with thick dark limbs; I was all bony angles and translucently tan freckled skin.

On the drive to my hotel I learned that she was originally from Guam, had married an American sailor twenty-five years ago and they had been relocated to Okinawa. Her husband, Lester, retired from the military, but they decided to stay here permanently.

"I'd never make it without inhaling ginger and fish guts every morning," she said with a wry laugh as she took off driving. We passed tall, gleaming buildings and crowded inter-sections. "Naha is the biggest city on Okinawa," she said. I was having difficulty taking in the busy scene; I'd expected Okinawa to be more rural, more like the remote island I'd read about.

"This has got to be the first time someone moved here just

to work for the paper," she said. We were at a stoplight and she turned her broad face toward me. "I mean, we have American reporters, but they always come from the bases. Military spouses mostly."

I was shy in the face of her straightforwardness, unwilling to share my secrets. I reached up a damp hand to try and smooth down my unruly curly hair. It was an ineffective and inelegant habit I'd developed when my anxiety spiked. As if flat hair would translate to calm nerves.

When we started moving again, she dodged in and out of the narrow lanes, avoiding sideswipes here and there on the jammed roads. We zipped past gambling parlors, clothing stores, cell phone shops, restaurants, nightclubs and peep-show bars with red, green and electric blue signs blinking their invitations to come in. The neon flashed brightly, standing out against the pale-yellow sunlight. People crowded every street corner, and many had one foot off the curb ready to step into the intersection. If the crowd had accidentally shifted forward, they would have been pushed into oncoming traffic. There were more people than I expected, and they were sardined all around us. I cracked my window and inhaled whiffs of sulfur, spices and sweat.

"So, what's your story?" Amista persisted.

"I've always wanted to live in Japan," I said, still looking away.

"Japan, I get," she said. "But didn't you do your research and see that Okinawa is the least Japanese place of all Japanese places?"

"I guess I read that," I admitted. I'd read textbooks and news articles that described the friction between Japanese mainlanders and the Okinawans who were sometimes treated as peasant cousins by those more affluent on the mainland. I'd also read about the simmering tensions between the Okinawans and the American military, which gobbled up the island's land and resources.

"Still, this is a first. Just saying." She didn't seem unfriendly but was insightful enough to know a woman from Illinois doesn't end up in Okinawa by accident or happenstance. I changed the subject.

"Do you visit Tokyo?" I asked her. She told me she did, once in a while, but that she preferred the island's slower, calmer pace. I mentioned that so far, Okinawa seemed anything but calm. She gave a husky laugh and said we were seeing a fraction of the whole and that I'd be happily surprised when I saw the more natural parts of the island. I admitted I'd applied for jobs in Tokyo, but this was the only offer I'd received, and she said, "Ah," as in, *that makes more sense about how you ended up in Okinawa.* She seemed open enough, so I nonchalantly asked if she'd heard of Suicide Forest, *Aokigahara.* She shot me a surprised look.

"Horrible place. Why do you ask?"

"Just curious. I read an article about it on the plane," I fibbed.

"I don't know much," she said, "just that people go there to kill themselves." I told her the article about Suicide Forest, "*Aokigahara*" it's Japanese name, had piqued my interest. "Morbid," she replied, with a raised eyebrow and a sideways glance. I dropped the subject.

I asked what it was like working at *Okinawa Week* and she said there was a pecking order that I'd learn about right away. "Reporters with the most tenure get the best story assignments," she said, "and you'd be smart not to buck the system." She went on to say that she, an older fellow named Jed, and the staff photographer were the ones with the most seniority. "You and our photographer, Hisashi, are the only people I know who moved to Okinawa just to work for *Okinawa Week*. He left a fancy family in Tokyo."

For a second, I debated telling her about Owen and that I knew Hisashi was his brother. She was friendly, but the previous weeks weighed heavy on me. I was too tired and spent to delve into it, plus she'd probably think I was nuts. I thought so myself at times, but it was too late to turn back now.

She steered the car down a tiny alleyway between ramshackle buildings and storefronts as we crawled along. The crowds thinned but the buildings closed in, pressing toward us from pocked sidewalks. We snaked past a group of suited men sitting at an open patio bar, a woman chopping fish in a small store, a young couple kissing on the sidewalk. Tall concrete towers flanked tiny shops in a mishmash, so unlike the zoned organization of my Illinois hometown. We crept along, our pace slower and slower in the narrowing alley. A tan dog darted in front of the car, followed by black one. I peered between the buildings to see where the dogs went but couldn't track them in the dimming evening light. Amista stopped the car in front of a bright glass double-doorway with a sign above it that said, "Seaside Hotel the Beach."

"Shouldn't it be 'Seaside Beach Hotel?'" I asked.

"You'll get used to it. Japanese-to-English translations can be awkward. By the way, this plush hotel is a bribe. The boss wants to make sure you'll stay," she said, trying to be funny. "Another thing. You might be surprised by how close people get to you. Okinawans don't need as much space as Americans."

"I noticed that in the airport," I said, and told her what happened with the boy who grabbed my hair.

She laughed her husky laugh and said some locals had never seen foreigners. She told me technology had been slow to spread here, so access to media from outside Japan was limited.

"It's not like we don't have the Internet, but let's just say it can be sketchy." She spoke with motherly patience, giving me time to process her words. "Oh, and here's a tip. If you tend to blurt things out, you'll want to watch that."

"Thanks," I said, pricked by a new stab of anxiety. In school I had learned about the Japanese practice of being agreeable and never confrontational, especially at work. In my haste to take the job, I hadn't focused on my new workplace, what the people would be like, how things might be different. Now with this unexpected scenery and this new information about Okinawa, I cringed, my stomach sunk. My office at the *Sun Times* had been a modern cubicle farm with rushing reporters and instant access to information. Before I arrived, I couldn't have imagined a newsroom any other way, but now just an hour in, Okinawa already felt like a different world. Who knew what *Okinawa Week* would be like?

Amista checked me in to the hotel, speaking fluent Japanese with the front desk clerk. Then she left, saying she'd see me in two days, and although I liked her, I was relieved to be alone. My best friend Rose told me I was a "pathological" loner, but I defended myself. I didn't seek solitude all the time, just enough to un-fray my nerves. I wasn't antisocial, but after long days at work, or long hours on a plane, a few quiet hours appealed to me more than happy hour.

I exhaled and scanned the lobby. It was clean and modern, with mirrors, glass tables and leather couches and I was startled by its shininess. I declined the help of a bellman and rode the elevator to my tenth-floor room as layers of jet lag, tension and sadness took their toll. I played Leonard Cohen on my phone and collapsed on the bed, blanketed in cool darkness and cold sweat.

. . .

When I awoke thirteen hours later sunshine streamed in through tall windows, cutting angles and shadows across the wrinkles in my blue jeans. The room was padded with white carpet, white pillows, white armchairs, and white curtains. I shook my head to clear my cobwebbed mind. Then, with a start I remembered I'm finally in Japan, but Owen's not here, not in Okinawa. Dizzy, I stood.

Out the window was a scene from Southern California, *The O.C.,* come to life. There was the sparkling blue ocean with surfers floating beyond the break and gliding on top of white crests. A crosshatch of grey concrete pylons and a sturdy seawall fenced in a boardwalk where people walked dogs, skateboarded, and sat eating and laughing. There were no simple traditional wooden buildings, like the ones I'd studied, no raised homes, with *shoji* panels encircled by *engawa,* veranda-like corridors. This wasn't a hip *Harajuku* scene from a music video either, with eccentric teenagers in colorful costumes. It wasn't gleaming, sophisticated Tokyo, and it wasn't the rural farmland dotted with military bases I'd expected in Okinawa.

I showered and went downstairs. The wet heaviness of the air slapped my skin as I stepped onto the boardwalk. It was July with subtropical heat more oppressive than any summer afternoon in Illinois. Clothing stores crammed the beach boulevard and English-language signs advertised sundresses, bikinis and toe rings. The people were mostly American, moms and dads with kids and beach towels, young men with short military haircuts. There were only twenty or so Japanese amidst this throng of Americans. Thousands of American military people lived on the island, I knew that, but with a million and a half residents total on Okinawa, both Japanese and American, this ratio had to be off. The Sunabe Seawall, with its surfers and tourist shops, couldn't be representative of Okinawa. I fought off the urge to sprint back to my room and away from this crowd.

It had been twenty-four hours at least since I'd eaten, and my tired legs and growling stomach propelled me into the first takeout restaurant I found. It had plastic menus in English, along with a photo of each dish. The small dark woman behind the counter pointed to "taco rice" and indicated I should order it. "Eat?" she said and shot me a dismissive smirk when I ordered salmon sushi instead. Did the hair-netted cook shoot a scowl at me from the kitchen? The restaurant sold half-size bottles of wine, so I bought two of those, then hurried back toward my hotel. Already, Okinawa was too much to take in.

A splashing commotion caught my attention and a crowd gathered near the seawall. A black dog bobbed in the water, fighting to climb onto a pylon. The tide sucked him out, then threw him against the concrete. Two men hung off separate pylons and grabbed for the flailing dog. One guy finally got ahold of the dog's collar, yanked him up and carried him over to the boardwalk. He set the dog down; the dog shook himself off and trotted away. The man stood dripping in front of me, an American flag tattoo across the breadth of his bare chest. I asked if that was his dog.

"That's Gogan. He's the neighborhood dog." I was incredulous. "Everyone takes care of him. He's the Sunabe Seawall dog." I pressed my lips together, didn't respond. "Don't look so worried, he knows how to get along." The man had a kind tone and warm eyes. He extended a wet hand, introduced himself as Nathan.

"Lucy."

"Military?" he asked.

"No."

"Well, nice to meet you, Lucy. And nice to meet someone

not in the military. Not many of you around. Do you live on the Sunabe Seawall?"

"I don't live anywhere, I guess. I'm staying in a hotel until I get a place." I could see where the conversation was heading and didn't have the energy to make small talk. "Good job saving Gogan," I said, and started to walk away.

"The word *gogan* means seawall, by the way. Um, want to grab lunch?" I stopped walking, uneasy, and he spoke before I could answer. He promised he wasn't trying to hit on me but was happy to meet an American on Okinawa who wasn't in the military. He had a familiar Midwestern accent with flattened vowels and polite manner. Still, I declined, and told him I needed to focus on my new job.

"Oh, okay. Where do you work?" he pressed, unwilling to let me leave. He stood in a wide stance with his hands on his hips. Water dripped down his muscular legs. He was attractive, but no match for my resolve. I'd been sexually reticent since I was a teenager, "non-loosy-Lucy," Rose called me.

Right when I told him I was to start at *Okinawa Week* soon, it dawned on me that it might not be the smartest thing to tell a stranger where I worked. But he seemed harmless enough.

"I'll look for your byline," he said, and I turned away. "Lucy, Okinawa is nicknamed 'Divorce Rock.' Did you know that?" I turned back, curious.

"No, I hadn't heard that."

"Are you married?"

"Nope. Why's it called Divorce Rock?"

Nathan smiled a bright white surfer smile and raised a sun-bleached eyebrow. "Because about fifty percent of the Americans who live here end up being divorced," he said. "It's a true fact." The legend, he said, was that because of America's bloody attacks on Okinawa during World War II and the many locals who killed themselves to avoid becoming prisoners of war, the spirit of the island absorbed the pain and anger of those who died here. The constant hot winds blew off the East China Sea and inflamed the hearts of the Americans who should've been happy, the young, married military folks, and they ended up divorced. "Broken by Divorce Rock," he said.

"My goodness."

"Good story, huh? Anyway, maybe if I email you at work, you'll let me take you to lunch one day." Nathan jogged down the boardwalk, jumped on a scooter, waved goodbye and zipped off.

I watched him go then turned toward the sparkling, glinting water. Divorce Rock. Suicide Forest. None of this had been in any history book I'd read. A wave crashed on the cement and sea water splashed on my face. I leaned into the strong ocean breeze and walked on, my thoughts muddled. I'd only been in Japan for twenty-four hours and every moment had been radically different from what I expected. In my imagination I hadn't pictured other Americans. I'd only placed myself in the picture, just me with Owen and a sea of Japanese people. Of course, that was ridiculous and of course many non-Japanese lived in Japan. But aside from my minor interactions at the hotel and with the lady in the take-out place, I'd mainly seen American faces. The Japanese I'd interacted with had either frowned at me or yanked my hair. No one and nothing, so far, reminded me of Owen or Owen's Japan.

Back in my room I ate the sushi, chugged wine, and checked email and texts. I emailed my mom to say I was fine and would call in a few days. I texted Rose. "So far it's like California," to which she responded, "Huh? Send photos." I took a shot of the glowing red and orange sunset out my window and sent it to her.

I sat at the desk and stared out at the horizon. "Disappearing men," was the designation I'd assigned to my dad and to Owen. They'd been ripped from my life like leaves ripped off a shrub in a storm, stunning in their sudden absence, the limbs bare where they had been plush. I'd given little thought to those I left behind in Illinois, Rose and my mom, probably because their existence in my life felt inevitable, non-malleable. I hadn't made other lasting ties during college or at the *Sun Times*. Maybe after my dad's death and Owen's departure, I knew I'd leave, and so I never locked on to anyone permanent.

Already, I'd had two teachers, *senseis*, in Japan, Amista and Nathan, who'd given me curious insights about the country that I couldn't have imagined. Owen had been my *sensei* too, my first true teacher after my parents, opening my mind and heart to a culture across the world.

In my semi-dark room, I read an email from Ashimine-san, the publisher of *Okinawa Week*, my "boss," to whom Amista had referred earlier. "Welcome, Ms. Tosch! Welcome to Okinawa."

"Thank you for this excellent opportunity," I emailed him back. "I've always wanted to live in Japan."

He responded with a joke. "Okinawa is only a little bit Japanese." He'd typed in a sideways winking smiley face, presumably so I'd know he was kidding. "See you soon," he wrote. "Amista will bring you."

I was to start at *Okinawa Week* in the morning and despite a head that felt waterlogged from heat and exhaustion, I plunked around online, through photos of the Sunabe Seawall, maps with the distance to my new office, and the locations of the many military bases up and down the island, which took up big swaths of land.

Without deciding to do so, I plugged *Aokigahara* into the search engine, Suicide Forest. I didn't want to admit to myself that I needed to see it, to understand what it was. Gruesome images popped up—skulls and leg bones on a thick forest floor, holey boots and clothes in a jumble, a lone Buddha statue amidst a tangle of branches. Photos showed overgrown trees, tangled into claustrophobic canopies and almost impassible pathways. I'd seen plenty of wooded areas in Illinois, but nothing as dark, as if no sunlight could sneak in at all.

By far the majority of photos I found online were of hangings, half-decomposed men, or the clothed bones of men, slung from tree branches or scattered on the dirt and leaves below. I flipped through four or five shots then flicked off the computer, rubbed the tears out of my eyes. It seemed impossible that such a place was real and yet here it was, fully documented online, as if "Suicide Forest," was just one of the many types of places one could go in Japan: grocery store, office, airport, restaurant, seawall, *Suicide Forest*. It also seemed impossible that my Owen, the man who radiated light like a bright star, could have walked into such an abyss, thrown a rope onto a tree, put it around his neck, and attempted to end his life. Two months before he'd done that, we'd been back at Northwestern, writing poetry, making out, sharing Japanese tea, falling in love.

I closed my eyes and forced myself to think about the next day when I would start my new job. I knew there would be differences in the way they handled things here, and Amista had warned me about the pecking order. In the best-case scenario, I'd immerse myself in interesting stories and perhaps find respite, a way to thwart my nagging thoughts about Owen. I'd been plagued by questions about what had happened to him after he got back to Tokyo, why he wanted to die. Why he'd do something so drastic as try to hang himself.

After a half-bottle of wine, I found myself scribbling, and wrote a few lines about the seawall, *gogan*, outside.

Gogan, breakwater, dam, bullwork, embankment,
smashed to sand, drowned and reformed,
prior shape as irrelevant as a wall of rocks,
sand again in no time at all

I felt like the seawall I wrote about, my former self, the one that existed before Owen Ota, irrelevant. My previous identity had been smashed to bits by the love of Owen and the enlightenment he'd shared about his home country. Now I was someone else entirely. I wasn't that girl who remained cocooned by small-town safety, I was now a woman who chased her dreams across the globe. I was braver than I'd been in the past, but perhaps more reckless too.

I curled up in bed. The ocean roiled beyond my window. I tried a different song on my phone, something sad about the death of a lighthouse keeper by Nickel Creek, but I soon switched it off and listened to the waves outside, to my blood course through my temples. I'd decided to move to Japan, and I was in the *least Japanese of all Japanese places*, on an island Owen probably never visited. My loneliness was deep and dark as the East China Sea, and it was stained with anger. How dare he dazzle me, woo me, invite me to his country and then desert me? What kind of wicked trickster had he been and how naïve had I been to trust him, to love him so blindly, and yearn so deeply to be in Japan? When I would finally tell Rose all of this, I could see her laugh first, at my stupidity, then realize how pathetic I was and put her arms around me in sympathy.

The wine disrupted my sleep and I tossed in bed and worried about the next day. *What am I really doing here?* Doubts flooded my mind, and after a few hours, I made a midnight decision. I'd go to my new workplace tomorrow and tell Ashimine-san I'd made a terrible mistake, apologize for wasting his time, promise to pay him back for the airline tickets and hotel. I'd book the first flight back to Chicago. I was certainly the most naïve woman in all of Illinois, to think that my life would change for the better by following Owen and his hollow promises all the way across the world. I stared into the night, hopeless, until the black waves shifted to shimmering grey under the rising sun and it was time for me to get up and quit my job.

CHAPTER TWO

W hen my alarm rang at six a.m. I hadn't slept. It was going to be a horrible day, turning in my resignation at *Okinawa Week,* disappointing the cheerful boss, Ashimine-san, with whom I'd emailed. I could only imagine Amista's frown as she realized what a flake I was. It would be a few hours before she'd pick me up.

I didn't turn on any lights but flicked on my computer. I was about to look up *Aokigahara* again, but local news exploded on my screen and I was sucked into an awful blast of information.

"Teenager Alleges Rape by U.S. Serviceman," the website, *Ryukyuchat,* said, "Assault on Manza Beach." A photo showed a white luxury hotel next to a sandy beach and aqua bay, captioned, "Scene of the crime." There was a black-and-white photo of a man in uniform, the accused, "Airman Reginald Stone," the caption said. There was also a soft-lighted color photo of the alleged victim, fifteen-year-old Midori Ishikori. She had thick black bangs and looked perfect and pure in a white blouse with powder-blue private school insignia on one tiny breast.

I was queasy; Stone's photo showed him to be a big man, and a black man. Midori Ishikori was so little, more like a preteen than a teenager. The idea of a two-hundred-pound man violating a ninety-five-pound fifteen-year-old gave the story a lurid, tabloid quality.

Along with the photos of accused and accuser, there were images from last night, when street protests had broken out spontaneously. I must have been in my room before the news hit because I hadn't seen or heard anything. As word about the rape accusation spread, the locals erupted with fury.

Snapshots showed fishermen, farmers, housewives and shopkeepers gathered in small groups of twenty or thirty in front of the locked and heavily guarded military base gates, illuminated by strobe lights and waving signs that said, "Americans Get Out!" and "Vanquish the American Menace." I was stunned by the images on my computer screen, so many locals out in force, no non-Japanese in any photo.

Now it was eight a.m., almost time for Amista to pick me up. A text dinged my phone. It was from her. "I can't drive you. Hotel will. Streets are jammed. Be careful."

I dressed quickly, slapped on some makeup. Since entering the workforce last year, I'd become skilled at feigning more confidence than I felt. A bit of tawny blush and eyeliner shielded me, acted as a barrier from those who would otherwise stare at my ghost-pale face. No one described me as beautiful, but with the right makeup, I was acceptable. And on that day in Japan, I'd especially need my makeup protection.

When I went downstairs the hotel car and driver were waiting for me. He got us out onto the main street easily enough but when he tried to make a quick right into a side street it was blocked. Construction workers were digging a hole in the middle of the asphalt. Signs directed us to a detour and as we turned the next corner, my breath hitched. Up ahead one short block, the street was packed. People spilled out of doorways and crowded on sidewalks with placards held aloft. A small line of cars had built up and we were boxed in. The only choice was to keep moving forward and drive past the throng. We arrived at a traffic light as it turned red. The crowd was across the street, their backs toward us, rows of white and red t-shirts. *Please don't turn around.*

The car behind us honked. A few protestors turned then quickly turned back. Except one, a teenager who turned all the way around, stood squarely on two black-booted feet and glared at me through the car window. He held a rock in one hand, and he didn't take his eyes off me as we turned through the intersection. He was reflected in the rearview mirror and watched our car as we drove away. When he turned back to the protest group, he raised his closed fist in the air and clenched the rock.

My hands were unsteady, and I grasped my cell phone as though it was a gun. I asked the driver to stop in the parking lot of a convenience store so I could calm down and call Amista. I told her about the rock wielding teen. She told me not to panic.

"Protests like this flare up every few years. It's as if the Okinawans want to remind us that we're trespassers," she said.

"Us? But *we* aren't the military. We're reporters, not soldiers. Do they know that?" I cringed at my use of the word "they," as if Okinawan rape protestors were in one category and Amista and I were in some vastly different one, *them* and *us*. I closed my eyes and sat back into my seat. Stone's face invaded my mind's eye or was it the face of the teen with the rock? Somehow, they melded together, and I couldn't quite picture either one. A creeping fear prickled my skin. Did I imagine hatred in the convenience store clerk's eyes? Did he glare out the window at me? I patted at my hair and ignored him.

I would probably be late to work on my first day because of the traffic, but what did it matter? My first day would also be my last. I asked the driver to continue on. We drove past a bright yellow breakfast diner, a placed called Pancake House that could have been plucked from Anytown U.S.A. I was glad for a few more minutes in the car to gather myself before I faced Amista and Ashimine-san and delivered my news.

As we snailed along, I read more news on my phone. Local gossip sites *Ryukyuchat* and *MoshiNaha* had published the first details about the accusation. Their reports provided snippets of conversations, glimpses of the accuser and the suspect reported by hotel staff and tourists just hours after the alleged crime, before officials made public statements and before charges were filed.

The dove-white sweet-faced girl and her parents weren't from Okinawa; they were well-to-do Tokyo people, visiting the subtropical island for vacation. Midori had come back to their Manza Beach Resort hotel suite damp and disheveled, her bubble-gum-pink swimsuit cover-up ripped and soiled, her face bruised and tear-smeared. She'd told her parents she'd met an American on the beach, Airman Reginald Stone, who seemed nice at first, bringing her a can of the soft drink, Pocari Sweat, and flirting with her in half-Japanese. But he'd turned vicious and when no one was looking, he'd dragged her behind the hotel, next to a shallow ocean stream, and there he'd beaten and raped her, threatened to kill her if she told a soul.

As I read the reports, I was rapt, amazed at the audacity of the journalists to assert such details before an official statement of any kind. It seemed incredible to me that the reporters could access such specifics so quickly, but here it all was in tabloid-type write ups.

One reporter wrote:

"Midori sobbed when she admitted to her parents that she'd

flirted with him too, as if what happened were her fault because of her unladylike behavior. Before the attack she had waved at him and smiled, so he came over to where she rested under her sun umbrella. After the assault, her outraged red-faced father bellowed at hotel security, who called the Okinawa city police and they'd apprehended the enlisted man on the spot. Stone had acted shocked when he was picked up from where he sat, on a towel on the white sand beach, as if he had nothing to fear and nothing to hide. He immediately claimed he wasn't guilty and said that Midori had consensual sex with him, said that she was probably ashamed and therefore crying wolf."

The tabloid went on to say by that night, Midori was already in hiding in her plush hotel, shielded from the public eye by her parents and a hastily hired local lawyer, on retainer until the Ishikori's family lawyer could fly in from the mainland. Airman Stone was being held in the Okinawa City jail, alongside subway gropers and pachinko debt defaulters and convenience store thieves.

Stone was the first American soldier to be detained in the jail since last year, I read. In two-thousand and seventeen, an intoxicated nineteen-year-old sailor had mowed down a streetside bento stand with his car, sending fried and curried pork patties, ginger slices and sesame rice raining onto the sidewalk. The proprietor was unharmed, but as is typical in such cases, the American was ordered to pay restitution, a hundred percent of the value of the destroyed stand and merchandise, along with another fifty percent as a sign of remorse, inflated numbers that would secure a comfortable future for the injured party. The sailor remained in jail for eleven months while his family in Indiana scrimped and borrowed to come up with the payment, a hefty get-out-of-the-military-early fee.

Aghast, I couldn't stop reading. I learned that over seven decades, there had been many accusations made by Okinawans against U.S. servicemen. They'd started around the time of the post-World War II occupation, an occupation many locals still considered illegal, and continued over many decades. There were reports of a multitude of assaults, robberies and thefts perpetrated by military men. But every few years, and again today, the American in the Okinawa jail was there for a much more egregious offense, an alleged rape of the very honor and spirit of the Japanese, in the form of a schoolgirl, a crime for which no remuneration would suffice.

The web buzzed with opinions about how the rape would finally force the Americans off the island for good, that this crime amounted to a fatal wound, an irreparably deep gash in the shared cultural and social center where American military, mostly men, and Okinawans, mostly women, intersected and intermingled; the restaurants, beaches, shopping malls and peepshow cocktail bars where they congregated, or had done, until yesterday.

And this morning, my second full day on Okinawa, Americans and Okinawans, previously civil and even social, sat on opposite sides of military barricades nurturing opposing views, almost to a person. Online forums revealed Americans believed Stone was innocent; Okinawans were sure he was guilty. Americans on Kadena Air Base, White Beach Naval Facility, Army Fort Buckner, Marine Camp Foster, Marine Camp Futenma, Marine Camp Courtney, Marine Camp Lester and Marine Camp Kinser—so many bases on this sixty-mile-long speck of land in the East China Sea—posted screeds about Stone's probable scapegoat status, the girl's likely motives for the accusation, either greed or to save face. Outraged Okinawans, on the other hand, urged people to escalate the protests.

At eight-thirty a.m., Kadena's commanding officer, Colonel Walker, released a statement on the base's official PR web page, and quickly republished everywhere, that prohibited Air Force personnel from leaving the base. Commanders of the other installations followed suit. Walker promised a full investigation, prosecution and punishment if Stone was found guilty. The Okinawa police simultaneously released their own online video, assured the public they were safe from the Americans, and that they'd be working on the case as a judicial arbitrator "in charge" of the U.S. military police's efforts.

"We assure our great citizens that justice will prevail and that Midori Ishikori's honor will be renewed. We will vanquish the American menace that threatens our peace and security." Police Chief Ito sneered into the camera as he read the press release. His awkward phrasing and the odd inflection of his spoken English gave his otherwise threatening tone an almost comic element, a detail not missed by mean-spirited bloggers who taunted him online.

Finally, my car arrived at *Okinawa Week,* which turned out to be a small concrete building at the dead end of a downtown road. I braced myself for what was to come and walked toward the front doors. In all the chaos, I'd almost forgotten I was about to meet Owen's brother, Hisashi, the staff photographer.

As I reached toward the door handle, Midori Ishikori appeared in front of me. Her image was plastered on the side of the *Okinawa Week* building, the words "Fuck Off Americans!" scrawled across the bottom. The skin on my arms and neck jumped and I tripped backwards. I righted my balance and saw that the photo was the same shot I'd seen online, with soft studio lighting and the girl's school insignia on a crisp white blouse, only now, captioned with profanity.

CHAPTER THREE

Amista came out the front doors to greet me, saw the sign, and ripped it off the wall. Stupefied, I didn't move. She asked me how my day had gone yesterday. I mumbled something about the dog rescue, meeting Nathan, and my impression of the Sunabe Seawall as something like Southern California.

"I should've told you," she said. "That area is an American hangout, not so much a place that Okinawans go. It's too expensive."

I couldn't believe we were engaged in small talk. "What about that?" I asked, pointing to the crumpled paper in her hand. Woozy, I took hold of her arm, and she steadied me. On top of the encounter with the protestors, the sign on the building and its hostile profanity felt personal, like a looming threat. She waited for me to compose myself.

"These things happen," she said. "It's not a big deal."

"Okay," I said, confused. She ushered me toward the front doors. I was fatigued, stressed and in semi-shock that rendered me passive.

A single stone *shisa*, painted in bright green, red and yellow, sat to the right of the *Okinawa Week*'s glass front-doors. I recognized the *shisa* from the many pictures I'd seen, traditional Japanese statues of lion-dogs that guard doors of homes and offices, usually stationed in pairs, one on each side.

"There used to be two *shisas*, but one was stolen," Amista said, "so we're only semi-safe." She meant this to be funny, but it wasn't. She pushed open the doors and nudged me inside.

The office was large and open with several wooden desks spread out in no discernable pattern. A middle-aged Japanese woman sat at a drafting table facing the front window. No one else was there, just me, Amista and her. I wondered if this woman had seen the frightening sign too, and I watched Amista crumple it and toss it into a trash can.

"Hello Lucy. I'm Rumiko," said the woman. "Graphic artist." She stood to greet me but didn't shake my hand. "Welcome to here." She had a pencil behind one ear and the cord to her glasses caught on the other. She wore jeans and a plain white blouse. Her round glasses and makeup-less face gave her the air of an academic. "Please seat. *Hai*." She said, and indicated a desk toward the back wall, empty except for a big desktop computer, a printer, and a gold gift box with an oversize red bow.

"Thank you," I said, opting not to answer in Japanese. I hadn't tried to speak to anyone yet in my limited Japanese. I was certain they'd be intolerant if I flubbed the grammar or pronunciation. "Nice to meet you," I added, as if I was happy to be there and planned to get to know her. Telling half-lies had become a habit for me, like hiding my face behind makeup.

"*Hai*, Lucy. Nice," Rumiko said. She pointed to the gift box on my desk, so I opened it. Inside I found a plump and perfect honeydew melon. "Fruit special mainland," Rumiko said. "Ashimine-san, for you." I had no difficulty understanding her meaning, but I did a little mental hiccup at the lack of verbs in her speech.

Hai, yes, turned out to be one of Rumiko's favorite words. I wasn't sure if she liked me or not, but she answered yes, "*hai*," to every question I asked. "Do you create the layout of the newspaper?" I'd asked her. "*Hai*," she replied, and showed me the computer mockup of the week's issue. "Have you worked here a long time?" "*Hai*. Long time."

She showed me illustrations from the last issue, including a pen and pencil drawing of the soon-to-be-built new terminal at the Naha airport—sleek in comparison to the old, dank terminal where I'd deplaned. I refrained from asking Rumiko why the paper didn't publish photos with the story, instead of her drawings.

Amista noticed my questioning expression. "We only have one photographer," she said, and explained that Rumiko's original drawings were used to fill in the gaps where photos might have been. "You'll meet Hisashi," she said, and a sprinkling of anticipation seeped into my stomach.

Meeting Owen's brother would be the only positive aspect of an otherwise bad day. I rehearsed my resignation speech in my head and spent my first hour in the office reading over *Okinawa Week* back issues at my desk. I realized that the quirky throwback nature of Rumiko's hand-drawn images was one of the paper's unique and popular features. Despite my intention to flee back to the U.S., this cozy old-fashioned office intrigued me. Amista already felt like a protective older sister to me and as the minutes clicked by, I grew more worried about how she'd take the news of my departure.

I jumped in my chair when a small, dark figure came down the hallway. I hadn't realized anyone else was there. It was a stocky man in a suit and tie who emerged from a back office. He bowed in front of my desk. "I welcome you to *Okinawa Week*.

Thank you for joining my staff," he said, and shook my hand. "*Watashi-wa* Ashimine-san."

"Thank you," I stammered. "And thank you for this gift."

"You're welcome. We are happy to have you here. And please don't be alarmed at the protests," he said, his eyes full of fatherly concern. His face was like burled oak and his voice was quiet and firm. He gave the overall impression of a Yoda, grizzled, wise and kind. He did another little bow and said we'd have a meeting after I'd gotten settled, then went back down the hallway and disappeared to where he'd come from. I almost called after him but refrained. My will to quit was waning. It was hard to imagine disappointing this sweet elderly man.

As the staff came in for the day, I was more and more sure I should stay. One-by-one Amista introduced me to the odd, mismatched bunch at *Okinawa Week*. Jed Conkright was a red-faced, pot-bellied American expat who'd retired from an export company to cover local business for the paper. Kei Naoki was a Japanese reporter, about thirty-five years old and either too shy to look at me or just uninterested. "Reporters come and go," Amista whispered. "Kei doesn't pay much attention."

Cece Hildebrandt was the wife of an Air Force pilot and the paper's culture reporter, and she squeezed both of my hands when she said hello. She was whisper thin and had perfect red lipstick and arched black eyebrows. It was dizzying to be in the company of so many personalities after more than a week of mostly solitude. Cece, in particular, couldn't get over the fact that I'd come to Okinawa voluntarily, and alone.

"You aren't married to a military guy?" She raised one over-plucked eyebrow in disbelief. "You *found* this job and just moved here? To Okinawa, on purpose?"

Amista interrupted. "We're lucky to have her. She came from the *Chicago Sun-Times*."

"Oh yes," Cece back-pedaled. "I'm sure we're lucky."

Amista shook her head a little but Cece didn't notice. "Can you believe what's going on today, with the protests?" Cece said, in a hushed tone. "Okinawa is such a hellhole. Of course, this had to happen to a lily-white mainlander," she added.

Amista sputtered, "What, as if it would be better if it happened to a dark-skinned Okinawan girl?"

I was rattled by this sudden angry exchange. Amista glowered at Cece and with a start I understood that the rape allegation was loaded with racial implications. Stone was black, Midori was fair, many Okinawans were dark-skinned. I wasn't sure what it all meant, but I recall in that moment, being forced to take note of skin color. Rape is rape, I'd thought at first. The colors and nationalities of the perpetrator and victim were irrelevant. I didn't know what I didn't know. The word "hellhole" echoed in my ears.

Everyone dispersed to their desks and I followed Amista to hers. "I was planning to quit today," I blurted out.

"There you go, spouting off," she said. "Didn't I warn you about doing that?" She shot me an amused smirk and said she was surprised, asked why I wanted to leave. I told her it had all been too much, that I was overwhelmed by how foreign everything was and by how hostile.

"After coming all this way, you'd just up and quit?" she said. "I wouldn't have taken you for a quitter."

Her words stung me, and she was right. If I ran home to Illinois, I'd regret it. Even though Owen wasn't on this island and even though Okinawa was an alien and hostile version of the Japan I'd expected, I'd gut it out. I'd stick with my new job and new country and face the unknown. I was miserable and scared and overwhelmed, but I wasn't a quitter and after all, I *was* in the country I'd longed for. So right then, standing in front of Amista's desk, I resolved to stay.

In all the drama of the day, I had almost forgotten the tantalizing prospect that soon I'd meet Hisashi, Owen's brother. "What about the photographer," I asked Amista. "Will he be here today?"

Just then someone barged through the double front doors in a flurry, like a cartoon character or superhero, in a wave of energy that rippled across the office. He towered over me, tall and muscular, with a camera slung over his shoulder. "Lucy!" he said, as though we were good old friends. He shook my hand and it was enveloped by his much larger one. "So great to meet you."

"You too," I said, and examined his face for any trace of Owen. His frame was much larger than Owen's. But, did Hisashi have the same neat, small teeth as Owen?

"You were friends with Owen." It was a statement, not a question.

Amista was looking on, puzzled. "You two know each other?"

"Not exactly," Hisashi said. "She knew my brother back in college."

She opened her eyes wide in surprise and turned back to her work.

Changing the subject, Hisashi said, "When time permits, I'll take photos for your stories." Like Owen's, Hisashi's English was perfect and could've passed for American. His friendly, forthright manner had a valium effect on me, dulling my razor nerves. I saw in him no trace of my subtle, skinny hipster boyfriend. "Oh, I have the tea set Owen wanted you to have. I'll give it to you later," he said, grinning at me. Then he blew out of the office in the same blustery way he'd entered. I sat at my desk reverberating like a ringing bell.

Throughout the rest of the day I compared mental snapshots of Owen and Hisashi. They were so unalike. Owen was slender and soft spoken; Hisashi's bulk took up a doorframe, his voice boomed. They were brothers, but I couldn't see it.

From my desk, I caught glimpses of Rumiko looking at me. It wasn't hostility in her expression, but a sort of disdain, her darting eyes narrow, thinking.

In the years since my father died, I'd taken on a fragment of my mother's invisible stillness, had taught myself how to be unnoticed when I wanted to. I could inhabit a crowded room and remain alone. But I felt exposed in Rumiko's observing glances, as if she saw me and didn't approve. I took to ignoring her, never catching her gaze.

Hisashi didn't come back to the office that first day and I wouldn't see him again until the following week. My curiosity grew stronger. Why was Owen's brother here, in Okinawa, instead of in Tokyo with his fancy family? He had mentioned the tea set as an afterthought, but the tea set represented Owen's broken promises to me; it was a symbol of what we had. Back at Northwestern, he'd promised to give me the tea set, told me it was a special gift. But he never gave it to me. And then he left. Had Owen told his family about me, that he loved me, and I loved him? I dove into work to occupy my time, stifle my unease, and pass the time until I could talk to Hisashi again.

My desire to get to know Hisashi and the possibility of seeing Owen again solidified my decision to stay in Okinawa. No way I could leave until I understood. Once I got the information, the closure I needed, maybe I'd be ready to head back to Illinois, start over at the *Sun-Times,* or maybe go straight to New York and try to get hired by *The New York Times.* If Owen was out of my life for good, Japan couldn't retain its ferocious hold on me.

. . .

Back in my quiet hotel room, I considered my first days in Japan. I ruminated on what Amista said about our office *shisa*, that it only kept us half safe, and I wrote a poem.

A pair of guards, fierce protectors, loyal and strong,
    always in twos, never stationed alone,
    as if solitude sapped their strength.
    Lion-dog-soldiers, one the keeper of good,
    one to cast off evil. But what of a single shisa?
    She waits helpless, to witness what befalls her wards.

I worried about the profane sign that Amista crumpled and tossed away as if it was unimportant. Wasn't it a threat? I hoped her joke was wrong, that I was safe on Okinawa, safe in Japan. I decided that on my first day off, I'd shop for a partner for our *Okinawa Week shisa*. Might not help heal the island's troubles, but maybe it would protect our little office.

CHAPTER FOUR
ILLINOIS, 2013

I was living with my parents, preparing for my senior year at Northwestern. The orange and blood August sunset washed the Oakville sky in a brilliant haze. We'd had a small pizza party celebration for my twenty-first birthday, just my family, Rose and her mom. At the end of the night, my dad, tipsy and happy, said, "Good for you, Lu. You're ready to fly where the wind takes you." His eyes were at half-mast and his skin felt clammy when he hugged me. Wobbling up the narrow stairs to his bedroom, he blew me a kiss. He was sweet like that, blowing kisses, speaking to me in optimistic clichés, especially after a few glasses of wine. My parents had offered me wine too that night, but I turned it down. In reaction to my father's over-drinking, I'd become a teetotaler early on.

I went to bed the way I did most nights, listening to "Hallelujah," the rumbling poem-anthem of a song by Leonard Cohen. I was asleep before the song's refrain, awash in anticipation of my final semesters in college, feeling more adult at twenty-one than I'd felt the day before. In what I first perceived to be a half-dream, I woke to my mom's panicked shouting. It seemed like it had only been five minutes since I went to bed, and I couldn't make sense of her yelling, the sounds of paramedics scuffling and bumping about, and the baritone "Hallelujah" still playing on repeat.

By dawn I was standing in an over-bright hospital lobby with my mom and Doctor—White? Brown? Black?—his name was a color, only I didn't recall which one. His mouth was moving, but his voice came from a tunnel somewhere else, saying that my dad had a stroke in the late-night hours and there was nothing to be done. My mom chimed in, robotic, and said that his skin had been blue-grey and cold by the time she noticed him, unmoving beside her. I was a block of ice, my nerves frozen in a state of alarm.

"He was intoxicated last night?" the doctor said, not waiting for a response. "We could do an autopsy...?" My mom declined the autopsy, unwilling to hear the results, saying what did it matter, he was gone now anyway.

A flurry of activity followed. Friends filled up the house, casseroles and cookies occupied every surface. Then came the small funeral and burial at the local Unitarian church. We weren't members, but they were kind enough to host us anyway. The thing I remembered most clearly from that day was the casket dropping down, slowly, mechanically, into a brown dirt rectangle. I couldn't reconcile my father with this wooden box and the white roses splayed on top. Since the night of his stroke, everything moved so fast until that moment at the hillside cemetery when it all slowed down. It took an eternity for the coffin to inch down into the grave. My mom threw another rose, red, down into the dark hole and I imagined it dripped its color onto the white ones, staining them.

I called my college advisor and told her I wasn't coming back to school. She offered me a delayed start to the semester, but I declined. Paralyzed by a chainmail of grief, I was unable to think or feel or venture outside our tiny tidy house. My mom, stuck in her own sorrow, didn't comfort me or ask comfort of me. She seemed still and far away, perched on the edge of her bed, like a baby bird about to tumble to the ground from a swaying tree branch. She clung to each day quietly, a beating heart her only moving part. I stayed in my room and watched Hunger Games movies and Kpop videos. Rose tweeted at me and texted me, but I told her not to visit. I didn't have the energy to talk, and if she had tried to hug me, I'd just start crying again.

Growing up, my mom had been a boulder, steady and strong, the solid ground under my feet, anchoring me and righting my missteps. My dad had been sky, open and limitless, urging me to any possibility. "Be an astronaut, be a singer, anything you do is good, Lu," he'd say. Now with Dad dead and Mom wholly changed, I was ungrounded yet bolted in place, staring into a dim unfamiliar horizon. Things carried on this way for a year, I didn't think of the present or the future, only wallowed in the past when my father was alive.

The weekend before he died, we spent Saturday morning on the public tennis courts. I finally managed to return one of his fireball serves and even won a few points. That afternoon we warded off pretenders and hogged the reflex tester at the Museum of Science and Industry. We liked to track our speed stats and maintain our status in the top ten. That night, we'd gone to the Oakville Pub, a raucous sports bar where most parents didn't take their kids. I ate chili with extra onions and cheese, and he guzzled beer. I relished time with him, and he loved doting on his only daughter. When his eyes began to look glazed and faraway, I called Mom to pick us up.

Dad was a minor-league alcoholic, the type who mostly

drank at home, became bleary and happy, and went to bed early. One terrible time though, he got drunk at my senior prom. He was a chaperone, which was embarrassing enough, and I was on a first date with a shy, smart boy I'd liked for a while. My dad either snuck alcohol in, something a student would've been expelled for, or he snuck out to his car to drink. I was slow dancing with my date and saw Dad slump down on the bleachers like a sack of laundry. Teachers and parents rushed to help him as a circle of students looked on. Two adults carried him out and took him home. I told anyone who would listen that he had the flu and a high fever, but my date and the other students knew the truth. For months afterward, I couldn't look anyone in the eye. My dad never set foot at my high school after that, not even for my graduation ceremony, and I never spoke to my prom date after that night.

Over the years I fought off my own urges to drink—oh how I wanted to—and only once, on the evening of Dad's funeral, did I succumb, guzzling white wine until I wept in the corner of the church parlor. For a long time after that I was as sober and cold and hollow as a tomb.

My pragmatic mom, I later learned, almost left my father because of his drinking. He passed out at their tenth anniversary dinner table and she said she was done. But in the end, she decided her life with him was enough for her. He was mostly a cheerful drunk and they shared passions for academics, civics and me, and so she stayed. I found this out years later, and when I did, I understood why she was so steady and quiet. She was holding on, staying on her chosen path, but without hope for more. "I love him. And that's that," she'd said.

My love for my father was complicated by being ashamed of him and afraid that it was genetic, and I'd become a drunk too. Still, his death left me bereft. Even though I was angry with him for messing up his life and probably contributing to his death, at the core of my heart I burned with love for him. At my young age, and despite my sheltered upbringing, I understood that to love someone meant to accept them, that if you knew someone fully, faults and all, and accepted them anyway, that was love. That's what my mom taught me, both by her words and be her steadfast commitment to my less-than-perfect father.

A hot day eleven months after he died, I sat listless, half-staring out my bedroom window at a plump robin who stared back at me from his perch on an oak limb. A gust curved the branch sideways and the bird clenched his claws, holding tightly to his leafy seat. When the wind stopped, he cocked his head to one side, eyeing me with suspicion. Though of course he didn't, I clearly heard him say, "Are you going to sit there forever?" It was the first coherent thought I had—maybe it didn't come from the bird, but from inside my own head, I wasn't sure, but it startled me into the present moment.

The robin gave me one more skeptical look and flew away as another breeze whooshed through the leaves. I squinted into the sunlight that danced through the branches of our old backyard tree; it was a different sun, brighter than on recent past days, more piercing. I'd deferred my senior year of college but in that sharp sunlit moment the chains fell off my limbs and it was time to go.

And so, I continued my scholarship at Northwestern in Evanston, several towns away from Oakville, my hometown, and from my mother who still sat in stony grief in her bedroom. Mom and I talked on the phone but it was like talking with a zephyr. She'd always been stolid; now she was barely a breath of air. "Lucy, be safe," she'd breathe, at the end of each conversation and I promised I would.

Good for you, Lu, I heard my father whisper on the windy morning I headed back to school. I hadn't been raised in any church, didn't adhere to any doctrine, didn't believe in angels or ghosts who whisper from beyond, but that day I heard him, and it pushed me along.

For the first time, I'd relinquish the faded familiarity of my childhood bedroom and live on campus, be fully integrated into college life. My dad and I had set it up before he died and I would follow through, despite the nudge of discomfort I felt when touring the dorm, surrounded by bodies and smells and sounds I wasn't used to, sour perspiration odors, unexpected clangs and clunks from down long halls. One girl snorted and babbled as she slept on the common room couch, and some annoying soccer players yelled as they ran up the stairs. It was way outside my Oakville safety zone, but I'd suck it up, the way my dad and I had planned. Just one more year until graduation and my life could begin. Next year, I'd get a job, take an apartment in the city—the whole adult works.

CHAPTER FIVE

Illinois autumn rolled in hot and thick the week I went back to school. On the first day, I meandered to my classes. I'd left myself extra time to wander around the campus and refamiliarized myself with its layout and architecture, its odd mixture of imposing nineteenth-century stone facades and modern, gleaming, window-walled buildings. Though my skin was sticky from the humidity, I didn't mind; it was a relief to feel anything after my year of bolted-down numbness. Evanston was just one-hundred miles from my hometown, but the muggy air was different from the oppressive air in Oakville; it was palpable and promising, like a kiss from a new boyfriend in a warm rain shower.

When I began, four years earlier, Northwestern was an intoxicating upgrade from my homogenous hometown. It was really *something* to be on a big college campus after eighteen years in a suffocating suburb.

From sheet-linen ivory to piano-key black and all shades between, a multicultural mishmash of animated, eager students strolled, skated and biked around, and bantered, debated and laughed. A year ago, I'd been one of them, lively and full of light. Now, I was a year behind schedule for graduation, but at least I was there.

I headed toward my English class, patting at my flyaway curls, pushing my hair behind my ears, off my sweaty neck. I arrived at the back of a dim, squat building I'd never been in before; it had Lysol-scented hallways and not enough windows. When I got to the classroom, Rose sat green-washed by the fluorescent bulbs, and I hugged her, inhaled a double noseful of her latest fragrance. She'd tried a new one every month for the past four years and told me she'd eventually settle on a favorite.

"Juliette Has a Gun," she said, as I took the seat next to her. "That's the name of the perfume."

Rose and I had been best friends for fifteen years, enmeshed by our shared passions for good books and bad T.V. We read highbrow contemporary fiction—Lorrie Moore, Louise Erdrich and George Saunders—watched lowbrow T.V.—*Real Housewives of Anywhere* and *Catfish*—and were superfans of K-pop music. She could be surly but accepted my insecurity and my compulsion to be nicer than necessary.

Her father was an alcoholic, like mine, and died of liver failure when we were in grade school. By unspoken agreement, we never talked about our fathers, and took comfort in knowing the other one understood. I felt guilty saying so, but I told Rose I hoped my mother would be happier now that my father was gone, perhaps relieved a little. Rose understood what I meant and commiserated.

Rose had taken a year off college too, not because of a family tragedy, but to work as a steakhouse waitress and earn more money to pay tuition. Her high school grades had been decent, but not the four-point-two-five marks I earned in advanced placement classes, good enough grades to garner me a full scholarship. Rose spent the summer after high school taking the remedial prerequisite to English 101 so that we could take it together; we'd studied English together ever since, always in the same classes. Her explanation for her poor achievement in high school English despite being an avid reader of difficult modern literature was, "I'd do better if the school let me read anything decent." She couldn't afford to room in the dorms, so we scheduled our senior year classes together and ate lunch together most days.

That first day, her eyes were dark with tired, puffy circles underneath. "I couldn't sleep last night," she said. "And you look even more pink than usual."

It was a reference to my cheeks, which blushed an embarrassing fuchsia when I was nervous. A teacher once asked if I had a fever because my face was so flushed after I gave an oral report.

"No. I'm good," I said. "Trying to be."

She nodded. Ever since we were little, we'd dreamed of attending Northwestern. During my year of concrete and darkness, I'd forgotten how this place could light me up, prompt me to visualize my future. Before my year off, I'd majored in journalism, and wrote for the student news website, *North by Northwestern*. I loved poetry and literature and would've majored in English, but my mother convinced me journalism was more practical.

"You can support yourself as a reporter," she'd said, "not so much as a poet or novelist."

My father had been my cheerleader. He said, "Follow your passion and it will lead to a living." He was prone to tipsy over-optimism, so I didn't completely believe him, but I hoped he was right. To be safe, I studied both literature and journalism, semi-expecting to become a reporter after college. I was anxious and eager to succeed, and generally chose safety over risk.

Rose started to ask how I felt but stopped when the door

swung open. A slouchy crepe-faced professor took his position in the front of the classroom, made a slow turn, checked out each student one-by-one. He was about to speak when the door flew open again. A slender guy dressed all in black, even black-soled sneakers with black laces, strode in. He was tall, maybe six-feet-three-inches, with spiky black hair and light olive skin. The front of his black t-shirt was emblazoned with red calligraphic characters. Rose and I caught each other's eyes and she raised one eyebrow.

"Cute," she mouthed.

I turned back and examined his striking shirt. He noticed, lifted his lips in a slight smile, and came over.

"Beware of perverts," he said, and his small smile expanded to a grin. I couldn't articulate a response. "That's what my shirt says," he continued. "It's a popular slogan in Tokyo. Perverts grope women on trains there."

I may have said, "Wow," but I can't remember. My face was hot. His knife-edge cheekbones were so much manlier than most baby-faced college boys, and his deep-set eyes shone with intelligence. I struggled to take in the whole of him, his sallow skin against the solid blackness of his attire, perfect small teeth, still smiling. He stood close to me and it was hard to form perspective, to put him into context. His energy, foreign and electrically attractive, raised goosebumps on my arms.

I was so surprised by his black-clothed coolness and his odd comment about perverts, I hadn't noticed he was Asian. Was he Chinese or Japanese or Korean or...? Wait, he'd said Tokyo, so maybe Japanese? My face was on fire, as if he were privy to my internal dialogue about his nationality, as if he sensed the wash of pheromones surging over me.

"My name's Owen," he said.

Rose barged in and said, "Hello." And I opened my mouth,

but before I could speak the professor cleared his throat and started class.

Owen took the only empty chair, across the room. I half-listened to class that day. Owen's directness and striking appearance had jolted me. I was sure the searing chemistry that coursed through me was visible and palpable to the whole room. Rose smirked as she noted my effort to keep my eyes focused anywhere but Owen.

Is this how things happened? Just like that, people fall in love, or lust? A stranger walks into a room and, well, that's that? This had to be more than lust, certainly, deeper, a cellular-level connection, I told myself, though what in our one-minute inter-action justified more than lust? I'd had boyfriends over the years—tepid, proper relationships that included first dates and first kisses, but no sex. My introversion and insecurity moti-vated me to abstain. When I was thirteen, I decided sex would have to wait until my heart, mind and body were all aligned, ready for such closeness on all the necessary levels. I knew I couldn't handle doing anything with my body that my spirit didn't agree with. It wasn't a popular stance, and Rose teased me about it, calling me "non-loosy Lucy." Rose and other friends followed contemporary norms and treated sex like the equivalent of sharing a soft drink, but I held out. I wasn't scared of sex exactly, but I wasn't ready. At least not yet. But none of my early boyfriends had spurred this type of searing poker stab in my gut.

The professor rambled off the syllabus; I continued to *not* look at Owen. I pondered what he'd said, *people grope women on trains in Tokyo,* the idea of public transit feel-ups, women fending off the probing, grimy hands of strangers. I was certain on-train groping happened in the U.S., too, though I'd never heard of it. Certainly, I'd have read about it if I needed to worry.

Rose texted me. "Perverts on trains? LOL!" Amused by the drama of my reaction to Owen, she strained not to let out a guffaw.

During class introductions Owen boasted he'd been educated at the best international school in Tokyo, that his mother was a bigwig at a wireless company, and his father and brother were still in Japan. "Northwestern is the best college in Illinois," he'd said with authority and no discernible accent, "and my mom had to move here for work, so I came too, to experience the United States. In Tokyo, some people try to dress and act like Americans. My parents named me Owen because it's an American name. They deny this, but it's true," he said with a wry laugh, and like teenagers mesmerized by reality TV, the other students laughed in unison. Humble-bragging was intriguing when Owen did it.

Standing tall, speaking to our small English class, Owen had the radiance of a sparkly minor league star. He was cool and sophisticated, not like other nerdy boys, with their baggy jeans and floppy hair. Owen was an exotic to my small-town sensibilities.

I left my first senior English class with my emotional landscape crazily tilted by this stranger from Japan, a country I'd rarely thought of before. Now I knew things I could never unknow, that Japan had a groping problem, some Japanese people wished they were American, and the country was inhabited by supremely hip and well-spoken men. When class was over, Owen gave Rose and me a little wave and disappeared out the door.

"Wow," Rose said, as if channeling my thoughts. "He's something."

CHAPTER SIX

Each day of the first two weeks back at school Owen Ota wore skinny black jeans and t-shirts emblazoned with Japanese sayings or names like, *Eat Aaaaaahiiii, Radiation Dolls, Red Zombies, Edo Warriors,* and other things or bands I'd never heard of. Rose and I waved hello to him each day, but he always rushed in and out, leaving no time for conversation, not that I was brave enough to start one.

Owen was the first bright thing to attract my interest since my dad died. I became intensely curious about him, which magnified my gut-searing attraction. I yearned to learn about his life in Japan and what he thought of the U.S., what he liked to eat, what he liked to do for fun, what his skin felt like. On the superego level, I found him different, intriguing. My id wanted to smell his lips.

He distinguished himself in class right away with an essay comparing F. Scott Fitzgerald and David Foster Wallace, which the professor had him read aloud. Owen slouched a little as he stood in front of the class, not stiff and straight or trying to stifle a twitching eye or lip like most nervous young men did.

"Both authors were hamstrung by mental illness," Owen read, with no trace of self-consciousness. "Fitzgerald with addiction, Foster Wallace with depression. Their illnesses may have served as creative fuel for their earlier work, but in the end, cost them their lives."

The deep masculine quality of Owen's reading voice startled me, and I felt conspicuous and awkward at my front-row desk, embarrassed by my giraffe-thin legs poking out from wrinkly jeans shorts. I was too skinny, and my face was unremarkable, but at least my eyes were pretty. One sophomore-year date had told me my eyes were, "ocean beautiful," a compliment I conjured up at times I needed more confidence. Anyway, I was sure Owen hadn't looked at me long enough to notice my aqua eyes or much else about me.

As he continued to speak, I caught Rose's eye and she gave a little nod. We were both impressed by his literary panache. He knew a thing or two, it seemed, just another reason for me to be intrigued.

After class Rose teased me. "Bet you wish you wore something cute today. But you're not ugly, so you have that going for you."

"Whatever. He's interesting, right?"

"Yeah. *Interesting.*" She pushed me on the shoulder, something she always did when teasing me, an affectionate jesting jostle. Rose kept her long auburn hair brushed in place and she wore chic Kate Spade sunglasses. She enjoyed poking fun at my unkempt curls and wrinkly denim. "Someday you'll grow up," she liked to say, meaning, if and when I grew up, I'd learn to dress better.

"I'm a bohemian intellectual," I'd say. "We don't care about appearances." Though in truth, I was starting to think about mine, the need for more attention to my apparel and grooming.

Later that afternoon I ran into Owen in the packed student

union hallway, our shoulders collided as we tried to pass each other. "Sorry," I said, then inhaled sharply when I realized he was standing in front of me, close enough to kiss. He grinned. Could he read my mind, perceive my nascent fixation on him?

"Hi Lu," he said, with no trace of the testosterone-jacked overconfidence of most guys his age. He edged us over to the side of the busy hallway.

"In your class introduction you said you write for *North by Northwestern*?" He rubbed his chin and I nodded. His breath was minty, and an unfamiliar spice wafted off his skin. "I will be too. Maybe we can work together?" From the way my heart jumped, he might as well have said, *I am in love with you.*

"Yes," I said, and looked down to fumble with my books so he wouldn't see my cheeks go pink.

"Seems like fun. At *North by Northwestern* you get to meet people and learn stuff, right? Like real journalism?"

"Yep." Just yep. I couldn't think of what else to say.

"Okay, well, see you Wednesday, Lu," he said, and walked off, and I stumbled away as if I'd been sipping wine instead of attending classes.

For the next two nights I cooped myself up in my stuffy dorm and refamiliarized myself with *North by Northwestern*. It was the university's well-respected online newspaper and I'd written simple campus news for it during my first three years—blurbs about the appointments of new deans, lists of academic award winners. But now I needed to get a better fix on all its sections, so I could start imagining what types of stories I could be assigned to co-write with Owen. I wrote an email to the editor asking for bigger stories than I'd done in the past.

Two days later, I got an email back from the editor, informing me that I was welcome to write for the "Life &

Style" section, in addition to my usual news blurbing duties. It was a letdown. At the little newspaper in my hometown, the "Life & Style" section was parties and fashion, topics I had no interest in. *North by Northwestern's* "Life & Style" had more substance, but not much. I combed through it until I found a powerful piece about students whose mothers or fathers were in the Army serving in the Middle East, and another story about a professor who spent his summers in Honduras building homes for the poor. So, there would be some small potential to write serious pieces, to show Owen I could string together sentences that contained more than one word.

On my walk to English class I cobbled together a plan; I'd make the most of every assignment, learn all I could, research every detail, interview anyone and everyone, and of course, spend time collaborating with Owen when possible. At best, I'd get to work with him, at worst, I'd gain some valuable experience that might help me land a job when I graduated.

As I took my seat, I tamped down my sweat-frizzed hair and dabbed at my face with a Kleenex. Owen took the seat next to me, the first time he'd done so. Usually he sat across the room.

"Hi Lu," he said. "Hot enough for you?"

He sounded just like anyone from Oakville, both in phrasing and inflection. "Your English is perfect," I said, and immediately felt stupid for saying such an impolite thing.

"Good education," he said with a wink. "Nice hair, by the way. No one in Japan has such interesting hair."

Interesting. Heat rose up my neck. It was the same word I'd applied to Owen when I talked to Rose. I couldn't stop myself from patting at my hair to settle my nerves.

"Did anyone ever tell you your eyes are a pretty blue?"

I thanked him and turned away, but he thrust his cell

phone toward me. The *North by Northwestern* site was on his screen.

"I made it on to the 'Writing' team.'"

"That's great," I said, adding an upbeat inflection to my voice.

Owen had been assigned to the most intellectual section of the publication, the one students who considered themselves writers wanted to work for. In the "Writing" section, there were stories about poetry and literature, poems, personal essays and short stories. Everyone knew that only the most creative, smartest students got to write for "Writing." A stab of jealousy poked me. Then I reminded myself that a year ago I was sitting morose and silent in my Oakville bedroom and now I was on the verge of, I wasn't sure. Everything?

"They have me in 'Life & Style.'"

"Good for you, Lu. That should be fun."

"My father used to call me Lu," I told him, and before he could respond I added, "I doubt we'll ever get to do a story together."

"Not unless someone throws a poetry-writing party," he said, with a teasing tone.

"You're funny."

"You're funny too, Lu. And I don't just mean funny looking."

Surprised by his silly joke, I burst out laughing. "You should talk. What's that on your t-shirt today? A two-headed dog? Talk about funny looking."

He laughed too and shoved me gently on my shoulder. The gesture was similar to the one Rose always did, but his small nudge sparked my skin. It was progress. We were having an entire conversation and I'd strung together words into full, clear sentences. Emboldened, I said, "Do you like living in Illinois?"

"I do. But, I'm a *gaijin*. People look at me funny because

I'm a foreigner. That's what *gaijin* means in Japanese, foreigner."

Later, I looked up *gaijin*, and was surprised that Owen referred to himself with a word often considered a slur in Japanese. It meant foreigner, but its common usage was more like unwanted alien than welcome visitor. Of course, I knew people at Northwestern stared at Owen because he was magnetic, not because he was a *gaijin*.

For the next two weeks Owen and I walked together to the dining hall after English class. The awkwardness I'd felt in his presence started to ease and I was relieved to be able to focus on this intriguing newcomer, instead of on my grief about my father. Our conversations centered around *North by Northwestern* and our English class, and one day, I had a bone to pick with him.

"In your first presentation, you said Fitzgerald had mental illness. Do you really think alcoholism is a mental illness?"

"Did I say that?" He stopped in front of the student union, a serious expression on his face.

"You did. Alcoholism isn't a mental illness. It's a disease," I said, more aggressively than I intended.

"Okay then. I guess you're right." He pursed his lips and did a small eye roll. "Are you an expert on this?"

"No. Just pointing it out." No way I'd tell him about my father. Never.

"Okay," he said. "I misspoke." We threaded through the crowd, changed the subject to our upcoming interviews and essays and articles. When we entered the dining hall's side door, he said a quick goodbye and zipped off to who knows where. I kept hoping he'd stay and have lunch with me, but he never did. After two weeks of this routine, I found the courage to ask him to stay.

"Thanks, Lu, but I've gotta run." Dejected, I watched him weave through the throng of lunchtime students and out the door.

"Hey." Rose stepped in front of me, dabbed on lip gloss. "C'mon," she said and dragged me off to the cafeteria, trailing a wave of musky perfume. "Don't worry. You'll get your chance with him. Besides, you practically gave up dating after senior prom."

True enough. I hadn't dated much after the incident with my father, but no one dated much in Oakville, they mostly just hooked up. Even in college, though I'd had a few casual boyfriends, I hadn't considered any of them serious, as if I knew all along that Oakville and Northwestern guys were not going to be a part of my future. With Owen it was another story. I burned with rejection from the offhanded way he'd turned me down for lunch. I'd already spent hours fantasizing about him as my boyfriend, willing it into reality.

Rose and I were sharing a plate of tangy Lake Michigan whitefish and rice when my phone chimed through the din of student voices and clattering dishes.

"Who's that?" she said, grabbing my phone, bobbling it and almost dropping it onto the fish. "Knew it. Owen."

I took my phone back. Owen had texted, "Wanna do the book project together? The one for English class? At my house?"

"Yes," I replied. We'd been assigned to read a poetry book of our choosing and attempt to write a similar poem.

"Start soon," he wrote. "Next week?"

"Sure." One-word texts, Rose reminded me, would make me seem casual, not over eager.

"Here's your big chance," she said, twisting a small bit of

her hair through three fingers, a tic she usually did when she flirted.

"We'll see." I hadn't told her about the electricity I felt when Owen touched my shoulder. I didn't want to jinx it. "I don't know if I get a romantic vibe," I said. It was a half-lie. I knew how I felt, but I hadn't been able to read him at all.

"Yeah, right," she said. "You're a terrible liar."

Rose and I had shared everything since we were kids. Unlike most girls back home, we didn't have any bitter breaks where one of us got mad over something silly and pulled away for a time. We'd stayed tight all the way through. She was the hip fashionable friend and I was the academic nerd, but it worked for us. But I didn't want to discuss Owen. I wanted to keep him to myself.

"Keep me posted about how things *progress*," she said with theatrical emphasis, "with Owen."

The heavy hot air pressed on me as I exited the student union. I inhaled the scent of wet grass and squinted in the shafts of afternoon sun that slanted through the leaves of the tall oaks. When my phone rang, I couldn't see the caller ID through the reflected sun on the screen.

"Hi Lu." It was Owen. Another jolt under my ribcage. "My mom asked if you'd like to come to dinner Friday. At our house. And since we have to work on the book project anyway...."

I agreed and the next few days were a dreamy blur. Not even Leonard Cohen's sultry poetry could lull me to sleep on Thursday night.

CHAPTER SEVEN

I rummaged around in my matchbox dresser trying to select an outfit. It wasn't a date, I told myself, it was a study night and dinner with Owen *and his mother* at their suburban Evanston house. Owen didn't live in the dorms like the rest of us, but a shared bunk room and a moldy, soap-glazed group bathroom would not have constrained his urbane coolness.

I took a swig from my water glass to cool down and splashed a little on my cheeks. I put on a yellow dress that displayed my shoulders and neck but wasn't too revealing. I took pains to hide what I considered my worst flaw, my scrawny arms, which made me look like an anorexic or a refugee from some foreign starvation. My legs weren't much better, but at least they were toned and tan from walking around campus every day.

The sun set purple grey as I walked the ten blocks from campus to Owen's house, and the air held the first stages of autumn decay, sweet green leaves bleeding tart orange and brown at their edges. The further I got from school, the more elegant the streets became. Neighborhoods morphed from faded wooden duplexes fronted by scraggly bushes, to large well-kept homes with flowering dogwoods shading rolling green yards. It was nothing like my Oakville cul-de-sac where each tract house was a mirror image of the next one, with white aluminum siding and prefab front doors.

As I walked further from campus, homes mirrored the diversity of the student population; big, small, messy, tidy, colorful, plain, ornate. One had a gunmetal Pi sculpture in the front yard, another a white rocking hammock, and another a tumble of children's toys. I took slow breaths to compose myself.

"No need to be nervous. Not a date," Rose texted, as if reading my mind.

When I arrived at what turned out to be a mini mansion complete with perfect hedge rows, I stopped in front of towering front doors with inlayed, etched art deco glass. Suddenly they swung inward and a striking woman was squeezing my hand.

"I'm so glad Owen has a friend in Illinois," she said, with warm formality. She had on chic black eyeglasses and a red silk blouse, and her skin was the smoothest I'd ever seen. I stared at her too long and she smiled. "Welcome," she said. "Please come in." She pushed the door open wider, to reveal glowing white marble floors. Unlike Owen, Mrs. Ota had a slight accent.

"Thank you," I said, handing her the small bouquet of pink spray roses I'd picked up at the corner market. I tried not to stare, but I'd never seen the luxurious shade of red silk she wore or skin that shone like glass.

She ushered me through a high-ceilinged foyer into a large dining room, where Owen was seated at a black lacquer table, much too long and wide for just three of us. My heart jumped as it always did at the sight of Owen.

"Lu!" he said, more loudly than necessary. He stood and

stiffly half hugged me, more of a shoulder bump than an embrace. Cold air slapped my face as it tumbled down from open vents up in the wall. Owen's face was blank, as though he'd never seen me before, his expression guarded, semi-friendly. Not knowing what to make of this, I took a seat across from him and commented that his house was beautiful.

"Yeah, it's fancy, I know," he said, sarcastic.

I assured him that I meant it as a compliment, told him I had never been in such a nice home. His face softened then, and he stopped looking through me. Finally, he smiled his perfect smile, and a wash of relief trickled over me. There was Owen, not the robotic stranger who'd greeted me.

He told me I looked "nice" and reached for one of the tiny pink teacups on the table, handed it to me. We sipped warm green tea while his mom jostled around in the kitchen. The dining table's edges were ornately carved with swirling vines and it was decorated with delicate white orchids and votive candles. I almost giggled aloud at how different this was from my parent's functional Pier One dining set, pressed wood with plastic hinges, and store-bought pizza as its centerpiece. I couldn't identify the tangy scents wafting around. Aside from kitchen rustlings, Owen's house was quiet, as if pausing so we could have a private moment before his mother joined us. I wanted to say something to draw out his perfect smile again. But we didn't speak, we just sat sipping our tea. I burned with anticipation about the evening and what might happen between us.

Finally, Owen broke our silence, not with something romantic or personal, but with talk of schoolwork. He asked if I'd be okay doing our report on *haiku*, told me he had two copies of an excellent *haiku* book. I'd never studied *haiku* before and I paused, unsure.

"I'll teach you," he said, in a lowered voice, reaching across the table for my hand. "It will be my honor to show you this Japanese art."

His mother came into the room carrying a platter and she noticed our clasped hands. Owen was slow to release my hand while his mother's eyes were on us. A tinge of unease hit my back and suddenly I was unsure. *What were we beginning with this dinner and why was he so cold at first? Not a date, but do people not on dates hold hands?* I pushed my questions away, decided that anything was possible. He'd held my hand and that meant something.

Ms. Ota started by serving thin slices of raw tuna. "*Ahi,*" she said, a delicacy. My parents had taken me to the only sushi restaurant in Oakville and my Northwestern dining hall served it sometimes, so I wasn't unfamiliar with it. "In Japan," Mrs. Ota said, "the most highly regarded chefs in Japan get their picks of the best quality fish." The chefs at the bottom of the ranks get the dregs, she added, with a sly smile. Like Owen's, Mrs. Ota's teeth were small and perfect, her eyes dark and deep-set, attractively framed by black eyeliner. The *ahi* was sweet butter and salt on my tongue.

"It's delicious," I said, trying to be nonchalant. Owen told his mother that I was "willing" to learn about *haiku,* that we were doing a *haiku* project together. "Yes," I added, unnecessarily, and she remarked that our choice to write about *haiku* was "wonderful."

"Such a beautiful art. Did you know that Owen is a published *haiku* poet?" she said. Owen threw me a small, self-conscious smile and pointed out that it was just a local publication in Tokyo, nothing big. I was floored, told him he was the only person I'd ever known that'd published anything other than in a school paper or website.

"Owen is modest," Mrs. Ota said, beams of pride brightening her beautiful eyes. I pictured my own mother, a mouse in her bedroom back in Oakville. She hadn't said she was proud of me since I returned to college, since I'd unwrapped myself from my leaded blanket of grief. She'd mainly worried me with silence and when she did speak, she warned me to be "safe." How wonderful it must be to have a mother like Owen's, so glamourous and open and radiating raw maternal love.

The next dish was a steaming platter of *tempura* vegetables, carrots, sweet potatoes, string beans and onions. I ate more than my share of soft crunchy potatoes dipped in ginger and soy sauce. She brought in the main course on a gleaming black lacquer tray, a heaping bowl of rice and cuttlefish smothered in pungent yellow curry. I struggled through half a bowl with my nose running and then put my fork down, trying not to clink it on the plate, hoping Mrs. Ota wouldn't notice.

"Not to worry, Lucy. Dessert will clear out the burn," she said, and replaced the curry with a little square, like a tiny pineapple upside-down cake. I don't recall the name of the cake, only that it tasted cool and fruity. The rest of our conversation during the meal was light. Mrs. Ota asked me questions about Oakville and asked how I liked college. I avoided talking about my father, didn't want to throw wet wool over this shiny, laden moment.

Mrs. Ota said she hadn't planned to come to Illinois but was willing when her company sought to transfer her. "Luckily Owen's school records were strong enough for late acceptance to Northwestern," she said.

"Lucy's mother is a teacher," Owen said, shifting the focus away from himself. I'd forgotten I'd mentioned my mother in class introductions. My dad had been a teacher too, but I hadn't mentioned him in class.

"Ah. We call that *sensei* in Japanese," Mrs. Ota said. "Teachers are treated with utmost respect in Japan. You must be proud to be the daughter of a *sensei*." Pride hadn't been on my radar. My parents' jobs were respectable, nice, stable, but I hadn't considered them as worthy of high honor, and my dad, well my feelings were a mixture of love and shame. "Will you be a *sensei* too?" she'd asked, and I'd said journalism was my probable plan.

Mrs. Ota wanted to know about my travels, where I'd been and what I'd seen. I was embarrassed to admit I'd only traveled in the Midwest, places my parents and I could go by car, Michigan, Indiana, and around Illinois, mainly. I didn't want to talk about my meager life, my limited worldliness, so I asked her how she liked Illinois.

"We won't get too attached since it's our temporary home." I was struck by her use of the pronoun "we," as if she and her son not only shared a home but felt the same feelings, an agreement not to become attached to Illinois. My full belly gurgled with unease at the thought of Owen leaving Northwestern. She continued, "Owen tells me you might consider a study abroad program. You'd love Japan. We have a graceful and unique culture."

Owen rubbed his chin and smiled at me, asking for commiseration. "Yes," I lied. "I've been thinking about it." Up until that moment, I'd never thought about it, never discussed with Owen or anyone else the idea of studying in Japan. Of course, since I met him, I'd been pondering the country, picturing myself there with Owen, but not really considering how I might get there. I shot him a questioning look.

When his mother carried dishes into the kitchen, Owen said, "I don't know why I told her that. I guess I thought it would make her happy."

"Happy that I'd want to study in Japan?" I whispered, keeping our secret. "Why?"

"She likes anyone better if they like Japan, that's all." The chair felt hard on my tailbone and I shifted my weight. Owen stood, said something about being tired, preferring to start the *haiku* project tomorrow instead of tonight. He shouted to his mom that I had to go.

She poked her head out of the kitchen. "Goodbye, Lucy. See you again soon?" Her elegant voice held a tinge of hope.

Owen guided me to the door. He didn't hug me goodbye, but instead touched my shoulder in the same spot he'd touched in the hall at school. He promised me we'd work on the project the next day and then he said, "I'll show you my fort too."

In my hustle out the front door I didn't think to ask him why he had a fort, why anyone twenty-one years old would have a fort. I did say, *"haiku,"* as if confirming a private deal we'd struck. "Yep. *Haiku* tomorrow," he said. "Bye." He didn't offer to walk me back to campus and I was ejected out into the night.

I hurried to the dorm under the inky sky. My skin grew damp from the heavy hot breeze after the air-conditioned house. My right hand, which had held Owen's, was warm, as if blushing, and my shoulder was tingly where he'd touched. I tiptoed past the common room and climbed into bed, closing my eyes hard, muting my phone so I wouldn't have to talk to Rose if she called.

I tried to sleep but instead I pondered my time in the gorgeous house, the spicy Japanese food, and Owen's beautiful mother gazing at him with such pride. Owen's behavior had been a little off, cold and then warm and then cool again, but maybe he was nervous. I turned on Rufus Wainright's version of "Hallelujah." As the chorus rose and fell, I repeated little mantras in my mind in hopes that they'd take hold in my sleep and I'd dream them into reality. *Owen and me, in love, in Japan.* Such juvenile fantasies, but at the time, I didn't know.

CHAPTER EIGHT

The next day Rose pried relentlessly for details about my dinner at Owen's house. "Did you kiss?" she asked. "Did you do more?" I refused to tell her anything, not that he held my hand and not that he mentioned the idea of me studying in Japan. "I know you like him," she said, "because you've never been this quiet." It tortured Rose that Owen and I may or may not have kissed, may or may not have done more. But I didn't want to talk about the fact that nothing happened between us and that he'd ushered me out the door with one small tap on the shoulder. Today would be different and after today, maybe I'd want to tell her.

Since last night, a beansprout notion of Japan, of going to Japan, had been germinating in my brain, working on me. I started reading about the country. I hatched the notion of going to Japan to see Owen. I could study in Japan. I could live in Japan with Owen later, as adults, in love. Was this fantasy or a real possibility? I wasn't sure, but it was the start of a longing like the beginning of a hunger pain, a hot, hollow hole in an empty stomach. My future-self beckoned to me, from a shady spot next to Owen on a tree-lined street in a Tokyo suburb, from a crowded downtown corner with well-dressed workers rushing to and fro, from a tall corporate window, where Owen and his mother shared a corner office and I was joining them for lunch. Somehow it all seemed pinned on today, on what happened between us with the *haiku* project and in his fort, as if our future together would be confirmed by one charmed afternoon.

Owen drove his electric-blue Volkswagen Bug up to the sidewalk outside my dorm, where I stood with Rose and a few other students. I shielded my eyes from the sun and focused on Owen's hand, extended from the car window. He handed me a paperback with Japanese and English on the cover. *Beautiful Haiku* was the title. Its cover illustration was a rounded cherry blossom tree with a shock of pink flowers haloed around leafy branches. "It's a quick read. Get in."

As we drove away, Rose and others watched us. I sat tall in the passenger seat relishing being Owen's chosen one, tamping down my urge to kiss the side of his olive cheek. The cool guy had selected the nerdy girl. I almost forgot about his odd treatment of me the night before, yin and yang, close to me and far away at the same time. Today we would work on *haiku* and I'd see his "fort." The word "fort" conjured up all manner of sneaky spaces in my mind, hidden shacks where high school kids made out, underground bunkers for hiding time capsules. I didn't ask him what his fort was because I didn't want to spoil the surprise or let on what I hoped might happen there. Rose gave a little wave as we drove off.

I asked Owen if he we had enough time to read an entire poetry book and complete the project. "Don't worry," he said. "Trust me." And I did trust him, to teach me about *haiku*, to take me to his fort, to drive me anywhere. We didn't have to define this as a date or something else. In that moment, being

62

together was everything and it was enough. The Bug's windows were down, and the wind whipped my hair wildly. Owen's hair must have been gelled into place because it didn't move. I wanted to touch his hair or put my hand on his long leg, but better judgement told me this wasn't the time. My arm stuck to the car seat and my clothes stuck to my skin. I yanked at my gauzy tank top in quick moves so he wouldn't see.

When we got to his house it loomed even larger than it had yesterday. A sudden steamy downpour threw sheets of water down the tall front windows and we sprinted in the front door, bumping into each other as we ran. Once inside, Owen dropped his backpack on the floor and drew me toward him and kissed me, full and long. My legs actually buckled; rainwater slipped down them onto the clean marble. He touched my fingers, still clenched around my damp backpack and took it from my hand, kissed me once more. Then as if a switch had been flipped, he stepped back and said, "Let's study."

Dazed, I steadied myself, asked if he was sure. He said he was sure and that his mom was probably home, somewhere in one of the far-flung rooms and besides, we *had* to do our project. "We'll have more time together. In the fort," he said, his brown eyes soft, and I agreed.

And so, just like that, we got to work. We spread our computers and books on his large low living room coffee table. "I've been writing *haiku* since I was little," he said. "Let's write one together to go with our report." His voice had an infectious delight, as if the idea of co-writing a *haiku* with me was the best idea he'd ever had.

I'd tried my hand at poems in the past and my results were mediocre, certainly not fit for publication the way Owen's *haiku* had been. But his enthusiasm was intoxicating, and my thought processes were chemically diluted from our brief make out. If Owen thought we could write something worth sharing with the class, then I believed we could too. I asked him if I could see the *haiku* he'd published in Japan. He said, "Not now," but I persisted, asked to know where it was published. My curiosity was piqued. He would only say that it was published in a tiny literary journal in Tokyo and that he'd show me "later." If Rose or anybody else had been so elusive, I would have called them out, but with Owen, I acquiesced, agreeing to wait until later to read his *haiku,* to kiss him again, to see his fort. My boundaries were wiggly and weak when it came to Owen.

He walked me through the history of *haiku.* Speaking in a professorial tone, he told me that in 1892 Masoaka Shiki established *haiku* as a new poetic form with three lines; five syllables, seven syllables, and five syllables, and a seasonal theme from nature. Then Kawahigashi Hekigoto came along and furthered the *haiku* form to include two key concepts: the poem should have no center of interest, and it should be on a subject taken from daily, local life.

"The goal is to thrill people by writing about an everyday experience," Owen told me, "but create a new understanding about it." And another thing, he said, *haiku* have two parts. The parts must be separate but must enrich each other.

I enjoyed seeing Owen in *sensei* mode and I leaned in attentively, wishing for more kisses, but content for the moment to be close to him.

"Here's one of my favorites," he said, "by Murakami Kijo." He opened the book and set it in front of me. I read aloud.

First autumn morning;
  the mirror I stare into
  shows my father's face.

. . .

Simplicity, beauty, truth. This *haiku* captured so much. A tear popped into my eye and I turned so that Owen wouldn't notice, but he took my hand. I hadn't told him that my father had died a year earlier, but his face registered understanding. "Does this remind you of your father?" he said, and I nodded. "Is he gone?" I nodded again. "I'm sorry," he said. And we sat, hands entwined until my urge to cry had passed.

"This poem reminds of my father too," he said, finally. "For different reasons. Mine doesn't approve of me." His blunt statement filled up the space between us. "Lu, I feel accepted by you. You respect me." This sudden change of subject, from our fathers to us, to our relationship, startled me. His voice was choked.

"Of course, I respect you. What do you mean, your father doesn't approve of you?" He dropped his head into his hands, slumped over. I moved closer, slid my hand up and down his back. It was probably wrong that I tried to turn a comforting moment into a sensual one, but he stayed there, head in his hands, leaning against me. After a few moments he straightened, gently pushed my hand away.

"My brother, Hisashi. He's the one my father loves," Owen said sadly. "He's successful, a photojournalist. But, even Hisashi doesn't have my dad's full acceptance. Hisashi lives far away from the family, on an island, Okinawa. That bothers my dad."

I wanted to ask questions to understand more about Owen's family dynamic, but he steered our conversation away from his family to mine. "Tell me about your father," he said. "Talking about mine is no good."

I felt connected to Owen in that moment, safe to share my secrets, and so I told him my father had died, that he'd been an alcoholic, and that my mom hadn't recovered from his death or been fully happy in their life together. Pained, he leaned in touched my face, sending new sparks across my skin. He kissed me ever so lightly. I heard a door open somewhere, maybe the kitchen.

"Hello?" Mrs. Ota called out. I moved away, but Owen didn't. He held our gentle kiss in place. When he finally let me go, Mrs. Ota stood nearby, smiling.

"Studying?"

"Yes. We are." Owen sounded irritated.

"Keep it up," she said, with a little laugh.

She left, and Owen said, "Lu, I'm sorry about your father."

"He wasn't perfect, but...." I swallowed the lump in my throat, didn't want to feel the grief anew, fresh because of acknowledgement by Owen. "He was a teacher like my mom, they taught at the same elementary school. I look just like him."

"Then he must have been beautiful," Owen said.

The ceiling could have split wide open at that moment and sucked me up into the galaxy, I was as high as the moon and stars. "I hear him talk to me sometimes." I paused, then said, "Sometimes, especially when it's windy, I hear his voice."

Owen's eyes widened. "Ah, what a gift. To hear the loving words of a father from the spirit realm." Our thighs touched, and I felt my face grow hot. He continued, "In Japan, we honor the dead as though they are alive. We give them gifts and speak to them too. Ancestors can speak to us, that's what Japanese believe. When you come to Japan, I will take you to my ancestral shrine."

And just then I felt Owen rein himself back in, the way he'd done the other night, and after kissing me in his foyer, like flipping off a bright flashlight. He stood and said, "We should finish the report."

"Right," I said, confused by the scene that had just played out. I was torn between wanting to kiss him again and wanting to show restraint. We ended up spending the next two hours writing our report, which we titled, "How to *Haiku*—A Creative History." We wrote our own *haiku* to read to the class, with the requisite nature reference and a twist to illuminate something new.

Evanston is still
trees pause, awaiting a storm
downpour never comes

I was proud to have written even the simplest little poem and giddy about writing it with Owen. "If anyone had told me I'd be sharing *haiku* with a woman from Illinois, I'd never have believed it," he said, echoing my own feelings about writing poetry with a man from Japan.

"It's late," he said. "Tomorrow, I'll show you my fort." And he drove me back to school, dropped me off on the curb, and was gone as quick as a thief. I stood for a moment, awash in moonlight, then went in and waited for tomorrow to come.

CHAPTER NINE

For a second time, I stood waiting for Owen in the dorm parking lot, while the September sun seared the top of my head. When he finally arrived, students watched us drive away and I pretended I didn't notice them. Everyone looked at Owen always. He was exotic, magnetic, cool, with not a drop of sweat on his brow despite the pressing heat. I felt conspicuously plain sitting next to him in his car, certain he could feel the hot flush radiating off me.

We drove straight to his "fort," a term that struck me as odd, not something that most men had, but that's what Owen called it. We bypassed the main house and arrived at a grey wooden shed that he'd turned into a sneak-away space. Inside, my eyes strained to adjust to the dimness. There were two lumpy beanbag chairs, a small television, and a tea set sitting on a tray on the floor. The pink roses I had given his mother a few nights before were on the tea tray and they blanketed the enclosed space with their perfume. I was pleasantly dizzy, tipsy with the scents of sugar and must. I sank down onto a beanbag and

Owen cracked the door so that the afternoon sun shone fiery crimson on the tea set.

"My grandmother gave this tea set to me when I was twelve," he said, "a month before she died. She told me it's infused with love and that it's impossible for tea served from it to be bitter."

"That's nice," I said, fidgeting in my uneven seat, leaning forward for a better look. The set was four small red teacups, a matching pot and bowl, each painted with delicate pink flowers, and a small ivory cloth, arranged neatly on a matching tray.

"Those are *sakura* flowers, cherry blossoms," Owen said. "The traditional flower of Japan. When you come visit me in Tokyo, I will show you," he said. "Until then, this tea set will help you remember me. I'd like you to have it."

Stunned, I didn't respond. He wanted to gift me his grandmother's tea set? And he was speaking to me about flowers and infusions of love? I was floating outside myself, and Owen glowed in the semi-darkness like an angel or a ghost.

"My family, the Ota family, has always been successful in business. We are well-known in Tokyo," he said, in a new proud tone. "We have interests in wireless, media, transportation and fishing. Japan's strongest industries," he said.

Wireless, media, transportation, fishing. The imaginary construct I was starting to build about Japan was a jumble of crowded trains where girls got groped by perverts, glamourous people like Owen's mother wore rich red silk and had glass-smooth skin, where the food was spicy and squishy, trees sprouted delicate pink flowers, families had eloquent, generous grandmothers, and now, also a place where big buildings housed important people who dealt in wireless, media, transportation and fishing. *Fishing?* The only fishing I knew was in a rowboat on Walloon Lake, Michigan, where my dad had taken me one summer. Owen's Japan beckoned me, gorgeous and sparkly and shrouded and mysterious by turns.

"Wow," I said, chagrined by my ignorance, thrilled he was willing to share bits of his world with me. I was desperate for him to show that he loved me at least a fingernail as much as I already loved him.

Owen laughed and his small perfect teeth shone shiny white. His face was half illuminated by the sun sneaking in. "Wait," I said, struggling to keep my thoughts square. "You said the tea set would help me remember you. But I don't need to remember you. You're here."

The fort door creaked shut in the breeze and now it was darker, the air thick between us. "Mmmm," he whispered, and reached around me and rested his arm on my shoulder so that his fingers lightly encircled the side of my neck. Then he leaned in and kissed me while I held my breath. I began to open my mouth, but he gently squeezed my neck, just below my ear, a gesture at once odd and intimate. He pulled back so that our lips were close but not touching and he breathed in a quiet and steady rhythm. My insides were compressed, contracted with the effort I was exerting not to grab him closer.

"Won't you visit me?" he said, still not releasing his grip on my neck; I could feel each of his fingers pressing their prints into my skin. Then he put his closed lips against mine, pushing flatly, a sensual moment turned steel by a concrete kiss. A bubble of alarm popped into my throat. His first kiss was too soft, his second too hard. I was wobbly with confusion.

Panic and attraction washed over me in a simultaneous double wave. Off-kilter, I hovered over the scene, seeing it at the same time as experiencing it. Owen and I alone together, just as I'd wanted, kissing and building up to more, just as I'd wanted. We were sitting close, our legs touching like they'd done the night before, but there was a chasm between us, a blank space. I'd longed for the chance to be with Owen to slide his shirt over his head, run my hands over his taut torso. But his kisses seemed careful, choreographed, not what I'd anticipated after a month of waiting, hoping. He was holding me, but he was uneasy too.

"I want you to visit me in Japan," he said, trying to salvage the moment.

I blinked a few times, calming myself. "I'll visit you," I said, and closed my eyes, exhaled my disappointment. A visit someday? That's all? It didn't compute. I was in love, believed he was falling for me too. But we'd just agreed to a visit, someday, nothing more definite.

"Good. Now, tea," Owen said, forcing a light tone. "Let me do a little tea ceremony for you." He squeezed my shoulder hard and I jolted. Bewilderment rippled the lines of my logical thinking and I sat still in my beanbag.

I shifted my focus to the tea set in front of us, recalling what I'd read about Japanese tea ceremonies, and how methodical and elegant they were. Tea hosts would lay out cups and other items so that their placement was most convenient for their guests. To the Japanese, a tea ceremony was not only a way to share refreshments but also a beloved art form to be practiced and perfected. With the beginning of a tea service, the odd and romantic moment with Owen took on a formal, distant feeling.

He sat forward and removed his shoes, placed them off to the side on a little mat. After who knows how long, I did the same. In slow precise movements he scooped powder from the bowl on the tea tray into one of the cups, poured in hot water from the pot and whisked as steam rose in a wisp. He sipped from the cup, picked up the ivory cloth, wiped the edge, turned the cup around and passed it to me. I imitated him, sipped and wiped the cup with the ivory cloth and handed it back to him.

We continued in this way until the cup was empty. The tea tasted lemony and good and I began to believe he might kiss me again soon, that we might be more intimate before this encounter was complete.

"Tea is a special Japanese tradition," Owen said. "This was not an elaborate ceremony, but I am honored that you joined me." He spoke in a conspiratorial whisper.

My head felt foggy, sandbagged with the weight of my feelings for Owen, this dark, uncomfortable scene, and now a new and foreign ritual. "Thank you," was all I could muster.

After a few quiet moments, Owen leaned in to kiss me again. This time it was luxurious, passionate, and I was liquid with expectation. I moved closer, touched his neck, felt his pulse with my fingertips. Suddenly, he recoiled and yanked himself away from me. He dropped his head into his hands and gulped deep breaths. I was unsure of what had just happened. After a moment I reached out and touched his arm.

"I'm sorry," he whispered, his voice wavering.

But I told him not to be sorry, it didn't matter, that I loved him. "It's all too fast," I said, and he nodded. For the first time in my life, I wanted to have sex, was willing to. But Owen slid away from me.

With nothing left to say or do, I gathered myself, put on my shoes. We stood and he wrapped his arms around me. "I love you," he said. "You are a true friend," and the word *friend* sliced the edge of my heart like a precision paper cut.

I walked home and the stars kaleidoscoped around my foggy head and my heart pounded in my ears. What had just happened? Our lovely, intimate moment had gone sour. It felt as though Owen wanted to back away from me at the same time as he kissed me. Cooler night air did nothing to calm my hot cheeks as I stumbled back to campus. I was as jittery as the leaves fluttering on the trees around me, could have let go and tumbled to the ground at any moment. Owen had apologized. For what? The word *friend* bounced back and forth like a ping-pong ball in my skull. I almost veered into the bright entryway to NU Tap Room, but instead shuffled back to my dorm, a hunched and cowered zombie.

I lay on my bed, closed my eyes and tried to recast our encounter. Surely it wouldn't be like that all the time. I ruminated about the Japan Owen had revealed to me via the lovely tea service, the *haiku* lesson, his pride in his family business. And I pondered what he said about his father's disappointment with him. That was hard to clarify in my mind. How could any father not be proud of Owen? I stared into the dark of my lonely dorm room and considered his invitation to come to Japan, his intention to give me his grandmother's tea set, his comments that I was beautiful and understood him. That was love, wasn't it? To be understood by someone you considered beautiful? I grabbed on to these notions as if they were life rafts that saved me from an undertow or balloons that soared me up to a new universe.

The next day, Owen texted and asked me to go for a walk. I was eager to see him so we could talk about what happened in the fort, and what didn't happen. We met in downtown Evanston, shared turkey sandwiches at a little café. We reread our report and our *haiku*, and I started to believe the apprehension I'd felt in his fort was gone. He smiled and put his arm around me as we made our way past shops and restaurants. He was at ease, comfortable, and I felt warm from within.

"Lu, when you hear your father in the wind, it's not just in your head," he said, jolting me from my happy reverie. "It's really him. That's what Japanese believe and that's what I believe."

"Oh? I kind of thought it was just that I *wished* I could hear from him, so I imagined it."

"No, no. That's not right. When a strong bond of love exists, the loved-one's voice can travel from the other realm. The dead comfort the living in this way." He looked at me intently, seriously, then leaned over and planted a small kiss on my lips. "Be grateful for a loving father," he said. "He will always be with you."

Surprised by his mystical commentary, I didn't agree or disagree. I wanted to ask him more about his father, about why his father didn't approve of him. "What about your father?" I said, fishing.

"Nope, don't want to talk about him," he said. "But I do want to talk about you visiting me in Japan." He told me I could come over as a student, or possibly even get a job there after college. He would act as my tour guide and maybe I could even stay with his family in Tokyo. The city is cosmopolitan, he said, and decorated with temples and gardens. When he walked me back to my dorm, he kissed and hugged me in the doorway. I was giddy, excited about where the relationship was going, relieved it didn't feel off-kilter anymore.

"It would be amazing to go to Japan," I said, and he agreed. I slept soundly that night, peacefully, looking forward to our *haiku* presentation and eager to spend as much time with him as possible.

CHAPTER TEN

Then, nothing. No call, no text, no visit. Silence where Owen should have been. I knew something was wrong for him not to contact me at all, but I couldn't imagine what. For two days I was ill with dread, on the verge of vomiting. Owen and I had deepened our relationship during the past month and though it had been a bit off at times, I dreamed of everything. Not just sex with Owen at some point, but a life with Owen, a future in Japan with him. What happened in his fort was because we were nervous. We had already started to fix it with our lovely walk, hadn't we? But the following days, which should have held more whispers and kisses, were barren. I struggled with the impulse to run to a package store and buy bottles of wine, and instead passed the weekend sulking inside.

And then it was Monday and he didn't show up for English class. "Where's Owen?" Rose said, and I shrugged, wouldn't look at her. Reluctantly, I presented our paper to the class and read our *haiku* aloud by myself. I fought back tears as my concerned peers looked on.

That afternoon I texted and called Owen, but he didn't

answer. I started to walk to his house but turned back. Instead, I hid in my room and tried to concentrate on homework but mostly half-watched Japanese music videos on my computer. In the early evening, after an eon of waiting, I finally got a text from Owen. "I'm downstairs."

I hurried down and found him near the dorm's concrete courtyard fountain. Students walked and talked around us, ridiculously upbeat and happy. The evening air was chilling down. Fall had tiptoed in to replace summer all in one sad afternoon as I hid in my bedroom.

Owen stared at the ground, pushed browning leaves around with his foot, and then said, "I have to move back to Tokyo. Now." A pile of dead branches blew across the courtyard, scattering across the stone.

"Oh." A strum, like a discordant guitar chord, rippled through my gut. "But you just got here." I sounded stupid and small.

"My mom is quitting her job to run the Ota family's media businesses. My dad won't let me stay."

Not understanding, I said, "But, it's not like *you* can run the company."

"My father says I have to go back. He already dislikes me. I have to do what he says." Owen sounded defeated, older, deflated.

I hesitated, then, "Why does your father dislike you?"

"I'm just different...." His voice trailed off. "A *gaijin* in my own family."

"You've said that before, but it's not true. I've seen how your mother loves you."

"In Japan, father's approval is most important."

The chilly breeze tousled my hair and I shuddered. "I'll visit soon, or take a study abroad program," I said, repeating the ideas we'd discussed, though I hadn't any idea of how one could get to Japan from Evanston or Oakville. I didn't even know if there was an academic program from Northwestern to Japan. Everything had happened so fast I hadn't had time to research the possibilities.

"My life in Japan is complicated." His vulnerability was palpable. "Just know, I do love you." Again, he'd said it. "It's just, I'm sorry." Another apology. For being so affectionate and awkward by turns? For being about to leave me? He stared past me into the distance and pain floated behind his eyes.

"Owen, I don't want you to go..." I started, and he stopped me.

"I can't. I can't discuss anything more," he said. "Sorry, Lu." Then, a quick, hard half-hug and he drove away, gone in the same startling way he'd arrived a month earlier.

I stood for a time in the cool stone courtyard and felt lonelier than the empty year after my dad died. Upstairs I burrowed into my bed. I was flooded with regret and my chest was needled with pain. Why hadn't I soothed Owen in the fort when he was obviously distressed? Why didn't I make him explain why he had to leave? And anyway, why would he woo me, entice me with poetry, and exotic food and tidbits of the life we might share, the gleaming wonderland of Japan, and then abruptly leave me? Owen's departure left me in pieces, with the throbbing regret of lost potential and a list of unanswered questions. He had mesmerized me while he was with me, then snapped me in half with his impersonal brush-off.

Over the next weeks I slipped from sad to inconsolable. Owen inhabited both my waking thoughts and my subconscious, especially as I fell asleep each night. Owen came to me as a semi-illuminated figure in his fort, hovering over me as I tried to sleep, both alluring and threatening. Several times I reached up to touch him only to be stunned awake by the chilled dormitory air blowing on my outstretched fingers.

I had dealt with the death of my dad. But Owen vanished and I didn't understand. He was gone, yet still here, alive on the other side of the earth. His vanishing could be undone, he could come back, or I could go there, not like my father who was nowhere or somewhere I couldn't access. Owen had given me a lame excuse for why he was returning to Japan, something to do with his mom being called back to the family business. But why couldn't he have stayed at Northwestern to finish college? There had to be some *real* reason for his hasty departure, but I couldn't figure out what it was. Why would his rejecting magnate dad call him back to Tokyo so soon after he'd arrived in Evanston?

I refused to text, email or look him up on social media. I'd be damned if I was going to be one of those girls who chased after guys who showed no interest. I slogged through my classes and homework for the rest of the semester. All young women fall in love, but for me, my love was magnified and intertwined with an exotic foreigner who was out of my reach, in a faraway place, one that up until recently, I hadn't thought of at all and now, thought about constantly. *Owen. Owen in Japan. Owen and me in Japan together.* And now a layer of mystery. Was the family business the real reason for their sudden departure? Why did his father disapprove of him? And why all the push-pull, hot-cold behavior with me? He said he loved me, but, even those simple words seemed more complicated than they should have been.

I walked around aimlessly one evening as the semester drew to an end. The bitter wind from Lake Michigan cut through campus. I thought about how deliberate Owen had been about holding my hand until his mother saw. And our time in his fort, not only the abrupt end to our kissing, but also the strange aggressive way he'd grasped my neck. Had I felt anger oozing from him? Maybe it was chemistry I'd felt, burning through his fingers on my neck.

He contacted me once, two months after he left Illinois, by text. "Sorry Lu. Sorry." Another apology, but no explanation of why he hadn't been in touch. Nothing hopeful or promising, just those sparse fragments of sentences. I texted him back, asking when I could visit. He didn't reply. I was destroyed. I'd believed him and now, more silence. Thoughts of Owen clutched at my chest and burrowed into some side space of my brain, where they remained, confounding me. I grieved again as I'd done after my father died, but this time my sorrow was tinged with shame at the incomprehensible way he'd abandoned me. I hoped his grandmother's tea set had gotten smashed to bits on the trip back to Japan.

My pain lingered into the holidays, until Rose threatened to call my mom or take me to a psychiatrist. When Chris Tidy, the captain of the men's tennis team, asked me to a New Year's party I accepted. Since Rose thought that was normal behavior, she didn't force me to visit the campus shrink. But I only went out with Chris one time. I hated dancing close to him and I jumped back when he tried to kiss me on the dorm's snowy doorstep at the end of the night. I could only imagine two kisses I'd ever want again, from my father or from Owen. All others seemed irrelevant, wrong.

It was the same story for the other dates during my last year of college. When a boy tried to hold my hand or give a goodnight kiss, I turned to ice. Rose dated, went to parties and movies and dinners out, told me about her kisses and more. She snapped sexy selfies and posted them online or sent them to boyfriends. But I was not only celibate after Owen left, I was utterly uninterested. Nothing in my Illinois world could live up to the mysterious appeal of Japan, the memory of Owen and the fire I felt when he touched me.

It was the mystery of Owen's departure and the alluring, alarming nature of my love for him, comingled with the appeal of exotic Japan, of Owen and me in Japan together, that drove my decisions, good and bad, for the following years. A catalyst, I guess that's what you'd call it, a force powerful enough to alter the trajectory of my life. Like the mist that rises off of Lake Michigan and dissipates into the open sky, magnetic Owen and his beautiful mom had flown off into the ether, away from Evanston toward their rising sun homeland, the place where I longed to be. Without fully or even partially comprehending all the "whys" of my behavior, I was driven forward by Owen Ota.

Partly, it might have been that the raw combination of losses, losing my father then losing Owen in such quick succession, pushed me over the edge into obsession about Owen, about Japan. Or that Owen's and my shared status as fatherless —me, because my father was dead, him, because his father disapproved of him—caused me to fixate on him as my male "other," a man to fill my emotional void, while I believed I could fill his need for love and respect.

On a snowy evening before my last semester I tried to look up the *haiku* Owen had published, to find it online, but couldn't. Each promising link said, "content removed," or "link broken." Frustrated I told myself I didn't care what he wrote in his stupid *haiku*. But the fact was I couldn't stop caring. And in my memory, more than the fancy dinner at his house, or the hand holding, kisses or the time we spent in his musty, rose-scented fort, the heat of his fingers on my neck is what stuck with me most. Owen Ota had burned himself into me.

CHAPTER ELEVEN

In the spring semester I enrolled in "History and Culture of Japan," "Japanese Language," and "U.S. and Japan, Military Ties," and declared Japanese history as my new minor for my journalism major. It would be a crunch to squeeze in the requirements during my last semester, but I was determined. "An unusual combination," my mom said. "When did you develop an interest in Asia?"

"Japan, Mom. Not all of Asia. I read about it and it's fascinating. Since they offer it as a minor, I figured why not?" It was a fib. My mom and I didn't talk about meaningful things anymore and I'd never told her about Owen.

"Okay. Whatever you say, Dear. As long as you're happy." I pictured her on the other end of the phone, smaller and skinnier than she used to be, curly hair like mine—the only trait she, my dad and I shared—pale skin from months inside, perched these days on a kitchen stool.

Though I'd been wallowing in self-pity over the past few months, I'd also been tracking my mom, calling her three times a week. She'd become as predictable and routine as the sunrise;

up early, work hard teaching her second-grade class, eat dinner alone at the kitchen table, call me once a week. It used to be that she and my dad would drink too much wine at home on Friday nights and go out with friends on Saturday. But she didn't see friends anymore and spent her weekends volunteering at her school, at the women's shelter, at the church thrift shop, at the senior center. I worried about her, but only when I wasn't wondering about Owen. How was he? Where was he? Did he miss me as much as I missed him? He'd said he loved me, and I clung to that notion. Maybe his father wouldn't let him contact me. Stubbornly, I still refused to search for him online or contact him by phone.

I immersed myself in my Japan studies and in *North by Northwestern*. Rose and I drifted apart over the winter, she with her new, serious boyfriend Marcus, me with the journalism clique. As the snow drifts piled shoulder-high on the edges of Northwestern's campus, I dug myself into a cave of loneliness, busying myself while keeping social interaction at bay.

I found slight relief in *North by Northwestern* and worked my way up from the "Life & Style" section to front-page stories. The editor assigned me a headline piece about the dean's sudden and surprising resignation. I located the dean's near-campus house and waited for him to return, then persuaded him to answer a few questions. My story, "Dean Heads Home to Montana Ranch," garnered good reviews from my peers. I found that story research and writing gave me a glimmer of peace. Journalism was the only thing other than Japanese studies that could hold my interest.

I tackled a story about accusations of racism in the Greek system, and another about the lack of adequate funding for low-income students. By researching topics and especially by interviewing people—a student who believed he didn't get accepted to a fraternity because he was from Sudan, a woman from Rockford who had to drop out because her loans and scholarships weren't enough to pay her tuition—I got a worldly education without taking a beating from the real world. Through college journalism I matured in a specific, limited way. Being a college reporter gave me a view of the broader world, but at a safe distance from real-world conflict, protected by the incubator of academia.

I finally learned to put together a presentable outfit—I had to, so I could conduct in-person interviews for my stories. I had the dim realization that I might be a grown up, with two broken hearts behind me already, one from my father and one from Owen Ota. And there was the burning hope that Owen would unbreak my heart, if only he'd contact me, invite me to Japan again. I'd happily graduate and move to Tokyo.

On one of our infrequent dinners out Rose asked if there was anyone special and I told her that men were boring. *Compared to Owen Ota,* I could have sworn I heard her say, though she didn't say anything.

As senior year ended, my mother hinted that she'd been trolling back home for boyfriends for me. "The Winkler's son, Gregory, he's moving back to be the bank manager," she said. "He was always so polite. Good-looking too." Her voice was loaded with shaky hope. Most small-town girls like Rose and me tended to stay close to home and marry salt-of-the-earthers like Marcus, who came from a nice family in Springfield. That was the safest path, the expected trajectory.

"Mom, I don't know that I'm moving back to Oakville when I graduate. I'm looking for jobs in Japan."

"Oh."

"I've got applications out to ten newspapers there." *Good for you, Lu,* my father whispered in my ear.

"Okay, Dear." Sad, tolerant acceptance. That was the best I

could hope for from Mom.

She would have been aghast had she known the relentlessness of my fixation on Owen. She'd hadn't a clue about why I'd minored in Japanese history. Admittedly, it was a somewhat unusual combination. A major in journalism and a minor in Japanese history didn't seem like an obvious combination. And I hadn't been able to use my growing knowledge about Japan at *North by Northwestern*. The demand had been for stories about politics, and issues of interest to the Middle Eastern student population, stories about their religious practices or their immigrant families, their opinions about North Korea and Isis. No one in my Illinois world talked about Japan at all, outside my classes. "Japan isn't really on the radar these days," the editor said.

A month before graduation Rose and I reignited our friendship. "You actually learned how to dress," she said, poking me on the arm, fingering the red silk blouse I was wearing, the closest I could find to the luxurious color Mrs. Ota had worn. Rose was incredulous when I told her I'd changed my minor to Japanese history. "You're fixated on Owen. You realize that," she said.

"I don't think about him," I lied.

"You don't have to *think* about someone for him to be part of you," she said. "A person or a memory just sits inside you and you have no choice about it."

Rose married Marcus right after graduation and moved to Springfield with him when he got a job at the community college. While searching for jobs in Japan, I got an offer from the *Chicago Sun-Times* as an education reporter. To save money, I stifled my pride, moved back in with my mom and took the L downtown every day.

And so, my life after college was much like my life during college. Writing stories about people living in the broader world—teachers, union activists, low-income students struggling to thrive in school—while I remained cocooned in the familiar shelter of my Illinois home. On days off I continued my Japan job search. I concocted a plan to show up in Tokyo, as a professional woman by then, and confront Owen. I'd tell him I forgave him for leaving me and hoped, against hope, we'd pick up where we left off.

Every day after work, I combed through newspapers, magazines, online publications and blogs in Japan. I'd taken to sipping wine at the kitchen table the way my father used to do. I never got drunk but was often pleasantly blurry when I shuffled up to my bedroom. My mother would come by my room, see me on the bed with my computer and a wine glass on the bedside stand. She'd roll her eyes and I knew what she was thinking, but she never said anything.

For a year, things carried on this way, more or less the same daily routine: work, job search, drink, fall asleep. Then one night in May, exactly a year after I'd graduated from college, I sat at the computer, tipsy, and found a small English-language newspaper, *Okinawa Week,* with a promising opening, "local reporter." I scrolled through its content, mainly stories about American military and their interactions with the Japanese: "U.S. Marines Host Naha Schoolchildren," "Dragon Boat Races, U.S. Navy versus University of the Ryukyus."

Okinawa was an island south of mainland Japan, more rural and less developed than cities like Tokyo, and full of American military people. Owen had mentioned that his "successful" brother worked in Okinawa. I wondered how many newspapers there could be on the island. I scanned the masthead and boom! there it was, the name of Owen's brother, "Hisashi Ota, Photographer." I could hardly believe it. Knowing I'd never get the job, I filled out the online application anyway, attached my resumé and clicked "submit."

One day later, the publisher of *Okinawa Week* e-mailed me with an offer. "We don't usually get applications from the U.S. Your credentials are excellent," he'd written. He didn't even ask for a phone interview. Stunned, I emailed my acceptance. The company would pay for my move and in one short month, I'd be in Japan. It was almost too much to take in.

I called Rose to tell her about my new job in Japan and she laughed. "You're going to hunt down Owen?"

"No. I studied Japanese history and culture. I want to experience what I read about." I realized my voice was soaked with defensiveness. I decided not to tell her about Owen's brother.

"Okay. Whatever you say. I'm happy for you then."

When I told my mom, she was silent. In the year since I graduated from college and moved back home, we'd managed a predictable routine as roommates. We ate dinner together most nights and watched TV news before she went to bed and I'd stay up later, prowling for jobs online, drinking. Mom hadn't perked up much in the three years since my father died, but seemed okay with her quiet, small life, with just two years to go until she could retire. Her face went blank when I told her I'd be living on the island of Okinawa.

"Are you upset that I'm leaving?" Our roles had reversed, and I fussed over her well-being as if she were my kid. I worried she'd become more depressed when she was alone in the house again.

"Not exactly. Surprised, yes, but not upset. Your focus on Japan has been a surprise to me since it started."

I'd never told my mom that Owen existed, much less that I was willing to move to Japan in part so that I could find him.

She'd treated my interest in Japan with amusement, and she'd humored me when I talked to her about news from the country or showed her photos of pretty tea sets.

"Hey, maybe I'll meet a nice military man there," I joked, but she didn't laugh.

"If you're happy, I'm happy," she said, her lips trembling. "I mean it." She hugged me and I felt her tears on my neck.

Startled by her unusual display of emotion, I mumbled, "Thanks." I headed to my bedroom. It must indeed seem strange to her that I would pick up and move around the world, especially since I'd never been out of the Midwest. Pity poked my throat. My mom was where she'd always been and where she'd always stay.

Okinawa wasn't Tokyo but it was Japan and I couldn't believe my luck at landing a job there, especially since so many of my journalism peers were unemployed or only had part-time gigs. I fought off my desire to call Owen. I wanted to wait to contact him until my arrival in his country was imminent. Waiting was excruciating – I was nervous he wouldn't be happy to hear from me. When my move to Japan loomed a week away, I gave in and texted him. My hands shook as I told him I'd be moving to Japan. "Will be living in Okinawa," I texted, "working with your brother. See you soon?"

For an entire day, there was no reply. I was incredulous that he was ignoring me. Could he be mad that I'd be at the same newspaper as his brother? Maybe that was weird. Should I ask Rose if it was weird I'd be working with Owen's brother? She'd tell me the truth.

I sat in my bedroom on the verge of panic. Then, my phone rang. It was Owen's cell number. I composed myself, took a deep breath and answered.

"Lucy?" It was a woman's voice, not Owen's. "Is this Lucy?" The sudden realization that Mrs. Ota, not Owen, was on the other end of the phone.

"Mrs. Ota?"

"Yes, Lucy. I'm sorry to call you, but I saw that you texted Owen."

"Yes," I stammered, dumbfounded.

"Lucy," her voice cracked. A long, silent pause, then, "Owen's not well. He won't be able to see you. I'm sorry."

I sat down on my bed. The walls of my room were undulating, liquid. At some point Mrs. Ota repeated, "He's not well." I managed to get out one question, why? "He's not a happy person. He tried to take his own life."

Ice washed over my skin and tears burned down my cheeks. I don't know what I said to Mrs. Ota in that moment, but she said to me, "I have the tea set Owen wanted to give you. When you come to Japan, it's yours. My husband and I don't want to leave Tokyo right now, but my older son has promised to deliver it to you in Okinawa." So, Owen had told his mother about gifting me the tea set and his brother, my soon-to-be coworker, knew that I was coming.

"Where is he?" I had to ask.

There was silence, then her voice, barely audible. "Owen is in Tokyo, but he won't tell us where he's staying. We know he recovered, but he doesn't want to see his family."

"I'm so sorry," I said, and added I hoped to see her in Japan.

We hung up and I slumped on the bed. Mom called for me to come down for dinner. But I couldn't get up. *Owen tried to kill himself.* The heavy truth throbbed in my skull with the rush of my pulse. *Why? Why didn't I call him after he left?*

I berated myself for being stupid and stubborn. How could I be so shallow and full of pride? What if I had called him? Would it have made a difference to know I still loved him? I recalled his empty eyes in my dorm courtyard the day he left, and his strange push-pull behavior with me all along. I should have known something was wrong. I was stupid, assuming his erratic behavior was about *me*.

I don't know how long I stayed on my bed, but the room was dark, and the house was silent. I opened my computer. In a few clicks I found a link to a newspaper article in the *Japan Times*. "Ota Heir Attempts Suicide in *Aokigahara*." It was dated December 20, 2016, two months after Owen left Illinois. Needles ripped across my skin.

"Owen Ota tried to hang himself on a dismal November day, a day that saw suicides by a gunshot to the heart, an over-dose of Percocet and another hanging on another dark tree limb. Busy, even for Suicide Forest, Aokigahara," the story began. I could barely breathe. *"A source close to the family said that Ota's mother, Mika Ota, and father, Kenzo Ota, would take a short leave and then carry on with the family business. Ota has a brother, Hisashi, who lives and works in Okinawa. Ota's father released a statement. 'Mika, Hisashi and I are deeply ashamed by the actions of my youngest son.'"*

His father said Owen brought *shame* to the family. I'd read about the Japanese culture of shame, so many reasons for people to feel ashamed. Poor performance at work, financial troubles, relationship issues, it seemed that anything could cause a Japanese person to be riddled with shame. But Owen?

It was too much. He'd not only abandoned me; he'd brought *shame* to his family. My throat clutched shut and tears soaked my already wet pillow. Another thud of sorrow hit me. Owen had gone into a Japanese forest and tried to hang himself, in *Aokigahara*, Suicide Forest.

The name caused a chill to roll up my spin. How could such a place exist? In all my talks with Owen, all my studies at school, I'd never heard of it. A new image of Japan swirled and bubbled through my brain. It was a country with a forest devoted to suicide. I didn't dare look it up because I wasn't willing to learn where it was or what it was. My imagination painted it in dark green and black with heavy, threatening trees and quicksand mud on the ground, and my sweet Owen swinging from a tree branch. I choked back another flood of tears.

I started to compose an email to the publisher who'd hired me, to tell him I wasn't coming to Okinawa. My mom padded down the hall past my door, slowed, then kept going downstairs. A Japanese island without Owen was not a place I had ever considered. All my imaginings of Japan featured Owen by my side. I let fly one primal yelp that drew my mother half-way back up the stairs.

Through tear-blurred eyes I surveyed my bedroom, with its mismatched assortment of furniture, the faded poster of my childhood hero, Martha Gelhorn, over my bed. She was a female war correspondent during World War I, was married to Ernest Hemingway. Now she stared at me from the wall, daring me to stick with my plan to move to Japan, chiding me not to remain cloistered at home, wallowing. *Go and find out why,* she seemed to say. *Go to Japan.*

Hisashi, the "successful photojournalist," would bring me the tea set, Mrs. Ota said. Maybe he'd be willing to talk to me about Owen, to help me understand. Maybe he knew where Owen lived and would take me to him. On the other hand, he might think me an interloper, a stranger crashing his family's private pain.

I didn't confide in my mom. It was better not to worry her with my convoluted emotional life. When Rose dropped me at the airport, she said, "Good luck finding Owen," and I swallowed my tears. My father, who had been silent for a while, whispered, *"Go, Lu,"* from a distant rush of jet stream.

CHAPTER TWELVE
JAPAN, 2016

The street protests raged on. There was no violence, but the rhetoric became more threatening; in one news photo, a protestor held a placard, "Death to Americans!" My driver mapped out a route, so we'd pass the crowds from a safe distance. I watched local news on the television in my hotel room, sipping cool white wine to dull my sharp edges. Outside every American base, Okinawan citizens raged, waved signs and chanted calls for Americans to leave their island for good.

As senior staffers, Amista and Hisashi were assigned to cover the rape story. I'd seen little of Hisashi so far, had no chance to talk to him about Owen.

"Did you see that sign on the outside wall last week?" I asked Rumiko, the only person in the office when I arrived on my second Monday at *Okinawa Week*. Her disdainful glances during my first week there had irritated me and emboldened me to be more direct.

"*Hai*." She smiled reassuringly at me. "So sad. Such shame."

Had she meant to say, "Such *a* shame," meaning that the

situation was a shame, or had she actually meant to indicate the shame that she believed Midori must be feeling? Rumiko's face was polite and blank, unfazed.

"Wait," she said. She took the pencil from behind her ear and pointed to the sketch on her big drafting table. "Ah, Lucy. Look. Midori," she said.

I leaned in close. Rumiko had replicated in pencil the school portrait of Midori, but had filled Midori's eyes with tears, and had somehow drawn her adolescent face so the cheeks, eyes, and contours were weighed down. "Ah," I said, not sure what I meant exactly, just imitating Rumiko. "Ah, I see how sad she looks."

"Ah," Rumiko agreed, turning back to her desk.

I wanted to ask Rumiko if she thought the protestors were right and American military should leave Okinawa. I wanted to know if she considered me part of the group of Americans responsible for sullying the island. But if she did feel resentment or anger, she wouldn't tell me or let it show.

Then, "Stone should be shot." Her words rang as if fired from a gun.

I paused, stunned by her bluntness. I didn't expect such a frank comment from Rumiko. Still, it would be impolite for me to question her. I knew people didn't have debates or even open discussions at work in Japan. But I couldn't stop myself. "You're sure he's guilty?"

"Always guilty," she said, turning her computer screen away from me. "Sorry Lucy, I work. Excuse me."

Injured by her abruptness, I went to my desk. So, Rumiko believed Stone did it—the American was de facto guilty. I called over to her. "Well, I hope Stone didn't do it. And I hope Midori wasn't raped," Rumiko pushed her glasses up her nose and picked up her pen, as if I hadn't said a thing.

My other colleagues trickled in, but no one spoke. We kept

our heads down, avoided each other's eyes; none of us knew what to say in light of the charged atmosphere. Being an American suddenly felt more conspicuous than usual. I half-heartedly plunked around online and emailed my mom. She emailed back immediately. "Lucy, are you okay? I've seen the news. Do you want to come home?"

I assured her I was fine and that it wasn't as scary here as the news made it seem. The protests were peaceful, I told her, nothing violent. I didn't know if the non-violent protests would stay that way, but I didn't want to alarm her.

Rumiko's drawing of Midori had touched me and now I couldn't stop picturing tiny Midori, how terrified she must have been, how a beautiful beach resort had become a horror spot (if her allegations were true). I resolved to go to Manza Beach when I got the chance, to see the place for myself.

It was time to start my first assignment, a story about a retired Marine and his Okinawan wife, who'd launched a controversial new dating website, *MarryAmerican.com*, devoted to hooking up local women and American men. I'd read that some Okinawan women wanted to marry soldiers or sailors and move to the United States, and some servicemen wanted shy and subservient Japanese wives. I found these notions repugnant, but they also piqued my curiosity. Would I be able to find men willing to go on the record about this? Would Okinawan women be willing to be interviewed? Wasn't this akin to American sites like *Sugarbaby.com* or *MarryaMillionaire.com*, where daters chose each other for money or sex? And in light of the unrest on the island, was it okay to highlight American-Japanese couples who met this way? I texted Amista with my worries. She said *Okinawa Week* covered all kinds of stories, not just the biggest news, and I should consider myself lucky to have a fluff piece amidst all the strife.

During my research I came across a reference to "Bride

Schools," a set of classes put on by the American Red Cross for Japanese women marrying American men after World War II. In the nineteen-fifties, forty-thousand Japanese married G.I.s during the post-war occupation, and in the most patronizing, belittling way imaginable, the Red Cross took it upon themselves to offer to train the Japanese women on how to use washing machines, cook pot roast, host social events and so on, the way American housewives of that era did. It was sanctioned, gender-based brainwashing. That was more than a half-century ago, but to my surprise, in addition to MarryAmerican.com, I also found present-day social groups and nightclubs that existed specifically to connect American men with potential local spouses.

With that new information, the knowledge that as in the fifties, American-Japanese hook ups were a "thing," I wasn't surprised that it took only one day for me to find men and women to interview. I contacted the PR man from the website, and he gave me names. The first two couples I contacted were more than happy to be interviewed for my story. Since I didn't have a car yet, Ashimine-san hired the hotel driver to take me to the appointments.

The first interview was at a modest concrete apartment on a residential street with a *tatami* mat at the front door for shoes. The mat jolted my memory to the mat where Owen and I placed our shoes in his fort during a makeshift tea ceremony. At the time, I hadn't realized it was a traditional straw *tatami*. I was becoming expert at ignoring my nagging questions and memories while I was at work. When I was off work, I was a mess, drinking, worrying. Owen invaded my thoughts and I was itchy to see Hisashi again.

The door opened and I was greeted by the jowly, retired

Marine who'd launched MarryAmerican.com, along with his pretty Okinawan wife. He wore faded jeans and shook my hand too tightly. We sat on a tattered couch and before I could ask a question, he said, "I suppose you want to know why we launched this site." I didn't have a chance to respond before he continued. "I'm so happy with Kimiko here, I figured other couples could be happy too. She's the best cook and look at how clean our house is." Kimiko nodded and stared at the floor and the Marine patted her knee. "She never leaves my side and only talks if I ask her to."

I held my face in expressionless sincerity, tightening my lips to hide my disgust. "May I ask her a few questions?" I said, trying to look indifferent. He agreed to translate.

I asked if she'd always wanted to marry an American and she said yes because they were "nicer" than Japanese men. I wanted to know if she'd dated Japanese men before and she said no, only Americans. I asked if that was a common choice and she said she didn't know because she doesn't have friends.

The Marine jumped in. "She doesn't need outside friends. We're happy with each other."

I asked the Marine if MarryAmerican.com was successful and he said there'd been more than thirty dates set up in the first few weeks. "I'm not in it for the money," he said. "Just to help guys like me find gals like this." He again patted his wife's knee and kissed her on the top of the head. She shot me a serious look I couldn't read.

I was curious how this rough man had managed to woo this lovely woman, but no way I could ask that. "Your site didn't exist when you and Kimiko got married," I said, "where did you meet each other?"

"She was a stripper. I liked the bar where she worked, and I liked her better." As if she understood what he said, Kimiko looked away, ill at ease.

I left the suffocating house and took a gulp of air. I collected myself and headed to the second interview in a similar small beat-up home. There, a young Okinawan newlywed with bright blue eyeshadow told me, "Ray is sweet. He lets me go out for coffee with friends when he's at work." I cringed at her use of the word "lets." I knew some Japanese still adhered to traditional gender roles, but it was hard to fathom the type of patriarchy I'd encountered at the two homes. My own parents had been strictly egalitarian, and I wasn't prepared for such stereotypes as these.

Back at work, I slogged through the writing process, trying not to sprinkle the piece with my cynicism. My story was published two days later along with photos of the happy couples that I'd taken myself. "How to Marry an American," earned me a set of disgusted emails. "Since when is it news that Japanese women try to steal our men?" said one email, from a woman who called herself "Flyboy Wife." I showed this email to Amista.

"Obviously that's a woman whose husband is an Air Force pilot," she'd said. It hadn't been obvious to me. Across the room, Cece typed with her French-manicured fingers. Could the email have been written by her or someone she knew?

I also received an email from Nathan, the man I'd met at the seawall. "Nice story. You really nailed an *important* cultural subject. HA! How about lunch?" I didn't answer and flagged it, so I'd remember to respond at some point.

During my first weeks, Ashimine-san promised that I'd get a chance to cover bigger stories, but that I had to be patient. "*Chotto matte kudasai*," he'd said, a phrase he often repeated: "Please wait a moment." It was a bit of Japanese that could fit any number of circumstances: a delay in earning the attention of a waiter, a too-long hold on the phone when trying to schedule an interview. In Okinawa people said the phrase constantly, *chotto matte kudasai,* and Ashimine-san said it most of all.

"May I cover Prime Minister Abe's visit?" I'd asked, after reading that Japan's leader would be coming to Okinawa to address the protestors' demands.

"*Chotto matte kudasai,*" he'd said. "It's not yet your turn. You will earn your way to cover top stories." He smiled with such kindness that if I hadn't heard him, I would have believed he'd said *hai.* He asked why I didn't have Hisashi take photos for my MarryAmerican.com story. "You can call Hisashi any time," he said, but I hadn't been sure I was supposed to.

I wanted to talk to Hisashi, to see him again, but I didn't want to bother him. Amista had told me she'd been with him lately, covering press conferences related to the rape allegation. The trial date hadn't been set yet, but reporters from the mainland and from the U.S. were swarming the island and there were media events scheduled every day, different members of Midori's camp and of Stone's, making their cases to the journalists. Amista asked me if I'd like to tag along with her for those events when I was free. It would be a good experience, she said, for me to participate in such a major story. I wanted to go with her, but I was uneasy, not sure I could handle the anti-American hostility on top of the sadness I felt for the alleged victim.

Amista took on the role of my local guide and I was grateful. She was a friendly respite from the drama all over the island. She drove me around until we found a small, tidy apartment I could afford. "Typhoon-proof," read the rental sign out front. "Low price." We surprised the apartment manager when we turned up at the rental office. He was watching a TV game show with the volume up loud. He introduced himself as "Dah-tay-san," that's how I heard it, on the papers it was written as "Date." He took us up to see the apartment and, in the elevator, said, "New walls," and pointed to the gleaming mirrors on each side. I caught him studying my reflection, his expression a disconcerting mix of condescension and lasciviousness. I avoided him after I signed the lease.

Once I was in my new place, I spent evenings at my kitchen table with a fan pointed at my face, watching news with the volume off since I couldn't understand what was being said anyway, basically killing time until I could see Hisashi again. Tipsy on local saké, I composed texts to him then deleted them. Amista took me to cheap hole-in-the-wall restaurants and helped me buy a car, an old white Nissan with ivory interior. "Never buy a black car when you live in a subtropical climate," she'd said. "Burn your ass off."

"Hi Hisashi! Any chance you could help me with my next story?" I wrote but didn't send the text. I texted Amista instead. "Are you working with Hisashi soon?" She replied that yes, she was, and did I need him to help me? "No. That's okay." I wanted to see Hisashi when it was organic, not forced.

Ashimine-san hadn't yet assigned me a second story and Amista told me he was giving me time to settle in. During my free time I kept tabs on the rape case and avoided clicking on Suicide Forest again. I did look up news about the Ota family and found photos of Mr. and Mrs. Ota in tuxes and gowns at charity balls. Aside from the article I'd found before I'd come to Japan, the one that announced Owen's suicide attempt, it was as if he hadn't existed. Mr. and Mrs. Ota carried on, it seemed, with a busy social schedule. When I'd met Hisashi the previous week, I'd seen no hint of anger or pain in his friendly eyes. Did Owen's whole family, including Hisashi, believed he brought "shame" to the family? The word *gaijin* kept popping into my mind. Owen had called himself a *gaijin* both in the U.S. and in his own family. Maybe I understood now, a little, because of feeling like such an alien in Okinawa. So much was going on around me, so much conflict and drama, but I was on the outside of it all, an observer more than an active participant. Little by little, since my father died, and more since Owen left, I had sprouted a hard snail shell, a barrier to more pain.

At the office, Ashimine-san spent much of each workday in the basement with Higa-san, the grizzled, ink-stained pressman who ran the enormous, antiquated printing machines. They were the only people in the building whose first names were never uttered by the staff. It was always the surname with *san,* the equivalent of "Mister," Ashimine-*san* and Higa-*san.* All afternoon the presses growled and spun spools of paper at skin-ripping speeds and spit out newspaper pages, which Higa-san and Ashimine-san loaded into a separate enormous machine for collating. I figured Ashimine-san opted for such low-tech printing equipment because it was cheaper, but Amista corrected me. "He doesn't discard things that have value. Those machines may not be like the *Sun Times',* but they work."

Every day at two p.m., Rumiko got up from her drafting table, rustled around in the kitchenette and served hot green tea to Ashimine-san and Higa-san. She placed two unembellished brown clay cups and saucers on a faded grey lacquer trey and padded downstairs to Higa-san's basement machine room. And for that half-hour teatime, those machines clicked off and the office went still. No one spoke or made unnecessary clatter. After serving the men, Rumiko made a third cup of tea for herself and stared out the front window as she sipped it, turning her back to the rest of us.

Some days Amista and I walked up the street to a little

bento stand to get our own tea, iced instead of hot. "Don't be offended by the office tea service," she said one day as we walked. "Routine and rituals are the Japanese way."

I considered mentioning the sexist nature of the ritual, at least as it happened at *Okinawa Week,* and she must have read my face. "You'll go to a traditional tea ceremony sometime. They are quite beautiful. The Japanese culture is elegant," she said, and I recalled the same words from Owen's mother. The memory of the tea I'd shared with Owen percolated in my memory. "You okay, Lu?" she said, interrupting my reminiscence.

"You're only the third person who's ever called me Lu," I said.

"Who are the other two?"

"My father used to call me that, and Owen did."

"You knew him," she said, a statement, not a question. She'd seen my first interaction with Hisashi, so she knew. So, I told her we had been friends, more than friends, in Illinois. "You must be so sad," she said, motherly, kind. "When it happened, Hisashi was devastated, but he hid it and still does. Never mentions it at all."

"I think he's avoiding me," I said, hoping she'd offer insight. But we kept walking and she didn't say anything else about it. Her phone buzzed and she said she had to go to another press conference, so we hurried, and I worked up a sweat that soaked my snazzy pink silk blouse.

When we got to the office Amista pointed to the lone *shisa* stationed at the door and said, "Rub her head, for good luck." I ran my fingertips across her stone mane.

"We need to get her a partner. Our female *shisa* keeps the good luck in our office, but a male one would help keep the bad luck out." After what happened next, on my thirteenth night in Japan, I wished I'd already bought our second *shisa* protector.

CHAPTER THIRTEEN

I suppose I wanted to come face-to-face with Hisashi as a surrogate for Owen, so that I could begin to understand what had happened. It was possible that Hisashi didn't know why Owen had done what he did, and moreover that he didn't know much about our relationship. Maybe he thought I was just a friend Owen knew casually at Northwestern. He'd told me he had the tea set for me and I was eager to see it again, to see if its crimson glow was as beautiful as I recalled, if tea I made with it was sweet, and not bitter, as Owen promised it would be.

I sat on my futon sofa, sipping iced wine, inhaling the scent of cleaning fluid from the building's once-a-week maid. It was the thirteenth floor of a fifteen-story tower and my view was to the East, into bustling, tumble-down Okinawa City. There was a good-sized picture window at the back of the flat and I could see down to a row of small unkempt houses and a large grass courtyard where two cows slouched, tied to a tree. My apartment was also just outside Kadena Air Base, the largest base on the island, and close to a thriving shopping and eating district,

Kadena Gate Street, which Amista assured me was perfect for a "young, single person." Protestors were there, she said, but wouldn't get in my way.

I'd gotten up my nerve and finally decided to call Hisashi, ask him for photographic help with my next story, a piece about Okinawans who learned English so they could get jobs on military bases. I'd call him the next day right when I got to work. In the meantime, I had an evening alone and needed out of my tiny apartment where I bumped around like a pinball.

Though it was my fifth night in the apartment, I hadn't once walked around the Kadena Gate Street neighborhood. I'd gone straight to work each day, secretly willing Hisashi to be there, starting in my chair whenever the door opened, hoping he'd bluster in the front door again. I returned to my place each night, tired and disappointed. Amista had invited me for dinner a few nights earlier, but I pled exhaustion, which was true. I was limp from the lingering effects of jetlag, or more precisely the utter shock to my body and spirit of being in a new time zone, in a foreign and complicated country, and from the effort of learning a new job, along with the delicate navigation of an unfamiliar workplace with different norms. Owen's hollow eyes from the last day I'd seen him hovered around my consciousness, in bursts of sadness that were sandbags on my spirit. I'd taken to speculating, "What if?" What if I hadn't been so proud after he left Illinois and I'd picked up the phone and called him? What if, when he sent me his one sad text, "Sorry Lu," I had replied, asking him, "Sorry for what?" What if we'd stayed in contact? Would he still have tried to kill himself? I berated myself this way every day and my nightly drinking had become a slippery slope. I rationalized it by telling myself it calmed me and helped me sleep.

Amista had asked me several times lately if I was "okay." She'd given me a second message from Nathan. Since I hadn't responded to his first email, he'd tracked me down via the paper's general email box and asked me to call him. But I didn't want to. I changed my clothes and headed out to Kadena Gate Street. My sundress fluttered up around my legs and I inhaled the florid evening air. Creepy Date-san peered at me from his office window as I walked by. I figured he must sleep in the office because he was there whenever I passed by. He was leaning back with his feet on the desk, and the TV glow illuminated his sallow skin.

I rounded the corner onto Kadena Gate Street and squinted in the viridescent lights blaring over Aiko's Soba Shop. There was so much neon on Okinawa that parts of the nighttime sky lit up like a lurid rainbow. To attract the young soldiers into debauchery, Amista had told me, that's why so much neon. Protestors lined the street further up and I turned down an alley to avoid them.

The street was quiet, with the military still on lockdown and no carousing soldiers or loud music blaring from bars as I'd been led to expect. I started to open the door to a place called Airman's Ale House, but stepped back, confronted by a placard taped to the glass, "No Americans." Stung, I headed toward a curry shop up ahead that I hoped had no foreboding sign in the window.

A portly man with a baseball hat had been walking alongside me, and now he was too close, right beside me, so I picked up my pace. He dropped back but I could still feel him there, so I paused, pretended to browse a cell phone shop window. Infuriatingly, he stopped too, close on my left. I headed toward the curry shop and he followed. I lingered, as if studying the menu. I debated my options and remembered a self-defense class I'd taken in college. I recalled the instructor's advice to follow my gut. So, I turned ready to confront the man invading my space, to yell at him to leave me alone.

Just as I turned, four hands grabbed at the portly man's arms, yanked him to the side. I yelped and jumped the other way. Two police officers in powder-blue uniforms had the man in their grasp, and a third was putting handcuffs on him. A fourth approached me where I stood, frozen in place, unclear on what had just happened. "Miss, are you okay? Are you harmed?"

"Harmed? What's going on?" I was trying to process the purpose of this interaction.

"Miss, I am very sorry for this terrible intrusion. We are taking this man to jail for the camera on his shoe. Can you make a statement? Come with us to the station?"

"Camera on his shoe?" I said, letting his words sink in. The officer was young with round cheeks like a teenager. The concern in his eyes told me he didn't believe I understood the situation. He motioned toward a police car parked across the street. "Can you come to the station? This man was filming you. You didn't know this? Up your dress. I'm sorry to tell you."

I'd worn a new sundress I'd brought with me from Illinois. I'd chosen it that night because its flowy skirt wasn't binding and helped me stay cool in the heat. Why would someone want video of my scrawny legs?

"Miss. I'm sorry. Upskirt photos are somewhat of a problem. If you can make a statement, you will help us convict him."

Upskirt photos. The term rang a bell and I remembered reading it somewhere before, then felt a sickening thud in my head when I realized it had just happened to me. *Groping on trains,* I could have sworn Owen's voice whispered in my ear. The portly man stood ten feet away in his handcuffs, officers gripping his arms. He stared at me with no embarrassment on his face, no apologetic contrition. The relentlessness of his gaze made me shudder. "Yes, I'll come with you," I heard myself say to the policemen. My voice sounded like a shy child.

Inside the Okinawa Prefecture police station, the young officer hustled me through a large crowded work room and into a much smaller over-bright room with bare walls. He sat down on one side of a square metal table and indicated that I should sit on the other side. I felt disembodied, not fully connected with my physical self, seeing the scene from a distance. It seemed absurd that I was in an Okinawa police station; I'd never even been in an American police station. The room was like those I'd seen on reruns of *Law and Order* and *Forensic Files,* an old-fashioned interview room, claustrophobically tiny and cold, with uncomfortable metal chairs and a dark window that could have been a two-way mirror. Soupy with fatigue, the cumulative stress of the past weeks, and the sickness in my gut from what just happened, I almost laughed. I felt a crazy giggle welling up, pushing at the base of my throat, and I squelched it back with a swallow. The young officer would think I was nuts if I laughed at such an odd time.

Another officer, much older, came into the room, carrying a third chair, which he set down next to me. The words, *I'm surrounded*, leapt into my mind. And, *Maybe I should make a break for it*. Again, a giggle tried to burst from my throat.

"Miss Tosch," the kind younger man said, "we are very sorry to meet you under these circumstances. We apologize for your inhospitable treatment. Could you help us please, and make a statement about what happened tonight?" He spoke quietly, respectfully, his pen poised over a little notebook.

"Yes, we extend our apologies for your harassment," said the older man. His name tag said Daishi, and at some point, the younger man had introduced himself as Officer Tanaka. "We have called the American military police and they are on the way. We will ask you a few questions and then they will take you home, okay?"

"Military police? I'm not in the military."

"*Hai.* We know. You told us in the car," Tanaka said. "You are a reporter at *Okinawa Week.*"

I didn't remember telling him that, didn't remember the car ride. I was on Kadena Gate Street a minute ago and now I was here. "Okay."

"The military police are involved in all crimes that involve Americans," Daishi said. He sat upright, his hands on his legs. "When did you first see the suspect?"

"When you arrested him."

"You didn't see him following you?" Tanaka said. "On the street? For about five minutes?"

"Well, yes, I did. But I didn't get a look at him until you grabbed him."

"You were unaware that he took video?" Tanaka lowered his voice as if this was a secret.

"I only know because you told me."

"Miss Tosch," Daishi said, in an officious tone, "we would like to show you the video, so you can confirm that it's you in these images. The suspect hasn't admitted the crime, but we documented him filming you and two other women. Can you take a look?" I nodded that I could.

Officer Tanaka flipped open his computer and there on the screen in super magnification were my legs, the floral pattern of my dress, my underwear. My underwear, seen from a vantage point directly below. Pink cotton. Clearly mine.

I felt my face flush. I wanted to shrink away and disappear from this room, this island, to have the past few weeks erased. Humiliation mixed with the quiet recognition that I shouldn't be humiliated. Isn't this what they taught us as women? That being preyed upon is never our fault, nothing to be ashamed of?

I knew this to be true and yet still, the undeniable pressure of humiliation sunk down through my skin and settled into my bones as I sat in this tiny room watching my underwear on video along with the two officers.

"Yes. That's me."

Tanaka flipped the computer closed. "Thank you. Sign here. And again, please accept our humble apologies that you experienced this."

"Thank you," I said, not sure why I was thanking anyone, except that he seemed genuinely sorry.

Just then the door opened, and a man and a woman walked in. They were wearing white shirts with the letters USAF MP printed on the sleeves. "Miss Tosch?" The woman extended her hand. "I'm Officer Penn and this is Officer March. We'd be happy to drive you home." Officer Penn's hair was slicked back on the sides and she had a burgundy lipstick line in place of an upper lip. "We work together with the Okinawa police." I shook her hand and she continued, telling me that it was quite common to feel traumatized in these types of cases. She spoke with forced enunciation, as if to a child or someone with compromised mental function. When she dropped me at my apartment, she gave me her business card. "Captain Gayle Penn, U.S. Air Force, Sex Crimes Specialist," it read. "Call me any time. I'll call you tomorrow to check up on you."

Now I was someone who needed to be checked up on because some strange man followed me on the street? Wasn't that an overreaction? It wasn't *really* sexual assault, was it? I hadn't even been aware it was happening. The humiliation only set in afterward when I realized what the man had done. Certainly, this was a short-term humiliation, one that I'd shake off after a good night's sleep. If I didn't think I was a victim, I wasn't. Wasn't that right?

Date-san wasn't in his office as I passed by, thank goodness.

If he had leered, I probably would have punched him in the face. I called Amista right after I locked my door. "Lucy, he's just some pervert with no life," she said.

I lay awake all night, the words "sexual assault" rattling around in my brain. I had suffered the most minor type of sexual assault and my body felt pounded by a wrecking ball. Poor Midori Ishikori, if her accusation was true, must have crumbled into a pile of dust and ash.

CHAPTER FOURTEEN

I woke up groggy and cranky, in dazed disbelief about the upskirt assault. I shook myself awake and headed for work. The sun blazed through my car windows and I cranked the air conditioner. At this point I was adept enough at driving on the other side of the road and sitting on the other side of the car that I could manage talking on the phone at the same time. With the thirteen-hour time difference, I assumed Rose would be home after work.

"Lucy! You haven't called anyone in a week. Your mom's worried."

"Sorry. There's been a lot going on." I told Rose I was fine, just busy with work. I didn't tell her about last night.

"Have you run into Owen?" Rose thought teasing me was funny. She still had no idea what he'd done.

"I'm focused on the job."

"Fine," Rose said, in an impatient tone. "Well, how's work then?"

"Interesting."

"Did you find an apartment?"

"Yep."

"What's it like?"

"Small."

"Alrighty," Rose said, annoyed with my laconic responses. "I'm good too, in case you were wondering."

We chatted for a few more minutes. She told me about her latest hullaballoo with her jerky boss at the animal shelter where she worked. With nowhere in town to put her engineering degree to use, she'd decided on nonprofit work. We commiserated about the irony of a boss who was kind to animals but a jerk to people, and it was a relief to talk about ordinary things with a familiar person.

After we hung up, I realized I hadn't thought about Owen, or Hisashi, for twelve hours. With a sad rush, I also realized if my dad had been alive, he would have flown over to take care of me. Although he mortified me at times, he also protected me. He shooed away boys who bothered me, defended me if a teacher was critical. It would have helped so much to be able to call him. I didn't plan to ever tell my mom about the upskirt incident, didn't think she could handle it.

When I walked into work Amista said, "How're you doing?" I was so dazed I hadn't noticed Hisashi standing by Rumiko's desk. His face was ruddy, and his neck was fire-log thick. He looked gigantic next to diminutive cricket-like Rumiko.

I told Amista I was shaken up, but fine. "Hard to say I feel assaulted, although that's what the police say happened. It was so strange and so fast. The lady officer kept calling it an 'incident.'"

My coworkers gathered and I told them about the miserable unrepentant man, the camera on his shoe, the embarrassing video in the police office. Cece gasped and hugged me. Jed put his hands on his hips and shook his head. Rumiko's eyes clouded, and she said, "Sorry, Lucy." Even quiet Kei was visibly disturbed, frowning and putting his palm on his forehead. I was uncomfortable telling them about the incident, but in that moment of commiseration, my coworkers' supportive responses took away a bit of the overwhelm I'd been feeling.

Hisashi wrapped his trunk of an arm around my shoulder as though he was my best friend. He smelled sweaty but pleasantly so, like salt and sand, and his breath was minty, as Owen's had been. "I'm going to help you with your next story," he said.

I'd forgotten that my next assignment was about Okinawans who had jobs on the American military bases. A tiny wave of relief wafted across my skin. He grinned and put his hand on my arm. I felt a sedative rush from his touch, which was soft for such a large hand. He pulled a chair up to my desk and we spent the morning making calls and scheduling afternoon appointments. He stayed by my side, like a human guard *shisa*. With his connections, he helped me arrange three interviews by noon. For the first time in two years, I was more focused on the solid, bulky presence of the man next to me, than on the fleeting emotional apparition that was Owen Ota. Hisashi wasn't handsome, really, but his imposing size lent him a powerful masculinity. Owen had been mystery and nuance and skinny hipness, Hisashi was solid and easy to read. I still couldn't reconcile them as brothers.

After lunch Hisashi and I headed out for our interviews, the first was to be with a male student who worked at Camp Foster, the U.S. Marine base. He'd agreed to meet us at the Jusco department store down by the Sunabe Seawall. On the drive over, Hisashi pointed out his favorite restaurant, Sushi Ota, down a side street, the best sushi on island, he said. Then, "Owen loves sushi."

His voice was quiet, ripe with emotion. I wasn't sure what to say, what question to ask. My throat clutched and I rubbed my eyes. "I'm sorry. I don't understand what happened to Owen. Why he...." I paused, didn't have the proper words for my question.

"You were friends, right?" His voice was soft, sad. "That's what my mom told me."

"More than friends."

Hisashi glanced over at me, eyebrows raised in question marks. After a silent mile, he said, "It's been hard, especially for my father. Not easy for my mother, either. Or me." His sadness welled in my own chest, a lead ball of pressure on my clavicle. No way I could bring anything up now, to ask more questions. Again, I told him I was sorry. Another silent mile. He changed the subject. "Tokyo has the best sushi, best in the world."

This gave me an opening to ask about something else I hoped wouldn't be as sensitive. "Why did you move here from Tokyo?"

He smiled, relieved for the change of subject. "I'm of Ryukyu descent. My family is originally from Okinawa," he said. He explained that when Japan conquered the tiny island back in the eighteen-hundreds his family migrated to Tokyo, or Edo, as it was originally named.

So, the fancy Otas from the mainland were Okinawan. "Do you have family here still?"

"No. All in Tokyo. My father doesn't approve of me living here. He's a snob."

I recalled Owen telling me his father didn't approve of him, and now Hisashi admitted he was subject to his father's disapproval too. "You're a rebel, then?" I said, "different than your parents?"

"Not a rebel. Not a snob either." Hisashi told me he wanted to see what life was like here, to know how island life differs from city life, to experience what his ancestors experienced. A simple desire to know his roots. Now in his hulking frame, vulnerability, a man seeking answers, something we had in common.

"We both came here to find something, then," I said.

"What did you come to find?" When he smiled, I again noticed that his mouth was a larger copy of Owen's with small perfect, symmetrical teeth.

"Japan. I've wanted to live in Japan since I was in college."

"Why Japan? It's such a big world, how does a woman from Illinois choose Japan?"

Here was another opening, a chance to admit that my admiration both for Owen and his country had driven me to come to Japan. I could ask Hisashi where Owen was now and why he'd done it. Instead I told a half-truth, "I was fascinated by Japanese culture."

"Okinawa is the least Japanese place in Japan."

"That's what people keep saying. I understand it, kind of. But what do *you* mean?"

"Okinawa was its own country," he said. He explained that historically, Japanese looked down on Okinawans and Okinawans didn't necessarily feel like they were Japanese. "It's not a happy relationship, even one-hundred-and-fifty years later, there are sore feelings."

We turned toward the Sunabe Seawall and the ocean glittered in front of us, blinded me in a burst of sparkling pinpoints. I asked him if he felt Okinawan or Japanese.

"I'm both," he said, and then we arrived at Jusco, the six-story department store where our first interview would be.

I snapped into reporter mode. We hustled inside the enormous building and walked past a dizzying array of products for sale. Window fans, clothes, lobsters, antique tea sets, furniture, fishing gear, Macy's, Nordstrom and Chicago's Navy Pier all in one place. My nose started itching, assaulted by the odors of chemicals, fish, and other pungent unidentifiables. We took the escalators to the fourth-floor food court and Hisashi spotted our interview subject, Takayuki-san, sitting at a Formica table.

"You can tell that's him by the way he's waiting, looking around. See?" I did see a dark-skinned and muscular man with a dragon tattoo on his forearm, bouncing his knee impatiently.

Hisashi bowed to Takayuki-san and I dipped my head in what had become my version of a mini-bow, not a full and formal Japanese bow, but an Americanized head bob. I extended my business card as I'd learned was appropriate. Takayuki-san studied the card and didn't meet my eyes. Hisashi spoke to him in Japanese and we all sat. I set my digital recorder on the table. "He speaks English," Hisashi said. "You can conduct the interview in English."

"Thank you." I had my prepared questions on paper but was ready to go off my plan if he said something that veered the conversation in an interesting direction. I knew how to conduct a good interview, to ask questions with enough wiggle room to elicit colorful comments and spontaneous honest answers. I had been known at the *Sun Times* as a savvy interviewer, squeezing all I could from the dry education beat. Hisashi waited for me to take the lead.

"Takayuki-san, you work in the stock room of the Base Exchange on Camp Foster, what do you like about your job?"

Takayuki-san squeezed his eyes shut as if this question needed serious consideration before he responded. "I like making enough money to support my family. Before this job, I worked on a dairy farm and we were poor. Now we live in a nice apartment and have a car. That's what I like about the job."

"Is there anything about your daily duties that you particularly enjoy or dislike?"

"I like that I work alone, mostly. I stock shelves all day and it makes me tired, so it's better that I don't have to talk to many people."

"Do you have friends at work?"

"No."

"Are all of your colleagues American? Or are there some other Okinawans?"

"The stockers are all Okinawan, so are some of the cashiers. But most of my coworkers are Americans."

"Why did you decide to take English language classes? Your English is already very good."

"My boss told me that if I could prove that I'd taken a course, he would give me a raise."

"Even though you already speak English?"

"Yes. It's a rule. I had to take the class."

"How did you originally learn to speak English?"

"At the library, after my work at the dairy farm. I took courses online."

"So you could get a job on base?"

"Yes, it took three years, five days a week. But now, my family is happier."

I paused here and decided to go off script. "So, you studied for three years to get a base job and then you had to study the same thing again?" He averted his eyes and didn't answer, so I tried something else. "Do you enjoy working for the U.S. government?"

He shifted in his seat and put his burly arms on the table. I glanced at Hisashi, who was staring at this big, serious man with his near-perfect English. Takayuki-san turned to Hisashi. "Does it bother *you* to work with Americans?"

Without pausing Hisashi said, "No it doesn't. I'm happy to work with all of my colleagues."

"Well, then you are a traitor and so am I. I work on base because I have no choice. If I could work at an Okinawan company and earn the same, I would. I hate Americans. Defilers of our island." He shifted cold, suspicious eyes at me and sat back in his chair.

My skin went clammy and Hisashi sat forward defensively. Takayuki-san's words slapped my temple like another assault, and I wanted to run away, but I needed to ask him one more thing. "If you hate Americans, why did you agree to this interview? Didn't you know I was American?"

He glared at me now, coiled and ready to pounce. "I wanted to have the chance to tell one American how much I hate you."

Hisashi stood, took my arm and lifted me to my feet. "Thank you, Takayuki-san. Goodbye." He ushered me out of the store and to the car. My hands shook as I clicked on my seatbelt. Hisashi consoled me. "Listen, that guy is a typical worker. No respect for others. He probably waited his whole life to act like a tough man and tell somebody off."

"I could feel his hatred," I said. I tingled and burned all over, shot through with a blast of fear and adrenaline.

"He probably hates everybody." Hisashi reached over and pressed down on my shaking hand. "In Tokyo, people aren't anti-American."

"But you said they're anti-Okinawan?"

"It's complicated."

"Do you have any other American friends?" I surprised myself by referring to us as friends. He said he did and that we needed to push on to our next meeting, as long as I was okay. I told him I was fine, realizing with a start that utter overwhelm was my new normal.

The next two interviews were smoother. The director of the American Chamber of Commerce was an older agreeable man, who previously worked at the Naval hospital. He gave me stock answers, partly in Japanese and partly in English. He said learning English had been "invaluable" to his career advancement. The other interview was with a slender middle-aged woman who worked as a cashier at the Kadena Air Base commissary. She also gave pleasant, uninteresting answers, all in Japanese. When I asked her what she liked about her job she said, "All the people are very nice to work with." When I asked why she was taking English classes she said, "To be a better employee."

The interviews had gobbled up the afternoon and now the sun melted orange into the East China Sea. Being with Hisashi for the whole day comforted me some. We'd seen protestors off in the distance on parts of the drive, but the simmering battle on the island became background noise, at least for a day, and I hadn't dwelled on the uncomfortable upskirt incident.

Hisashi turned the car in to Sushi Ota, the restaurant he'd pointed out earlier. I was flattered he assumed I'd want to have dinner with him and didn't feel the need to ask me. It was comfortable, familiar somehow, to be with Hisashi. I had no idea why it was so easy to be with a relative stranger, a man like no one I'd ever known and certainly not like Owen. His energy was warm, like a favorite oversize blanket. As we walked into the restaurant, diners took in his bulk. He was imposing, towering over everyone, as magnetic because of his size and open-faced friendliness as Owen had been because of his cool confidence.

I was eager to talk about Owen, to dig for answers. But I thought better of it. For these few moments I would let go, try to unwind during a nice meal and a quiet evening under a full moon that illuminated the island with a phosphorous glow. With an illogical twinge of guilt that by quashing my Owen obsession for a few moments, I was disappointing him. I let

Hisashi wrap his powerful arm around my back and guide me to a table. He waved hello to the two chefs who smiled and brandished knifes.

The ornately carved knife handles shone and spun as the men skillfully assembled beautiful pieces of fish, rice and seaweed one at a time. Hisashi ordered cuttlefish, mahi-mahi and ahi, all fresh and delicious. Dinner at Owen's in Evanston popped into my head. I took a swig of saké and refocused on my surroundings. The restaurant was dim with twinkle lights adorning the sushi bar and candles flickering on the tables.

Hisashi and I sat across from each other and talked about the day. I told him I felt doused in antagonism from all directions, from the angry interview with Takayuki-san, the upskirt incident, the protests and profane sign at the office. He was attentive and listened without saying much. His broad open face sunk as the day went on; his eyelids drooped, giving him the appearance of a sleepy pit bull.

We were both tipsy by the time we left the restaurant, with me in far worse shape, tottering, leaning. He poured me into the car and drove me to my apartment instead of to the office to retrieve my car. In the parking lot the moon washed us in a soft glow, and muffled voices, engines and music wafted over from Kadena Gate Street. It was cooler that night with a caressing breeze. Hisashi put both hands on my shoulders and when I looked up at him his head was part of the galaxy above, surrounded by stars. "Do you dislike Japan now?" he said. "Now that so much has happened?"

"No." And being drunk I added, "Ashimine-san is nice to me. And you are too. Rumiko, not so much."

"Rumiko is traditional. She likes you."

"I'm not so sure. She looks at me funny."

"That's the Okinawan way, to be cautious of newcomers.

Historically, newcomers to Okinawa haven't been friendly. But don't feel the whole island is against you."

"I get it. Some guy upskirted me, another guy told me he hates me, but I can try to be optimistic about Japan. I know no place is perfect."

"We agree on that," he said, "no such thing as perfection." He didn't move, just stood in front of me and the night sky shimmered around his head. Then, "Do you like me?"

"I do," I said, surprising myself with my honesty.

"Would you date a Japanese man?"

"I already have dated a Japanese man."

Then there was an awkward pause where neither of us knew what to say and the moonlight was shadowed by a cloud. Obviously Hisashi didn't realize I was referring to Owen as the Japanese man I'd dated. And now how could I ever tell him I'd kissed Owen, had wanted to sleep with him, had come to Japan for him?

He straightened, stepped back. "Wait. Today you said you 'dated' Owen." He made little air quotes with his sausage fingers. "Dated?" he said again, eyebrows raised.

I told him yes, Owen and I had dated, and that though I liked him, Hisashi, it would be strange to date him too, and didn't he agree? He squinted, said, "Okay, friends then," and something shifted in him, an understanding flashed in his eyes. And then as if nothing had just happened between us, he became his big, friendly bear self again.

"Well, I need to take time off work and you want to see Japan, right? How about we do that together?" He'd salvaged the awkward moment with the smoothness of a salesman. "As friends."

I agreed but was uncertain, told him Tokyo was the place I'd most like to see.

"Tokyo is great," he said. "Different. Fancier."

"I'm also curious to see Suicide Forest," I said, straining in my fuzzy head for the Japanese word. "*Aokigahara*. I read about it," I added, lamely.

Even in my tipsiness I felt him pull his energy inward. "You know that's where Owen went, right?"

"Yes," I whispered; unsure I should continue. "I thought seeing it might help me understand, give me closure on our relationship."

"*You* need closure?" Hisashi exhaled a long deep breath. "I'm never going to that place." His affect was flat, deflated. "Owen tried to kill himself. My family was almost destroyed, but we survived. That's all the closure there is." His sorrow was palpable again and I was sorry I'd said anything at all about Owen, or Suicide Forest. I was Owen's girlfriend for a month. Hisashi was his brother. I had loved Owen desperately, but even so, I knew better than to compare our feelings at that moment. Hisashi graced me with more kindness than I had any right to expect after my blundering comments. He kissed my forehead, said we'd be good friends, and left with the moon bouncing off his car as it trailed off into the night.

I plopped down at my tiny kitchen table, too drunk to sleep. I again Googled *Aokigahara*, possessed with the doggedness of an investigator. The more I'd thought about it, the more I wanted to see it, to go there in person. So, Hisashi wouldn't go with me, but that didn't mean I wouldn't go.

Online, there were grim images of a skeleton partially buried in dirt and leaves and a weather-worn piece of paper by a tree stump. An article said, *"Mr. Taka lost his house in bankruptcy in 2015. His suicide note said he was too ashamed to face his wife. It's the eighty-ninth suicide in Aokigahara this year. Despite government warning signs advising people to 'think of their families' and 'go back,' Mr. Taka walked two miles into the forest and shot himself in the head. He was missing for nine months until hikers found his remains."*

I shut my computer and stumbled to bed. In a fitful sleep dark shapes chased me through thick, tangled woods, Owen Ota kissed my forehead, my father blew me kisses. And Hisashi Ota stood deep in the forest, beckoning me to come further. As I approached, he dissipated, and Owen took his place, urging me to follow. I started to follow him but tripped and fell into a mossy bed of leaves and branches, was overcome with the smell of dirt and blood. I jolted awake, shaking with the hangover I already regretted.

My head was a pressure cooker of sharp jabs and dull thudding throbs, the pain exacerbated by the subtropical heat. I swigged coffee and squinted behind my sunglasses on my way to work, prayed there'd be no weirdness between Hisashi and me. I was warming to the idea of touring with him, my personal local expert on all things Japan and I hoped he wasn't upset with me.

As I Ubered to work, the street protests seemed smaller, more distant. I walked to the door and ran my hand over the head of our single guard *shisa*. Touching her as I went into work had become my secret ritual, an everyday gesture to sand my sharp edges. I hadn't forgotten about my plan to get her a partner, but in all the crazy busyness I hadn't had the chance. As I lifted my hand to the door handle, I froze. Red cardboard covered both glass doors, splattered with black painted lettering. "GO HOME OR DIE."

I glanced around to see if anyone else was on the street, but no one was there. There was no wind, no salty or fish smells wafting by, just florid stillness. Something brushed my arm and I jumped sideways. Hisashi stood over me. He reached up and yanked the cardboard down. The speed and aggression of his movement made me jump again. "Don't tell anyone about this," he said.

"What?" I scanned the bushes, the street, expecting to see someone lurking there, about to attack.

"It's just words." He opened the door and held it for me. "Don't worry about it."

I felt chastised by his dismissive tone. "But what if someone wants to hurt us or kill us?"

Hisashi wore an exasperated expression, his thick jaw tight, tired eyes harder than they'd been last night. "These things happen because *Okinawa Week* caters to Americans. But it's words, that's all. I won't tell Ashimine-san because it would embarrass him." I was dumbfounded. How could he be sure the threat wasn't serious? "Lucy, don't tell Ashimine-san." His voice had a softer, pleading tone.

My head was lead, and I was too drained and befuddled to argue. "Okay."

"You need help with your next story, right?" he said. "I'm free tomorrow." I knew Hisashi was solidifying my vow of secrecy by offering to help me with work, a story about the new English language classes at University of the Ryukyus, a piece related to my earlier one about Okinawans who'd learned English to get jobs on military bases. "I'll take you to the appointments again. I'll call the university dean personally to make sure he agrees to the interview."

"Okay."

"Lucy, don't worry." He spoke quietly now, squeezed my arm and went to his desk.

My legs wobbled as I went over to the assignment chart. Ashimine-san wrote our story assignments on an old-fashioned whiteboard instead of using the scheduling software on the computers. I hoped he'd changed my assignment to let me help

Amista with the rape story, but I still had the fluffy feature about the university.

At my desk I shuffled through papers, pushed aside press releases and notes and took out a clean sheet. I forced myself to concentrate on my story despite the tornado of anxiety flying around in my head. As always, I began my research online and hand-wrote a list of the names, phone numbers, and email addresses necessary to schedule interviews with the dean and with students at University of the Ryukyus. I could feel Hisashi watching me from his desk, but I didn't look up.

"*Hai*, Lucy," Amista called out as she entered the office, a friendly imitation of Rumiko. She held two cans of cold green tea. She handed me one of the cans and used the back of her hand to wipe sweat from her cheek. By the end of the day, my research was done, and my interviews were set. Hisashi and I hadn't spoken more than the words necessary to get the work done.

CHAPTER FIFTEEN

At my kitchen table, I considered what Hisashi had asked of me, that I not worry about the threatening sign at work, not tell anyone. No one had seen it but him and me; he'd torn it to smithereens and disposed of it before anyone else had arrived. I had to bite my tongue several times when I almost told Amista. Everyone, including Amista, had told me that protests on Okinawa were usual and not to be afraid of them. I avoided researching them, scared of what I might find, but now I was deeply afraid, my skin always jabbed by stress needles and I needed to know more, understand the context of my new world. I Googled "Okinawa protests." Up popped a slew of reports on Midori Ishikori and Airman Stone, new photos of the protests, mushrooming bigger and louder each day. "JUSTICE FOR MIDORI!" screamed one placard. "EXECUTE STONE," said another.

I also found many photos of past protests, including a thirty-thousand-person protest five years earlier when a U.S. Marine Corps helicopter had crashed on the campus of Okinawa International University, killing and injuring local citizens. I found another photo, from just a few years back, of one-hundred-thousand screaming, swarming people protesting the local deployment of new U.S.-owned Osprey aircraft. What surprised me most was protests not only popped up any time a crime was committed by a U.S. service member, but small protests went on all the time, every day of the year, outside U.S. facilities. A few more clicks and I learned that in Okinawa, seventy-four percent of citizens felt the presence of American military amounted to discrimination and that the Japanese government had promised time and again to do something about it but hadn't. I was floored. I didn't realize the animosity ran so deep and protests were so prevalent. I tried to recall if I'd read anything about this in school and was sure I hadn't. One professor had said Japanese officials often hid or slanted negative news.

The last two things I found online before I went to bed were about a hip-hop artist, Kakumakushaka, who had rapped about the deadly helicopter crash, and about a clothing company, Habu Box, which sold jackets that depicted giant Japanese *shisas* clashing with U.S. Osprey helicopters. In the photos grinning teenagers modeled colorful bomber-style jackets covered with intricate illustrations, a contrast of political upheaval and edgy fashion statement.

Lying in bed, I tried to reconstruct the Japan I'd imagined during my time with Owen. That Japan had been a beautiful whirlwind of family heirloom tea services, cherry blossoms and exotic people, a Tokyo that whizzed with advanced businesses and towering high-rises, all comingled with the allure of my love for Owen. Now the terrifying Suicide Forest was part of the mix and all around me danger and unrest. I had yet to see or experience any of the sparkling Japan I originally imagined. So far, my life consisted of sweat, low-brow journalism, an upskirt assault, and a pressure cooker of hostility, fear and uncertainty.

I clicked one more time on the angelic school photo of Midori Ishikori and then on the military headshot of Airman Stone. I sought solace in my music, closed my eyes and concentrated on the familiar low tones and crescendos of Leonard Cohen. It was no use. I awoke the next morning, tired and more discouraged.

At work, I was surprised to see two police cars in the *Okinawa Week* parking lot and four officers inside. Ashimine-san was having a quiet conversation with them while everyone else pretended to work. I went to my desk and flipped on my computer. Amista, Kei, Cece and I exchanged glances. Rumiko didn't look up from her drafting table. Jed blew in the door and asked what was going on, and Amista took him aside. Soon two of the police officers left and the two others appeared to take up posts on the sidewalk outside our front door next to the *shisa*. Ashimine-san gathered us around.

"*Okinawa Week* is subject of threat," he said. "Some crazy person has left a phone message saying he will kill me. He didn't talk about anybody else. Only me."

CeCe's rose-rouged cheeks darkened. She tended to be emotional and now her face was crumpling as though she might bawl. "Do they know who made the threat?" she asked.

"No, but they will look at the phone record. Maybe then they'll know. Point is, you are not in danger. Okay?"

Hisashi wasn't there. Did Amista tell Ashimine-san about the profane sign on the side of the building, the first one? Should I tell him about the second one, the threatening red sign on the door? In light of this new phone threat, I couldn't hold my tongue.

"Ashimine-san, yesterday there was a black-and-red sign on the door." Everyone paused, turned to me. "It said, 'Go home or die.'" Saying these words gave them a more frightening weight. I'd allowed myself to believe Hisashi's and Amista's assurances that mere signs weren't to be taken seriously, weren't real threats. But now that I'd spoken the words aloud, they seemed even more ominous than when I'd first seen them. Cece started to cry, leaving wet streaks in her facial powder. Jed let out a big sigh and Kei plopped down in his seat.

"You tell the police," Ashimine-san said, his wrinkly face tightened with stress.

I went to the officers standing outside and told them about the sign, including that Hisashi had torn it up and thrown it away. Within a minute another police car arrived, and I had to tell the story to two new officers. Amista poked her head out the door and asked if I was okay.

"Miss Tosch won't need to come to the police station today," said one of the officers. "But we will need to speak to Hisashi Ota. Is he here?"

"No," Amista said. "Not yet."

The officer handed each of us his business card. "Please have Mr. Ota call me."

When I came back inside Ashimine-san summoned me to his office, motioned for me to sit on an upright wooden chair to the side of his desk. With a gnarled hand he sipped from an unembellished clay teacup.

"Would you like tea?"

"No, thank you."

His expression was thoughtful, fatherly. "Lucy, I'll get to the point. Why didn't you tell me about the sign?"

My gut twisted. "I'm sorry."

"Don't you think I should know when my employees and my business are threatened?"

"Yes. I'm sorry. It was a mistake." I squirmed and stared over his head at the painting hanging there, two white swans in a pale blue lake full of green lily pads. Anything to avoid the disappointment in his eyes.

"Why didn't you tell me?"

I ticked over the facts in my mind. Hisashi's pleading request. The shock of seeing both the threatening sign and the profane one. And now Ashimine-san's disappointment in me. But I couldn't give up Hisashi to my boss. "I'm sorry," I repeated. "I didn't know what to do. I'm truly sorry."

"I accept your apology," he said. "In the future, you come to me. You respect me and tell me. I know things have been difficult for you here. Maybe that affected your judgment." He dismissed me and I slunk back to my desk.

I sat in my metal office chair and shivered, cold for the first time in weeks, a wash of ice on my skull. I don't know how long until the shivers stopped, but it was Midori Ishikori who crept into my mind as I absently thumbed through the material for my assigned story. I kept picturing her sweet school photo and I recounted the sordid details of the alleged rape at Manza Beach, ten miles up the coast. Hisashi came in, bypassed me, and went straight back to Ashimine-san's office.

I struggled to concentrate on my assigned story, about English language classes at University of the Ryukyus. I found myself thinking of how my story could change in light of the rape allegation and protests. Would fewer Okinawans seek English-speaking jobs on base now? How would Okinawans get to work and pass by the protests without drawing the ire of the crowd? Did the unrest alter University's plans to increase its English classes? I searched online for "Okinawan employees, American military," and stumbled across more stories in which Shinzō Abe had promised to reduce the American military presence on Okinawa. I wasn't sure my story would work with any angle about the rape case and protests, but I kept notes on all I found.

Hisashi came out of Ashimine-san's office and towered over my desk. "I told him it was my fault. You don't need to protect me," he said in a low tone so no one else could hear. He left the office in a rush. Of course, the interactions with the police and with Ashimine-san were disconcerting for Hisashi, but I couldn't help feeling that my drunkenness the other night had contributed to his shut down. He was a blank wall to me now.

There was a purple orchid on Rumiko's table, and I got a waft of its sweet scent as the front door whooshed shut. I thumbed through my story notes, uncertain that Hisashi would come back to take me to the interviews as he promised.

At noon, I conducted my first interview, a phone call with an analyst on the mainland who researched English-language training across Japan. Just as I hung up, Hisashi came back in. "Let's go," he said.

On the walk to the car, Hisashi's big frame protected me from the sun, but fuzzy heat waves hung in the air, blurring my view of the cracked sidewalk. A car whizzed by and its draft caused me to trip. I clutched his arm for balance. He stopped. "I told you I'd help you. You didn't believe me." We were facing each other in the almost-empty parking lot and his eyes were dark, serious.

"Since we both got in trouble with Ashimine-san, I thought maybe you'd changed your mind." *On top of my drunken outburst about Owen and Suicide Forest,* I thought. Hisashi had essentially ignored me for two days and I didn't want to upset him again, but I had to ask. "Why didn't you just let me tell Ashimine-san about the sign?"

Exasperated, he said, "Lucy, there's a lot you don't understand about Japan. You're a junior reporter and it's not your place to confront the boss with such news."

I stewed, wanted to retort that not telling him had gotten both of us reprimanded. "Then why didn't you tell him?"

"I blew it. I thought it would be better to ignore it. And it would have been if he hadn't been threatened by phone. That's never happened before." He stood square and straight, his shoulders blotting out the grove of trees behind him. "But it's still something for you to learn. In Japan, junior staffers know their place."

Fuming, I shut up and got in his car. I was partly angry that Hisashi had chastised me, partly chagrined that I didn't understand Japanese norms. The sky was darkening, and it started to drizzle as we drove to the University.

"Typhoon Fred is coming, a category three," Hisashi said. "It's like the island itself is about to explode. Even the sky is angry."

I'd read about the fearsome typhoons that struck Okinawa with regularity. They usually passed over the island without doing significant damage, but once in a while they were serious, and wrecked buildings and sent people to the hospital. The rain fell hard now and plinked heavily on the windshield and roof.

I broke the glacier of silence between us. "How bad is Typhoon Fred supposed to be?"

"I'm not worried," Hisashi said.

"You don't worry about much, do you?" I was impressed by his stoicism.

"It's my experience that worrying doesn't make any difference," he said. "If you worry or if you don't worry what's going to happen happens."

"That's awfully fatalistic," I said, not wanting to show how impressed I was by his attitude.

"That's my experience. Anyway, I choose not to worry," he said, as if the matter was settled and there was absolutely nothing to be concerned about. Then, "The university used to be on the site of a castle, Shuri Castle. Did you know that?" His rumbling voice carried easily over the sound of the rain and the car. He told me that the U.S. had bombed the university in the Battle of Okinawa and then the U.S. helped Japan rebuild it. "Ironic, isn't it?" he said. "And similar to the current situation. American bases give Okinawans jobs, but Americans also cause Okinawa pain. American is both bully and friend to Japan."

I thought about this as we drove along but didn't reply. Even though he was irritated with me, Hisashi was willing to share insight with me, to help broaden my perspective. I was grateful for that. Owen had been my *sensei*; now Hisashi was too.

The University of the Ryukyus campus reminded me of city colleges I'd seen back home. It had several large brick buildings and lots of trees and it also had a view all the way to the East China Sea. We raced up the wide entry stairway of the administration building and shook off the rain. Hisashi led me down a long hallway to Dean Aiko's office, a cozy room with a fireplace, wood furniture and photos of a family on the bookshelves; it could have been a dean's office at any university. He greeted us with a lopsided smile and a deep bow, handing each of us his business card, which we studied, and then we gave him ours, which he studied. He was trim and small, with perfect posture and thin strands of hair threading his scalp.

"Welcome, Miss Tosch. Pleased to meet you. Thank you for taking an interest in our English-language program." His English was perfect and unaccented, like Hisashi's and Owen's.

I dove into my list of questions, wanting this day to be over so I could go back to my apartment, drink wine, and wait out the typhoon. *Why did you start the program? How many people are enrolled? What's the average age of students? Do they have similar jobs, or do they come from different backgrounds? How many teachers are there and are any from the U.S.?* Then I asked him if the protests thwarted enrollment or caused people to drop out.

"Miss Tosch, University of the Ryukyus considers itself to be a friend to Americans. That's why we offer English classes, to enhance our relationship with our American neighbors on the military bases. Certainly, the protestors deserve to be heard, but the majority of our students are more interested in furthering their careers than in political squabbles."

I went off script and asked, "But isn't this more than a political squabble? Rape is a serious allegation."

The dean's face held patronizing sincerity. "Americans commit crimes. Japanese commit crimes. At the heart of it, the protests are political. Some people want Americans gone, but not everyone. As a descendent of Ryukyus, Mr. Ota knows that we are simple people with a desire for happiness, not conflict. Right Mr. Ota?"

I glanced at Hisashi, who, as typical for the last few days, was silent. He was smiling at the dean. "Yes, you're right. I'm here to find simple happiness myself."

"That's what I thought. The famous Ota family is gone from Okinawa, but one of their sons has returned to his homeland." Dean Aiko paused, and his face softened. "I know I am very late in saying so, but please accept my concern about Owen." My recorder was still on and I clicked it off, respectful of the private conversation.

Hisashi stood to shake the dean's hand so I stood too. "Owen hasn't made it to Okinawa, but he would love it the way I do," he said, bowing to the dean, who bowed back. The interview over, Dean Aiko took us on a quick tour of the classrooms, standard college rooms with rows of desks, blackboards and projector screens. Hisashi snapped photos of him standing with some students.

"Miss Tosch," the dean said, extending his hand, "I hope you got what you came for?"

"Yes. *Domo arigato gozaimasu*," I ventured, for the first time speaking in my limited Japanese to a Japanese person.

"*Domo arigato gozaimasu*," said the dean.

We got soaked as we ran to the car and the wind flung my door wide as soon as I unlatched it. We sat in the car panting, shaking off the rain. I glanced at Hisashi and he smiled. "Well done in there, Lucy. You did a great job with that interview."

Surprised by the compliment, I thanked him, happy for the renewal of warmth between us. Here was another opening and this time I would leap into it. My heart started to thump. "Do you mind if I ask you why your family doesn't want you to be here on Okinawa?"

Hisashi paused, shook the water out of his hair, then told me that his family was successful, integrated into Tokyo society, with rich friends, dinner parties, country clubs and so on. His father felt that their Okinawan heritage was an embarrassment, or maybe that if his colleagues knew, they wouldn't hold him in as high regard. "This has to do with class and skin color." Hisashi said. "In the past, Okinawans were poor fisherman and farmers. My mother, she's from a long line of high-society Edo people. Anyway, my father didn't disown me or anything, but I don't talk to him much."

Up until that precise moment, I hadn't registered that Hisashi's skin was on the dark side, could be called brown. Most Okinawan people I'd met were around the same color or a bit darker than Hisashi, except for the chamber director. He was pale, like Midori Ishikori. "Your father hides the fact that he's Okinawan?"

Hisashi exhaled heavily. "Hides isn't the right word. He just pretends his past doesn't exist, never mentions it at all. The family has been in Tokyo for generations now, so no one thinks anything of it." He turned toward me in his seat. "And anyway, don't all cultures discriminate against the darker-skinned members of their society, and against those who they perceive as 'other?'" I nodded. "But not all Japanese are like that," he said. "It's mainly an affliction of the rich."

"I wouldn't know about afflictions of the rich," I said. Raindrops exploded on the windshield and a little droplet hung inside the corner of the window. I plunged ahead. "I was in love with Owen." Hisashi sighed and said nothing, gathered himself up and started the car. "Wait," I said. "I'm sorry. I should have told you sooner."

Hisashi side-eyed me, didn't face me straight on. "Just how well do you know Owen?" he said, skepticism masking his broad face.

"We dated." I was flustered. "No, that's not right. I guess it's right to say that I loved him, and he told me he loved me, but I don't know for sure how he felt. After he left, I only heard from him once. Just one text."

"Dated," Hisashi said it as though it were a four-letter word. "You *dated* Owen." Sarcasm or disbelief tinged his voice, like an icy wind slicing my heart.

"We were young. I don't really know what we did. Just spent some time together, I guess." I couldn't feel my face or my fingers. They'd gone numb.

Hisashi face was frozen in a grimace. The wind was picking up outside and hissed through the edges of the doors. "Do you know *why* Owen wanted to die?"

"No."

"That was online too. The reason he did it. Didn't you find it?"

Now my face burned. I couldn't meet his eyes. "I couldn't bring myself to read anything more. I really don't know."

"Someday, if we become better friends, I will tell you about it." He emphasized the word *friends* and I shifted down in my seat, crossed my hands on my lap, resigned.

We didn't speak the rest of the way back to the office. When he dropped me off, he said, "Lucy, I'm not angry at you for your relationship with Owen. You just don't understand."

I braced myself against the whipping wind, held my soaked hair against my head with one hand. "Then help me understand," I pleaded. "Why did he do it?" My shoes were waterlogged boats and my clothes wet rags stuck to my body. He must have heard the desperation in my voice.

"Being an Ota almost killed him," he said with finality, so I knew not to say another thing. He shot me a sad glance and I got out of the car. He drove off into the grey and ominous evening and I slogged to my car and back to my apartment. The entryway to my elevator was a murky pond and trickles had seeped below the shiny mirrored door into the compartment.

It was dry inside my apartment, but wind roared during the night and rain pelted my bedroom window. Snuggled in my bed, I held onto my phone, but didn't dare try to look for more information about Owen. Both he and Hisashi had been shunned by their family back in Tokyo. Their father's disapproval had driven Hisashi as far away from Tokyo as he could possibly be while still in Japan, and it had nearly taken Owen's life.

I wiped a tear from my cheek. I would call my mother in the morning, tell her I loved her. In all my parents had done or not done for me growing up, I could barely fathom what it must feel like to be outcast by your family. I had striven to leave my poor, grieving mother, who would have done anything to keep me around. Hisashi and Owen had been rejected by their own father. I knew there was more to the story, that Owen had been so hurt he didn't want to live. But I wasn't any closer to knowing what it was.

I downed some cold sake and tried to sleep, hoped my dad would whisper comforts to me over the howling storm outside. I prayed that Hisashi wouldn't reject me now, the way that Owen had done in his fort when he simultaneously kissed me and pushed me away, and when he left me for good. I wanted Hisashi as a friend. His warmth and upbeat demeanor had brought me what little peace I'd felt in Japan. And I still had hope I'd learn more about Owen.

CHAPTER SIXTEEN

By the time the sun rose everything was still. It felt like the electric Illinois air right before a tornado strikes, when the leaves on the trees stop moving, hovering in anticipation, and the silence is full of tension and we think the tornado passed us by. Sometimes it had, but other times we shelter in the basement and gut out the worst of it, which comes right after the calm of its eye. We stay below, handwringing, until we know our house hasn't taken a fatal hit. Typhoon Fred, the TV news said, had come in and out like a whirling dervish and small swaths of rural farmlands were now sodden rubble and ruin. But a major disaster has been averted and the storm raged out into the East China Sea toward its next target.

My part of the island, Okinawa City, was spared Fred's brunt and the typhoon-proof windows of my building were intact. The protestors were back at their posts. A few downed store signs littered the streets on my way to the office, shattered splotches of bright blue and electric green, winking up from the sidewalk. I drove to work and patted my *shisa*, silently thanked her for protecting me from Typhoon Fred. I was the only one in the office and I quickly typed up a draft of my university story.

I was preoccupied by last night's interaction with Hisashi. *Being an Ota almost killed Owen,* he'd said. There'd been a heaviness to his voice, an exhaustion, as if *being an Ota* was an unbearable burden. I reflected on my minor part in the entirety of Owen's life, and a thread around my heart slackened, floated loose. When Hisashi blew in to work, I shot him my best smile, hoping he'd warm up to me again.

Amista came in and said I should tag along for her coverage of the rape story that day, an interview with Stone's military attorney on Kadena Air Base. She'd hit a wall with Midori's attorneys, family and friends; no one in the Ishikori camp was willing to talk. But there would be an Ishikori family press conference in two days, as well as the preliminary court hearing, where criminal charges would be filed before a judge. I asked her if Hisashi was coming along for the interview today too and she said he was.

I clicked around online, anxious, but also eager to spend another day with Hisashi. *MoshiNaha* had published a new photo of Midori Ishikori on its home page, a shot of her standing next to a black sedan. According to the caption it was taken at her home in Tokyo, in the driveway of her gated mansion. "How did they get that, if it's inside the gates?" I asked Amista.

"*MoshiNaha* reporters have no ethics. They probably scaled the wall." Her tan face was puffy, her warm eyes swollen. No one, not even strong, sure Amista was immune to the effects of the drama all around us. I made three strong cups of coffee and gave one to her and one to Hisashi, who gave me a little nod of thanks. I tried to imagine scaling a wall to take a surreptitious photo, and frustrated, understood that I'd never be able to do something so daring, so against the rules.

By noon Amista, Hisashi and I were stuck in a line of cars trying to enter Kadena Air Base. Our car was flanked on both sides by throngs of protestors. Some of the marchers did close, glaring once-overs of our car, of Hisashi. He sat tall, unaffected, and gazed back at them with his usual sociable demeanor. They looked at me too and I squirmed and turned my face.

Ahead of us at the base gates the guards inspected each car carefully, asked questions and even opened trunks and shone flashlights in them. "That's not normal," Amista said. "Usually cars zip through."

She had all the windows open despite the ninety-degree temperature, so we could hear what was going on around us; shop door bells chimed, a vendor hawked food from a small stand, car engines groaned in the heat, and the protestors chanted over the sounds of commerce. Their signs were in English, for the benefit of U.S. media Amista said, and one in particular caught my eye, "Americans Go Home!" a red sign with a black X through the word "Americans." It was carried by a tiny bird of a woman with a face like wet sand. Its black scrawl on a red background reminded me of the red cardboard sign that had been on *Okinawa Week's* door.

I fingered the digital recorder I'd put in my purse. Amista would record the interview, but I'd record my own copy, so I could review the conversation and learn how she handled Airman Stone's lawyer.

"On the way out, let's stop and see if we can talk to some of these folks," Amista said. This struck me as a scary thing to do, to stand face-to-face with people who probably hated me and at the very least wanted me gone. She read my face.

"Lucy, these protests aren't violent," she said. "That's a big difference between the States and here."

I hoped she was right. I could see anger smeared across many faces, but their actions were controlled and calm, and they waved and chanted in choreographed unison. Police on foot and in cars patrolled the area but didn't wield tear gas canisters or rifles as they'd done when protests cropped up in U.S. cities.

When we finally made it to the gate, the guards, sharp in pressed uniforms, wore pistols holstered around their hips. The head guard asked our purpose for coming on base. Amista told him we had an appointment with Colonel Abdir, and he referred to a clipboard, handed us a card to display in the window, and gave us a map with directions to the office. "Carry on," he said and waved us through.

I'd never been on an Air Force base, but it looked exactly like in the movies -- clean wide streets, tidy matched houses with identical white siding, manicured lawns, and flower-lined walkways with American flags waving by the front doors. One hundred yards behind us Kadena Gate Street was a blur of people and business, with trash on the sidewalks in front of bars and knickknack shops. The same road was now a Stepford, squeaky clean version of itself.

Amista pointed out a long flat concrete building with a large parking lot. "That's the BX, the base exchange. It's basically a department store. Good deals on makeup and shoes." I hadn't put it together that Amista had shopping privileges there because of her husband's status as a retired Air Force sergeant. So many facets of life on Okinawa, I hadn't a clue about.

We arrived at Colonel Abdir's office, which was at the end of a long runway and adjacent to an airplane hangar. The corrugated metal building reflected shards of sharp sunlight. I was excited, eager to have access to any tiny part of such an important story. Inside, a tall uniformed man escorted us into a room with a long wooden table, black office swivel chairs, and an American flag and Air Force seal in one corner. The man instructed us to sit, then shut the door behind him. There was no art on the walls, no books anywhere.

Colonel Abdir came in, shook our hands and sat across the empty table from us. He was trim with a tall forehead and a thick jawline and nose. His eyes didn't reveal if he was kind or cruel.

"It's not my policy to grant interviews about pending court cases," he said. "But I know you'll write a story whether I talk to you or not, so I'd rather I tell you the facts than you get them wrong from somewhere else. *Okinawa Week* has always been a friend to Kadena and our military families." He didn't smile as he said this, and his gaze was level at Amista. She didn't change her expression and neither did Hisashi.

"Thank you, Colonel. We won't take much of your time," she said. "I just have a few questions. I'm going to record you, okay?" In one fluid motion, she set her recorder on the desk in front of him.

"Yes," he said. "That way we'll both know if you quote me accurately." His eyes were stern, but he smiled as if he'd told a joke.

Amista said, "As well, Hisashi would like to take a photo of you to accompany the piece."

"Fine. And her?" He gestured toward me.

"She's new, learning the ropes. Just along to listen." I slid down a little in my seat, to make myself inconspicuous. She flicked the recorder on, and I turned on mine inside my pocket. "What is your official position on the guilt or innocence of Airman Stone?"

"Airman Stone is innocent. He had a consensual sexual encounter with Midori Ishikori. I don't know why she accused him of rape, but I have to wonder if it's because she later regretted her decision." He spoke in a firm staccato.

"Midori Ishikori is only fifteen years old. Isn't that statutory rape?"

"Midori Ishikori told Airman Stone that she was nineteen. He believed her."

"Does Airman Stone make a habit of hooking up with teenagers when he's off duty?"

"Airman Stone has a commendable record of service in the United States Air Force. We have no information indicating that he's broken any rules or laws when he's off duty." Colonel Abdir was unflappable, rehearsed.

"So, the Air Force doesn't have any rules about its ranks' sexual behaviors?"

"The United States Air Force rules are the same as the laws of the United States, only tighter. Service members are not allowed to do anything outside the law and furthermore, they are not allowed to have extra-marital affairs and are subject to disciplinary action if they do so. It's fair to say the rules in the Air Force are stricter than U.S. law."

"What is your response to Midori Ishikori's allegation that she was raped by Airman Stone?"

"Airman Stone did not rape Midori Ishikori. They had consensual sex."

"Is there any chance Airman Stone is lying?"

"No."

"Because rapists always tell the truth?"

Annoyed now, he said, "You are out of line, Mrs. Noga. I have no comment on what rapists do or don't do."

Amista didn't falter, pressed on with her questions. "What is your response to the protests right outside the base gates? What would you say to the protestors?"

Colonel Abdir paused, thinking. "I'd tell them that Airman Stone is innocent. I'd also tell them that if they have other reasons for protesting, they should take it up with their own government." The colonel stood. "I have another meeting. Anything else?"

"No. Thank you. May I call you again if I think of something else?"

"Yes. But if you call again, it better be with new questions. I won't waste my time going over the same things again." Colonel Abdir was how I'd imagined he'd be—efficient, stern, articulate, off-putting but impressive. And Amista had handled the interview with ease and slick professionalism. Hisashi snapped a few quick photos of the colonel standing by the two flags.

"He's smart, really smart," Amista said, as we headed back toward the gate. "Didn't give me *anything* that wasn't perfectly stated to make his case. I don't know if he believes Stone is innocent, but he's unflappable. At least we got direct comments, that's more than *MoshiNaha* or anyone else will get."

"I guess I didn't quite understand that part," I said, straining to find the right words. "Isn't there something unethical about granting one news source an interview and not the others?"

Hisashi had been quiet but now he said, "No. It would only be unethical if he gave different information to different reporters. If he altered the facts of the case in any way," he said, from over his shoulder. "Think about it, Lucy, newspapers and websites get scoops all the time. If a reporter does a better job making contacts and finding information, he gets a better story. Happens all the time."

"Right," I said, turning this over in my mind. Hisashi caught my eye in the side mirror and shot me a look, his expression amused. I almost laughed. I was as green as a reporter could be. I turned to Amista. "I've never seen anyplace like Kadena Air Base before."

"What do you think of it? I lived on bases like that for twenty-five years."

"Stepford neighborhood? Scary sameness? *Twilight Zone* perfection? Something like that," I said. "Even my hometown, Oakville, Illinois, isn't that homogenous."

Amista glanced at me sideways. "Okay, but on base there are black people, brown people like me, Muslims, Christians and everything in between. Is that true in your Illinois neighborhood?"

"No. But, I wasn't raised to look at color or to judge someone's religion," I said, defensiveness tightening my neck muscles.

"Not acknowledging differences doesn't mean they don't exist," Amista said. "For all the trouble the bases cause here on Okinawa, they are also real-life, functioning melting pots. Think about it. Where else but in the military do you interact constantly with every type of person you could imagine?" I was chagrined. I wasn't just a green reporter, I was a green person, a product of my insular suburban upbringing.

"Don't be so hard on her," Hisashi said. He'd been listening to our exchange. "She's young." And now he grinned at me in the mirror, as if he'd gotten some sort of upper hand by recognizing my inexperience, then turned to Amista. "Do you think Stone did it?"

"I'm reserving judgment until the trial," she said.

"He's guilty," Hisashi said. "Ninety-nine-point-nine percent of the time they are."

I almost piped up and said that's what Rumiko thought too, but as I'd been admonished to do, I kept my mouth shut.

As we exited the base, Amista turned onto a side street and parked in front of a store with bikinis and sandals in the window. We walked back to Kadena Gate Street and Hisashi and I hung back while Amista approached a young woman holding a baby in one arm and a protest sign in the other. The two women spoke for a moment and then we went back to the car. I asked what the woman said.

"She said that she doesn't know if Stone is guilty, but that she wishes the U.S. Military would leave Okinawa. Also, that she has nothing against Americans in general."

Hisashi said, "Did you point out how much business these little shops would lose if the bases closed?"

"I did," Amista said. "I asked if she was willing to see business here shuttered because soldiers were no longer customers. She said Okinawans and tourists were enough to keep the businesses afloat. And she told me I shouldn't be allowed to live here."

When we got back to work, Ashimine-san went to Amista's desk. "How is the story coming? Did the Colonel make a useful comment?"

"He said that Kadena has a special appreciation for *Okinawa Week,* and that's why he gave us the interview."

Ashimine-san bowed to Amista. "*Domo Arigato.* You make me proud." It was an intimate scene, two old colleagues and friends. It was beginning to dawn on me how deeply Amista was integrated into life here, with dual roles as a local employee and also as spouse of retired American military, who'd opted to live there permanently. She could rightly claim Japan as her home; it was part of her history and she was part of its economy. That recognition of her status also reminded me of how much of an outsider I was, in every possible way.

After work, I took a back-road route to the Sunabe Seawall and sat on the concrete barrier above the waves, happy to be anonymous in the crowd on the boardwalk. The evening was warm, finally a break from the driving heat, and the ocean breeze blew my hair into a fluffy cloud. The East China Sea glittered in the slanting sun like sparkling, buckling glacier ice. I looked at my phone, considered calling Hisashi. At some point we'd be able to talk more about Owen, but it would have to wait. Maybe he would find it creepy that I'd come all the way to Japan because of my feelings for Owen and my attraction for the country, even though I knew so little about it. Maybe he'd never want to speak to me again if he knew I had been romantic with his brother. Maybe too, I didn't really want to know why Owen had done what he did, or how he was now.

My reverie was interrupted when someone said, "Lucy?" I turned and there was Nathan, the man I'd met at this spot three weeks earlier. He was muscular in a fitted t-shirt, swim trunks and sandals. "How's it going?"

"Too much going on around here."

"I read your articles. Wow. How to marry an American?" He winked at me and smiled as though we were sharing a joke.

"I'm a rookie. I don't get to pick the story topics."

"It was interesting, actually. So was your story about Okinawans who study English." He shifted his weight from foot to foot. "It's about dinner time. What do you say?"

I couldn't come up with a reason to say no. Dinner with Nathan might take my mind off of Hisashi, and Owen, and upskirting, and threatening signs, and Midori Ishikori, and the turmoil that had consumed my short time on Okinawa.

CHAPTER SEVENTEEN

Nathan and I ducked into a cool, dark, mostly empty Chinese restaurant. We sat at a corner booth and flipped through plastic menus. He kept glancing up at me and his eyes were fringed in thick lashes, a girlish detail on a masculine man with a chest-breadth tattoo peeking from the top of his t-shirt. He asked how my first few weeks had been, and I shifted in the wooden bench seat, already wishing I hadn't agreed to dinner. Banter and getting-to-know-you talk felt like another oddity, a burden that I might not have energy for. But I would make the most of it, try to come out of my hardening shell, talk and think about non-threatening things. I asked him what military base he worked on and told him I'd only seen Kadena so far.

"I work and live on Camp Foster, that's the biggest Marine base. What did you think of Kadena? Since you're a civilian I bet it seemed strange."

"Yes. Like nowhere I've ever seen before. Then again, Okinawa is like nowhere I've seen before."

He told me people always have culture shock when they

first get acquainted with military life. "It's an entirely different world," he said, and explained that when he finished boot camp, he was assigned to San Diego. At first, he was thrilled to be in a beach town but when he got there, he learned that an entire population of people live and work on base and rarely go to the beach or anywhere else. He said just as some civilians in the U.S. would never have a reason to step foot on a military base, there were military people who never leave their bases. They work, shop, eat and do everything else without going outside the gates. "I could never hole up inside a base," he said. "Especially in somewhere as beautiful as Okinawa."

I hadn't been thinking of Okinawa as beautiful. Sitting across from Nathan, I felt a plink of loneliness. He was pleasant and attractive, but what was I doing here? I didn't have the nerve to get up and leave. As a military man, Nathan was as foreign to me as someone from Mars. I remembered the announcement from Kadena's commander after the rape allegation, that service personnel weren't to leave base. I said, "I thought the military was on lockdown."

"That only applies to enlisted. Officers can come and go as they please."

"Officers? I know very little, nothing really, about military ranks."

Nathan was amused. "Enlisted personnel don't have college degrees. Officers do."

I digested this for a moment. The waiter took our orders and then I said, "So, military people are penalized for not having a college degree?"

"No, that's not right," he said, an edge to his voice. He explained that officers are in charge, responsible for the enlisted in their units and that likewise, there were enlisted people in charge of other enlisted people. He said those in charge are expected take responsibility for their charges. "It's like a CEO, or a manager, versus a salesclerk. Different levels of authority and freedom. Does that make sense?"

It did, but something about it seemed wrong to me. "I dunno. What are you?"

He told me he was a Navy lieutenant commander and an internist, that the people he managed were other doctors, nurses, aides, paramedics and administrators, that it was equivalent to running a small hospital in the civilian world. So, he was a doctor, another type of person with whom I had nothing in common. I'd never felt so alone while eating dinner with another person. He continued, telling me that he was a "lifer," someone who'd stay in the military until he retired, then he'd move to some small town near a beach, possibly even Okinawa or one of the other islands in Japan's Ryukyu chain. I calculated and realized he was probably ten years older than I was. In another life, one where I hadn't loved Owen, I'd have found Dr. Nathan attractive, as handsome and smart as he was.

"What brought an aspiring journalist all the way to Divorce Rock?"

"I get asked that question a lot. Apparently, I'm a bit of an anomaly. It's a long story," I said. I had no desire to share my feelings with him, changed the subject and asked for his story. Without skipping a beat, he said he'd been married to his college sweetheart and six years ago, right after they arrived on Okinawa, she had an affair with a Marine.

"We got divorced and she married him. End of story." I felt a twang of pity for him. He was so tough, but sadness floated around the corners of his pretty eyes.

"No wonder you call this place Divorce Rock."

"I'm not bitter," he said. "Quite the opposite. I work and when I'm off I tour around. I like it here so much I've extended my tour of duty twice."

"Don't you have to go to Afghanistan or Iraq or somewhere

terrible like that?" I asked, conjuring up one of the few details I knew about military life.

"Most Marines and sailors do, but they also need someone to run the hospital here." He told me that he had a mix of feelings about never deploying to a war zone. He knew he was lucky, but also felt guilty because most go and some don't come back. "It's complicated. But what's not complicated is how I feel about Okinawa. I love this place. What about you? Are you loving it too?"

I didn't want to dampen his puppy-dog enthusiasm. "It's not what I expected," I said. He asked what I meant, but I begged off, feigning tiredness. We finished our dinners and walked outside to the seawall. The sunset had turned the low drifts of clouds orange-white and his skin glowed golden. We stood at about the same spot I'd first seen him, rescuing Gogan the seawall dog, and I recalled what he'd said that day. "When we met, you told me that Okinawa's winds are full of angry and sad spirits."

"Did I tell you that?"

"You told me it's a local legend stemming from World War II. Angry and sad winds blow off the East China Sea in retribution for the war, causing Americans to be unhappy here. You know, Divorce Rock?"

He pushed his lips together in a wry smile. "Divorce Rock, that's a real thing. It's an offshore rock formation north of here, and it's also true that many Americans who come to Okinawa end up divorced. But I made up the bit about the angry winds in retribution for the war." I frowned at my own naiveté and turned my face to the ocean, tasted salty sea spray on my lips.

During our goodbyes, he wore a wistful expression, said he'd like to see me again, but I deferred, telling him I'd be busy covering the rape case. It was a half-truth and I was surprised at the ease with which I'd said it.

. . .

In my apartment I nursed a glass of wine on my futon couch. City lights twinkled up through my picture window, but the typhoon-proof glass was sound-proof too, so all was quiet. Dinner with Nathan had been both a revelation and a foreign experience. He'd enlightened me about military life, an encapsulated lesson about things I wouldn't have otherwise known. But in doing so, he'd increased my feelings of isolation. I was American, but not part of the many American military people on Okinawa. I worked for a local company but didn't fit in with the local culture. And I blundered through a Japanese workplace, alienating more than ingratiating myself.

For the umpteenth time since coming to Japan, I thought about fleeing back to Illinois, where all was familiar and benign. Nathan said angry ghosts weren't responsible for stirring up troubled winds on Okinawa. But the notion of furious spirits wreaking havoc on people's hearts seemed possible to me. Owen told me that in Japan people spoke to the dead. And that the dead spoke to the living too, couldn't it be possible that the dead had their say by causing typhoons and drama and difficulty? Until my father died and I heard him talk to me in the wind, I would have never believed such mystical nonsense. But now I was untethered, unsure, unclear about what to do or what could happen from moment to moment. Anything was possible, maybe even something good, if only I could muster the guts to stick it out and stay in Japan long enough.

I woke up to a glaring bright morning, not a cloud in the clear blue sky. I checked my phone and had missed seven calls from Hisashi. He had texted too, saying, "Lucy, the police are looking for you. Please hurry."

CHAPTER EIGHTEEN

Officer Tanaka, the baby-faced officer from the Okinawa Prefecture Police, waited for me next to the *shisa*. His powder-blue shirt was wet, and his forehead glistened under the intense sun, the hottest day so far on Okinawa. He told me I was needed in court that afternoon, that the upskirt criminal had hired a skilled defense lawyer and so his victims, including me, would need to testify in person to bolster the case against him. My written statement wasn't enough and without my appearance the culprit might get off. Fear stung my belly. I didn't want to go to court. I told Officer Tanaka I had a work deadline.

"Ashimine-san will let you out of it," he replied. "I've already spoken to him." It was news to me that Ashimine-san knew the police personally, but then again, what did I really know anyway? Everything surprised me. I was stone, went to my desk and sat, staring, vaguely wondering where Hisashi was.

Amista came in and I told her about my court appearance. She said she would've gone with me, but she was committed to a press conference by Midori Ishikori's lawyers. I couldn't believe my bad luck; I was going to have to miss the press conference, the first and maybe only one by Midori's team.

"I'll take you to court, Lucy." I hadn't seen Hisashi come out of Ashimine-san's office. I thanked him and instantly realized I'd soon be in a courtroom identifying my pink underwear on video in front of him.

It was a few hours until we had to leave; I summoned all my determination and focused on editing my university story. An analyst in Tokyo had given me pertinent data: Despite studying it throughout school, a majority of students scored at or below the equivalent of grade three proficiency in English. Thirteen percent scored zero in spoken English. That information put things in perspective. Only the most driven people will study English in University of the Ryukyu's new program, the analyst had told me. I incorporated the data and the most colorful quotes from the dean and ended up with what I hoped was a solid piece. The headline was, "English on the Agenda for Career Advancement," dry, but accurate. I'd have a little time to revise it later if I came up with something better. It was noon and time for court.

The car ride was the first time I'd been alone with Hisashi since he'd helped me with the university interview. That day hadn't ended well, with Hisashi incredulous that I dated Owen, his sadness palpable when he told me that being an Ota had almost killed Owen. I'd been mortified at the reality that my sadness over Owen's disappearance was a grain of sand, compared to the ocean of grief Hisashi had gone through in the near loss of his brother. I held my feelings at bay, tamped them down and concentrated on the task at hand. Hisashi asked me if I'd been in court before and I told him not even for a traffic ticket.

"I will protect you, don't worry."

Alarmed, I said, "I'll need protection?"

"I didn't mean 'protect,' I meant 'guide.' I'll make sure you get to the right rooms and so on." He said he'd been in the courtrooms plenty of times, covering stories and that they are quite safe, with police all around.

He weaved along a busy street to an interior part of the island, away from the coast. Even with the air conditioning on full blast, the heat pressed into the car and my legs stuck to the vinyl seat. Without Hisashi I wouldn't have known what building to look for, where to park, how to get to the right court-room or even how to ask for help with those things. It would have taken me twice as long to get there, floundering with my cell phone GPS.

Giant *kangi* letters identified the Okinawa Prefecture Courthouse. A Japanese flag and an Okinawan flag flew side by side, and two humongous *shisas* sat beside the tall doors. People bustled in and out, sweating, carrying briefcases, laptops and folders. Faces were lined with stress. Like in an airport, they screened my purse and we walked through a metal detector. Hisashi conferred with an officer and took me to the third floor, down a crowded hall where people milled about alone or in groups. We sat on a bench. Two women across the hall snuck glances at me.

After thirty minutes, the door opened and an officer called, "Tosch, Kato, Watanabe." The two women who had been watching me headed to the room with me, each accompanied by a man. One was a teenager with braided pigtails, heavy black eyeliner and bright pink high tops. The other woman was older, wearing the type of peach-colored business suit I'd come to recognize as standard attire in traditional Okinawan banks, where the women wore matching pastel outfits and the men wore black or grey suits and ties.

Inside the sterile and chilly courtroom, Officer Tanaka

stood near the front, along with grim-looking Officer Penn and another man. A judge with thick glasses sat behind a large raised desk and a court reporter sat below him to his side. There were two metal tables facing each other on opposite sides of the room, not positioned side-by-side as they are in U.S. courtrooms. And a small empty desk sat facing the judge. There were a dozen or so people in the spectator area.

"Who are those people?" I asked Hisashi.

"Lurkers. People who lurk at court proceedings. They probably don't have jobs and are curious. There's no rule about that. Anyone is allowed to come to open court."

Officer Tanaka instructed me and the other two women to sit at one of the metal tables and our companions to sit in the spectator area. I felt nervous without Hisashi next to me but focused on what Officer Tanaka said. If and when the judge called each of us up, we were to tell the facts. Just explain what happened and answer any questions from him, the judge or the defendant's lawyer. The defendant wouldn't appear in person today, which was a relief. I didn't want to see his smug, unrepentant face.

Officer Penn said, "You will have to identify yourself, Ms. Tosch," and she turned her pencil lips up into a smile that I assumed was meant to be comforting. "I know this might be embarrassing. I'm here to help."

"I'm not sure what help you can be," I said, in a sharper tone than I meant to. It was so odd, having a stranger offer emotional support, adding a layer of awkwardness to the scene. I was in a court, in a foreign country, being guided by a man I'd known for a few weeks who might not even like me, in a room where I couldn't understand most of what was being said, about to see my underwear on a large screen. It would have been funny if I hadn't been so overwhelmed.

My two comrades sat next to me chatting quietly and

peeking over at me. I decided to introduce myself. "*Watashi wa Lucy.*"

They both nodded and extended their hands, which I shook, while also giving my little head bob that I hoped they would construe as a bow. I didn't want to offend them by over-doing it, but if I omitted the bow completely, they might think me rude or ignorant. They head bobbed back. The young hipster said, "I am Rika, and this is Hoshi. Can you believe this guy? What a moron."

I was glad she spoke English. "He's a jerk alright. Could this be any weirder?"

Hoshi squirmed and scanned the courtroom, obviously uncomfortable. Rika said, "Hoshi doesn't speak English. She's embarrassed. I'm okay. Just want to see this moron punished."

"Will the judge speak to me in English?" I asked.

"I'm pretty sure there's a translator. I've been to court a few other times, once with an American, and there was someone there to translate."

I knew it would be bad form to ask why she'd been in court before and anyway the proceedings began before I could respond. I glanced back at Hisashi and he nodded at me.

Officer Tanaka stood and gave a short speech in which he said "Himura-san" several times and I figured that was the name of the upskirt criminal. He also said each of our names, pointing to us in turn, frowning and shaking his head. When he was finished, he sat down at the table with us and Himura's lawyer stood up. He gave a short speech without mentioning any names and sat back down.

Tanaka stood again and a screen lit up at the side of the room. First, blurry images of strong legs, shifting from foot to foot, and Rika's crotch, with black-and-red heart-covered undies. Next a veil of peach around stockinged legs and nude underwear. Then my legs, pale and skinny, ending at the edge of my pink Victoria's Secret panties. I snuck a glance at Hisashi, and his head was turned from the screen.

From the back of the room a spectator shouted, *"Gaijin,"* in a low growl of a voice. Murmuring rose up from the spectators and the judge shushed them. The man yelled it again, "Gaijin!" and I saw him this time. He had pudgy cheeks he stared at me with squinty eyes. An officer hustled him out of the room. My cheeks flamed. *Gaijin* wasn't exactly a slur, but it was an insult and it meant "alien," or "foreigner," a person who wasn't where they were supposed to be. Owen told me he felt like a *gaijin* in the U.S. and in his own family. I glanced back at Hisashi and he shook his head, indicating I should ignore the rude spectator. But just as I'd felt embarrassed after being upskirted, I felt embarrassed now, wished I could run out of the room.

Officer Tanaka stopped the video and called me up to the witness stand. I felt like I was floating, my feet off the ground, propelled forward by something other than my own volition. The court reporter turned out to be a translator too, typing at the same time as saying in Japanese what Tanaka and I said in English.

"Miss Tosch, can you confirm that it is you in this video?"

"Yes. That's me."

"How do you know it's you?"

I paused, considered the best way to phrase this. "Those are my legs and that is my underwear."

"Thank you. Do you have anything more you'd like to tell the court?"

This was unexpected. I had no idea I'd be able to ad lib comments and my mind went blank. I stared at Hisashi, hoping maybe he'd give me a hint, but he stared back at me, didn't offer an encouraging nod.

"Anything at all," Tanaka prompted, "anything about the effect this incident has had on you?"

Fury creeped in to replace my mental blankness. My face was on fire and my throat felt strangled. I swallowed and said, "The street protests are scaring me and so is the anger I see in people's faces. We're getting violent threats at my office." The judge was startled, and the courtroom had gone silent. "I thought I could go out for dinner and relax but then this moron on the street," I pointed to Himura's lawyer, "assaults me." The pitch and volume of my voice rose. "I came to Japan because I love this country, thought I did anyway. Now, I hate Japan," I yelled. A bead of sweat rolled down my chest and I stood shaking.

The court reporter had been translating, whispering to the judge as I spoke. Now she stopped, hands paused over the keys. No one moved. The room was a vacuum of silent expectation.

"Anything else, Miss Tosch?"

"No." I wanted to sprint out of the courtroom. I must seem like a crazy person. What had I just said? Why did I mention the protests and threats? They had nothing to do with my case. I was losing it.

"Thank you then," the judge said, and indicated that I should go back to my table.

Rika and Hoshi gave me sympathetic looks and then turned away. Hisashi's face was fixed in an emotion I couldn't place. Anger? Disappointment?

Officer Penn leaned over. "Miss Tosch, it's a difficult time for you. Call me."

I wanted to bolt away from all this strangeness. But I sat through the testimony of the other two women, which were shorter than mine and without personal diatribes. They identified their legs and underwear on screen and then the session was over. Officer Tanaka told me that the judge denied Himura's lawyer's request that the case be dismissed and set an arraignment date for two months later. In the meantime,

Himura would be on house arrest and would be fitted with an electronic anklet to monitor his activity. "At least he won't be able to assault anyone else," Officer Tanaka said.

In the hallway, Rika approached me. She wore a pained expression. "Japan isn't a bad place," she said. "We don't hate Americans." She squeezed my hand and left.

Hisashi took my arm in his powerful hand and jerked me out into the crushing heat and into the car. He got in the driver's side and slammed the door, shaking the whole car. "You just told an open courtroom that our office has been getting threats. Do you realize that? Someone is going to tell the media. Ashimine-san is going to be furious. You might get fired." He glared at me and a vein pulsed in his neck.

I felt dizzy and overheated, like I might pass out. "I don't know what happened. I'm not thinking clearly."

"Lucy, you know that the office is a place for discretion. You should at least know that much about Japan. Your comments might bring real danger to us."

"I'm sorry. I didn't mean to say all that." Tears soaked my cheeks. "It's just too much. I didn't expect Japan to be like this."

Hisashi gave me a hard look, then turned away. "Okay. I get that," he said, speaking over his shoulder to me. "Let's just hope the media doesn't get wind of this. It's not a good thing to publicize threats. It tends to bring more crazies out of the woodwork. Do you understand?" He was less angry now, speaking to me as if I were an incompetent child.

"I do. I'm sorry. It's just been too much for me. I'm going to leave, go back to Illinois." I struggled to catch my breath.

"Wow," he said, turning toward me again. "You'd quit? Already?"

It couldn't get any worse, so I asked the question. "Please,

Hisashi. Tell me why Owen did it. I loved him. I need to know." A sob clutched in my throat.

He paused, then looked hard into my eyes. "I'm sorry for all that's happened to you. I wanted to help you. And I liked you. But maybe you're right. Maybe you don't belong here."

Confirmation. I was unwanted, unwelcome. Hisashi, once my ally, had turned against me. His usually smiling face was stony, guarded. He paused, frowning, and sighed. "Lucy, Owen is gay. That's why he did it. He doesn't *date* girls. You and Owen didn't *date*. He almost died because my father couldn't accept him"

CHAPTER NINETEEN

I couldn't face anyone at the office. I drove home as fast as I could, crying the whole way. I flung myself on my bed and sobbed. I was immature, idolizing Owen and glamorizing Japan in my childish imagination, when really, I understood nothing about Owen or his country. How in the world had I let a silly crush and made-up construct about Japan drive me all the way to this Godforsaken island? What kind of provincial idiot decided to live in a foreign country after two semesters of studying it in books? I'd created and believed my own fantasy about what it would be like—glamourous, exotic, modern, romantic—and it was nothing like what I'd imagined. It was a gritty, dangerous, boiling hot hell hole. The man who yelled *gaijin* had recognized me for who I was.

And now the knowledge that Owen was gay. Hisashi had flung those words at me like daggers. "Owen is gay." *You idiot. How could you not have known?* My thoughts were muddy, but a bolt of understanding shone through. Owen had been hot and cold to me in his fort because he was gay. He probably hated kissing me and that's why he'd done it so awkwardly, holding my neck too tightly and then pushing me away. Why did he let me think he felt romantic toward me?

I quickly knew the answer to my question. Owen undoubtedly recognized my crush and didn't want to hurt me. My infatuation had forced him to act in a way that he didn't feel. He'd said several times that we were "friends," and now I understood, he meant it. Friends. Not lovers. We could have never been lovers. Owen's mix of affection and aggression toward me had been driven by his own internal conflict. I'd mistaken it for passion. So stupid.

"Sorry, Lu," my father whispered in my ear, or was that Owen's voice I heard in my mind? He'd tried to be a real friend. He taught me about *haiku* and tea ceremonies. He complimented me and told me I was beautiful. Just like a best friend would do. Only I was too blind to see the real Owen. He left Illinois knowing that I didn't know him at all.

I cried until I had no more tears. I would leave Okinawa as soon as I could make the arrangements. I texted Rose and she called me.

"What are you talking about? You're leaving?"

I told Rose the story. All of it. My love for Owen, his hot and cold treatment of me in his fort, my fascination with Japan that was spurred by Owen, my fantasy of finding him and being adults in love in Japan, of learning right before I moved that he'd tried to commit suicide in *Aokigahara*, and meeting his brother, my coworker, from a fancy Tokyo family and learning that Owen is gay. I heard Rose exhale.

"Wow. That's some story. I can't believe you never told me anything."

"I'm sorry. I thought you'd think I was ridiculous."

"It was a crush," she said, gently, which made tears spring back into my eyes. "I know you thought it was more, that it felt like more."

I had never thought of it as a crush. My feelings for Owen had been real. I had loved him. Even though I hadn't known him for long, our moments together were locked in my memory, emotionally laden, more real than any other relationship I'd had.

"Owen is a near-perfect memory," she pressed. "Nothing in the real world can compete. You'll be disillusioned by everything and everyone. You have to let him go." I didn't know what to say. She continued. "Did you tell him you loved him?"

"Yes." And there it was, the new emotional twist that had stabbed at my gut since I learned the truth. He knew I loved him and yet he still tried to kill himself. My love couldn't have saved him.

"Having a crush is sweet, Lucy. You're sweet. But you have to let him go," she repeated.

I stared out my window at a careening seagull, floating up and around in circles. I inhaled several deep breaths. Then I promised Rose I would try to let Owen go. And I told her about all that had been going on, the upskirt assault, Hisashi's disappointment in me after my courtroom outburst, the growing street protests and my chance to participate in a big, meaningful story.

"So, you'll stay in Japan, then," she said, more of a statement than a question.

"I was thinking of going to Suicide Forest. I just want to see the place."

"So, you're staying."

Another thread fell loose from my heart. Right then I decided I would stay. I was a *gaijin*, a stranger in a foreign land, isolated and lonely and afraid. But I would stick it out, get through this terrible time, grow up and follow through with my commitments. It was my first adult decision ever, though I'd been playing at being an adult for years.

. . .

During the night I dreamed about the time Owen held my hand and kissed me so his mother would see. In my dream she was angry and ugly, some distorted version of the proud, loving mother I'd met. Owen's father was in my dreams too, or maybe it was Ashimine-san, a small, dark figure with slumped shoulders, pointing a finger at me. I woke up in the morning with bleary eyes and a pounding heart.

I knew I had to go to work and face the music, whatever the fall-out would be from my outburst in court. Would local media really seize on a statement made by an American nobody in a small, unknown court case? Had there even been reporters present? I showered and tried to wash the stress and sadness out of my face. I dreaded facing Hisashi, prayed he wouldn't be there.

I drove past the protestors and it was clear the size of the crowd had grown. They chanted and waved their signs and as I turned off of Kadena Gate Street, there he was, the rock-wielding teen I'd seen before. I recognized his black boots and his youthful face. He swiveled my direction. I wasn't certain, but I thought he recognized me. He raised his arm and made a fist, shook it in my direction and I hurried on.

At work, I huddled at my desk and poked at my university story, avoided talking to anyone. Kei, Jed and CeCe came in and out, but didn't try to start a conversation with me. The day went by in a blur, with me fighting off tears. Rumiko shot me a concerned look. Amista was oblivious to me, concentrating on the rape story. I went over to her desk to ask what had happened at the press conference. She was too preoccupied to notice my swollen eyes.

The lawyers had made a statement saying that Stone must be convicted and put in prison for his crime. They refused to answer questions. At one point a group of Americans had stood up and yelled from the back of the press conference, "Stone is innocent!" They yelled five times in a row before the cops yanked them out of the room. Amista showed me her screen, images of the press conference disruption were already posted. The headlines said, "Americans Protest Press Conference," and "Ishikori Lawyers Call for Justice."

As we gathered our belongings to go home for the day, Amista said, "In court did you see the guy?" She stood close and spoke quietly, so no one could hear.

"No. He wasn't there, just his lawyer. Three of us had to identify our underwear and that was it."

"Lucy made her own protest statement," Hisashi said, from behind us. He spoke in that comfortable, known-me-forever way he'd had when we first met. I stiffened; sure that his friendliness was some kind of ruse. I had no faith in my ability to read anyone anymore. He had yelled at me the day before and told me about Owen, and now he was acting cordial.

"I was too hard on you. I'm sorry," he said. "I realize things have been difficult for you. I don't blame you for lashing out. And look, I don't know what happened between you and Owen."

"I didn't know he was gay." I bit my lip so I wouldn't start crying again.

"He was well-practiced at hiding it," Hisashi said.

Amista had been listening and now her brow was wrinkled in concern. She came over and stood between us, eyed us in turn. "Sounds like both of you could use a break. Come to dinner at our house," she said. "Lester is barbequing shrimp. You," she said to Hisashi, "pick her up and bring her."

CHAPTER TWENTY

I changed into jeans and a cotton blouse, sipped a glass of cold white wine. My drinking had been escalating, but I gave myself the excuse of all the stress I'd been under. Hisashi texted me that he was downstairs. When I got into his car, he said hello like he always did, warmly with a smile. I worked up my courage. "I liked your brother very much," I began.

"You said you dated him," Hisashi said.

"Well, I guess I wasn't sure if we were dating," I said, cautiously, not wanting to be insensitive. "I only knew him for a month. But I definitely cared for him."

"Owen has that effect on people. Everyone's attracted to him." Hisashi's fleshy profile bore no resemblance to Owen's, but his voice had a similar sweet intonation.

"You and Owen seem very different."

"I'd say." Hisashi glanced over at me, his eyes narrow. "You didn't know he's gay?" A tumble of memories washed over me. In his fort, Owen had been affectionate and hostile at the same time, holding me too tightly, making out with me and then pushing me away. I remembered how he held my hand and kissed me while we were studying, long enough so his mother would see.

"I didn't know. I don't think he wanted me to know. But we were more than friends."

"Okay," he said. "I get that's how you felt." The busy street whizzed by outside and our headlights shone dully into the grey night. A new filter curtained my memories of Owen. It all made sense now, his strange behavior. I had been so attracted, so mesmerized, but to a figment of my creation, not a real person.

"I decided to move to Japan because of Owen."

"Wow."

"Not just to be with him, but because his descriptions of Japan fascinated me. Now it seems so silly, chasing a man and an idea all the way across the world."

"No. I can understand. Everyone loves Owen, even my father. And even though my father told him he brought shame to our family; I know he still loves Owen. The thing is, he forced Owen and Mom to move back to Tokyo so Owen could attend some sort of anti-gayness retreat. Our dad wanted to drive the gayness out of him. Owen couldn't see a way out of his situation. Either he lived a lie, or he disappointed our father."

I fought back tears, not wanting Hisashi to see me cry again. It would be so cruel, me crying over someone I barely knew, sitting next to someone who truly loved Owen. More and more my girlhood crush revealed itself for what is was. Silly. Immature. Unrealistic. I said, "He told me once that he liked me because I respected him."

"I'm sure that was true. He was always looking for respect."

"I was heartbroken when he left."

"Owen breaks a lot of hearts."

I worried that Hisashi might think me a bit ridiculous, but I wanted to know more. "Why Suicide Forest?" I asked.

Hisashi grimaced. "It's a place people go to be anonymous. Owen wanted to disappear, to erase himself. Suicide Forest is an abomination, a place from Japan's past that should be plowed over." His voice was full of sorrow and anger and out of respect, I didn't ask anything more. Owen Ota wasn't mine anymore, and I knew really, he never was.

As if I'd been veiled for a year, my surroundings were suddenly stark, swathed in bright clarity. Palm trees and houses out the car window, and a friendly handsome man next to me. It was the first time since moving to Japan that I didn't feel like I was in a fog. We drove into a quaint neighborhood with picturesque houses. I asked Hisashi if he'd been to Amista's house before and he said he had, many times, that she invited him every few months. "Does she invite the others from work?" I asked.

"Sometimes Ashimine-san, but you're the first American."

Amista's house was a one-story brick building, painted white, not the typical typhoon-battered grey concrete of so many Okinawan buildings. There was a pretty rock garden and bubbling fountain by a narrow stone path to the front door, which was guarded by two small stone *shisas*. Amista was shoeless when she opened the front door and we slipped off our shoes and left them on the *tatami* mat. The house smelled like jasmine with a touch of Okinawa's ever-present ginger and simmering curry scents wafted from the kitchen. We sat on low-slung furniture, traditional Japanese minimalist black lacquer chairs, soft futons and cushions on the floor. Ex-Marine Lester turned out to be much smaller than Amista and he gazed at her, larger than him by two times, with adoration. He touched her any time he was close enough to do so. A hand on her arm, a touch on the back of her neck.

At dinner Amista and Lester served delicious grilled shrimp with fragrant curry sauce, fresh corn on the cob, and sweet melon for dessert. Lester kept filling up our glasses with white wine and we were all warm and drunk by the time the melon was devoured.

"I hear you've had a bit of a rough go," Lester said to me, as we moved from the dining room to the living room.

"I guess so," I said, not sure which rough thing he was referring to.

"I'm sorry to hear that." He sat back into the couch and his belly was up high and round, his hand rested on Amista's thigh. "The upskirt guy, well that's just awful. And no way to treat a newcomer."

"I don't think he picked me because I'm a newcomer. He probably picked me because I'm oblivious. Had no idea it even happened until the police told me."

"It could happen to anyone," Hisashi said.

"True," said Amista. "Lester, tell Lucy what happened right after we moved here."

Lester leaned back in his chair and told me that back in 2000, when he and Amista had first arrived, Okinawa was in the midst of protests then too. A guy from Lester's squadron was accused of beating to death a bartender at a local nightclub. It was the headline news every day and all anyone could talk about. Lester and Amista lived on Camp Foster at the time and one night as they rode bikes home from dinner, a kid on the sidewalk kicked Lester so hard it knocked him off his bike onto the pavement.

"I'll never forget that big black boot coming toward me," Lester said. "The fall didn't hurt much, but I was in shock about what the boy said." Lester paused here with a grimace.

"He said, 'Fuck you, *gaijin*.' A kid! He couldn't have been more than fifteen." Hearing the term *gaijin* again was like a punch in the ribs.

"Someone said that to Lucy in court yesterday," Hisashi said. "*Gaijin*."

I cringed and Lester continued. "Well, I knew there was something wrong in that kid's heart, not that there was something wrong with Okinawa. I never took it personally." He touched my arm. "And, I hope you won't either." Lester spoke with sincerity and kindness.

"What happened to the guy from your squadron?" I asked.

"He was guilty," Amista said. "Sent to Okinawan prison for a long time."

The word *gaijin* had been sitting in my mind for a few days. I'd been called a *gaijin* and of course, Owen had felt he was one too, both in the U.S. and in his own family. It was a poignancy I wished we didn't share.

The conversation around the table shifted to the big news, the rape allegation and protests, and I was glad to have the focus off me. Lester wanted to know if Amista had turned up anything new in her reporting.

"Both sides say the other is lying. Nothing new about that. But I did find out that Stone has a temper problem. Been arrested in the past for public fighting. I'm going to write that part of the story tomorrow."

We sat and discussed the case. Hisashi was certain Stone was guilty. Amista said it wasn't yet clear. Lester agreed with Hisashi. I wasn't sure about anything on Okinawa and certainly didn't know the answer to this painful question. We all agreed that whether a rape happened or not, both parties' lives could be ruined as a result of this court case. Airman Stone's reputation could be permanently damaged. Midori Ishikori could be scarred for life. Japan itself could be changed if the protests succeeded in getting military bases shut down.

Lester stood and put both hands on Amista's shoulders, rubbed them. "Anyone care for another sip of wine?" We moved out onto the back porch where glowing paper lanterns hung from a white wooden trellis overhead. The moonlight was muted by silver clouds. Lester gave a goodnight toast. "To new friends, Lucy and Hisashi, who we thank for coming to dinner." Did Lester think Hisashi and I were a new couple?

"He knows you're colleagues, not dating," Amista whispered. She poked me in the ribs with a teasing finger.

Hisashi drove me home and walked me up to my apartment. Creepy Date-san peered at us over a newspaper as we passed. Upstairs, we sat on my small futon couch and he leaned closer to me and put his arm around my shoulder. He smelled musky and I leaned against his warm bulk. Our discussion about Owen had created an ease, an understanding between us. He hadn't laughed at my naivete, about my belief that Owen and I had been in love, and I had a glimpse into the difficulties he was living with, the complexity of the Ota family. Sitting with Hisashi I recognized in him the same tender heart I'd seen in Owen and it softened and opened my own heart just a crack. When he left, he kissed me on the top of the head, like a brother would do.

CHAPTER TWENTY-ONE

It was the first decent night's sleep I'd had in weeks. I got to work early and wrapped up my university story. It was dry and full of data, "University Enhances English Language Curriculum." Amista handed me a copy of her next story on the rape case, telling me to read it when I had time.

On the white board Ashimine-san had assigned me a new story about the activities of Okinawan and American Women's Clubs. Apparently, there were groups in which Okinawan women and American military wives socialized and did charity work together. I was disappointed and wished he'd assigned the piece to Cece, after all, she was a military officer's wife. Nonetheless, I researched the piece for the afternoon, reading up on joint hospital fundraisers and *ikebana* classes, where together, Okinawan and American women learned flower arranging. Aside from an event called, "Blogs to Build Unity," the courses could have been offered in nineteen-sixty. Frustrated after being cooped up all day, I needed out of the office.

I turned off my computer, grabbed Amista's story, got in the car and headed west. When I arrived at Okinawa City Beach at the northernmost end of the Sunabe Seawall, I parked and walked on the sand. It felt soft on my toes and the water sparkled in the afternoon sun. There were only a few people around, a family tossing a Frisbee and a soldier jumping in the waves. Nathan was nowhere to be seen. I plopped down on the sand and let my eyes adjust to the reflections and bursts of light reflecting off the water. As if I hadn't seen it before, I took in the dark and light shades of blue all around me, the water that melted from aqua to navy, the turquoise sky and the shifting line where sky collided with sea. The air smelled pleasantly of salt and fish.

Amista's story was titled, "Okinawa Erupts as Airman Denies Guilt." The deckhead was, "Stone history of violence, Ishikori silent." I was about to read it when my phone rang. It was Rose. We spent the next thirty minutes chatting. She asked about Hisashi and I assured her I wasn't dating him. We both agreed that dating Owen's brother was probably a bad idea. During our conversation my text alert kept beeping, but I ignored it and called my mom after I hung up with Rose. I didn't tell her anything more than that I was fine, that work was going well and that I loved her.

After a few more minutes staring into the East China Sea I scrolled through my texts. "I'm in Ginowan Hospital." It was Hisashi. I jumped to my feet and landed on a sharp seashell. I pressed the hem of my dress on my foot to staunch the bleeding and called him. He told me he had been attacked in the parking lot at the office, early, before anyone else arrived. A group of boys or men, he wasn't sure, roughed him up. He drove himself to the hospital and they would release him soon. A shudder rippled down my spine, the peace I'd started to feel, seeped out of my skin. "What can I do?"

He asked me to meet him at his apartment. I GPSed it and drove fast, gripping the steering wheel hard, worrying.

Hisashi's place was swanky, in Ginowan, right on the ocean. The building was a gleaming high-rise, modern and glassy. I continued to marvel at how Okinawa went from ramshackle to sleek in the space of a few miles.

When he answered his door, I hugged him. He was hot and damp. His forehead and cheek were bandaged as was his hand. The apartment was three times as big as my own and decorated with modern furniture and a crystal chandelier. I inhaled vanilla, a set of three candles on his coffee table. I stood back to take it all in, including his injuries. His face was the purple and red hues of a professional boxer after a fight.

"I wish I could say the other guys look worse," he said, smiling, though he must have been in pain. He told me there were three of them with bandanas wrapped around their faces. "I didn't get a good look, but they were young, I could tell from their eyes." We sat down on his black leather couch.

"Please tell me you spoke to the police."

"The hospital made me report it, but I wouldn't have otherwise." *Such stubborn pride,* I thought. "The officer said it was probably a random attack on anyone who works at *Okinawa Week*, the police don't think I was targeted specifically."

Fear choked my throat. It could have been me, Amista or anyone who had been attacked. "Did you tell Ashimine-san?"

"No. He will feel responsible."

I exhaled, incredulous that he'd make that mistake again. "How can you possibly hide it from him after what happened with the signs? He's going to see your face."

"Lucy, there are things you don't understand about our culture," he began.

He was right, I didn't understand most things, but I couldn't hold my tongue. "If you won't tell him for yourself, at least consider that it could have been Amista, or Cece or me who was attacked, or could be attacked later."

Hisashi closed his eyes, pressed them shut. Then he said, "Okay. I will warn our coworkers. But not Ashimine-san. He's old fashioned."

"My God," I said, exasperated. I couldn't put myself into the mindset of someone who wanted to avoid embarrassment for his boss more than he wanted safety, or justice for that matter, to see the culprits thrown in jail. I bit my tongue. I commented on the luxury of his place, with its lively red silk throw pillows on the couch and a real dining room off to the side of the living room. Nothing like my spartan apartment.

"I like living on the water," he said, rubbing his bandaged hand. "Come look." Two sliding glass doors opened to the West, and the view was all twinkling aqua water and light blue sky. "Lucy, I want to talk to you, to put a few things out in the open." I nodded, wary about what would come next. "It must be strange for you to get to know me after knowing Owen. We are not at all the same."

"I realize that."

"And I can't say I understand what your relationship with him was." I didn't answer, kept my promise to myself not to deepen Hisashi's grief by talking about my unrequited infatuation. "I have our grandmother's tea set. My mom told me it's for you, from Owen." He brought me into his dining room and on a long, black lacquer buffet, there it was, the pretty red and pink tea set Owen had promised me. It was even lovelier than I remembered, with delicate pink cherry blossoms etched over paper-thin crimson porcelain. A ripple through my chest, its beauty stunning, my memory overflowing. *It's infused with love,* Owen had said, and impossible for tea served in it to be bitter.

I told Hisashi that it was too special, should remain in the Ota family, but he said no, Owen's wishes should be honored. He gingerly lifted it and placed it in my hands and another string fell away from the binding of my heart. This gift from Owen was a symbol, a sign that our relationship had been real, had life and weight. At one point, I'd hoped the tea set had been smashed to bits, and now I was grateful that it shone in my hands, as if Owen himself reached out to me, offered amends for hurting me.

Hisashi was tired and needed rest after his ordeal, so I got ready to leave. By the door, he stopped me and said, "I could really use some R&R. How about we take a drive around the island tomorrow. Go to a tea house, see some landmarks?"

"I absolutely want to do that," I said, and he gave me a ginger hug. I wrapped the tea set in towels from my trunk, to make sure each item was safely tucked into a soft spot. I drove back to the Sunabe Seawall and sat on the concrete barrier, until the only illumination was the reflection of the moon on the water.

CHAPTER TWENTY-TWO

The next morning, Hisashi and I headed north up Okinawa's West Coast Highway 58, the flat, bustling main road that ran the length of the island. We passed miles of metal fences on our right, surrounding the military bases. The runways, parking lots, fields and clusters of organized buildings looked bland and misplaced across the street from colorful local trinket shops and busy pachinko parlors. Hisashi turned into a small strip mall and parked in front of a store with blacked-out windows. The sun reflected hotly off the store front and I squinted.

Inside we were greeted by a tiny old woman wearing a vivid green kimono. Her hair was black in defiance of the years etched into her brown skin and it was twisted into an elaborate bun held secure by polished wooden chopsticks. The room was small and dim, with tatami mats on the floor and a cinnamon scent in the air. "We're participating in a traditional tea cere-mony," Hisashi whispered. "Usually they don't let untrained Americans take tea, but Honda-san makes exceptions."

We removed our shoes and Honda-san led us to a black

granite basin in the corner. Hisashi rinsed his hands in the basin and took a swig of water from a small decanter, so I did the same. Then Honda-san indicated where we should sit on one side of the low table. She then left the room through an almost invisible back door that was flush with the wall.

"She will use *matcha*, powdered green tea," he whispered. "She skips all the courses of food that go with traditional tea ceremonies. It's like tea ceremony 'light,' for Americans and their short attention spans. She'll perform it in twenty minutes, versus several hours." His description made me smile.

Honda-san reentered the room, and cleansed her hands at the granite basin, moving methodically. Then she sat on the other side of the low table and placed both hands on the semi-circular handle of a jade green and ivory pot in front of her. The pot sat on an ivory lacquer tray along with three matching bowls, a smaller stone bowl filled with the *matcha*, and a small whisk and a scoop. An ivory cloth was draped over the side of the tray. With slow gentle movements Honda-san scooped the powder into one of the bowls, poured in the hot water and whisked the tea as steam rose in a wisp. She presented the bowl to Hisashi who sipped it and said something in Japanese to Honda-san. Then he picked up the ivory cloth, wiped the edge of the tea bowl, turned it around and passed it to me. I imitated him, sipping, thanking Honda-san in English because I couldn't think to say *arigato* or any Japanese words. I wiped the bowl and handed it back to Honda-san, who stood, bowed, slid open the sliding panel that served as both wall and door, left the room.

"That sliding door is called a *fusuma*," Hisashi said, and I nodded. My mind flashed back to the intimate tea ceremony that Owen and I had shared so long ago, and I smiled again. Seeing my smile, Hisashi smiled too.

"Don't move, she will give us more tea," he said. I sat as still as I could, ignoring the urge to unbend my legs. Honda-san returned and prepared tea in each of the two remaining bowls, filling them almost to the top. She gave them to us, and we again thanked her. This time I gave a little bow too. Hisashi took his time in drinking the tea and Honda-san sat like a Buddha meditating. When our bowls were empty, Honda-san picked up the ivory towel and cleaned off the whisk and scoop, and handed the implements to Hisashi, who said, "These are beautiful objects."

To my surprise Honda-san replied in English. "Thank you. They were first used by my great-grandmother who commissioned them from Naoto Kadekaru, a brilliant artisan. My great-grandmother passed them down to my grandmother and so on. They aren't as fancy as some, but to my family, they are precious." She turned to me, obviously expecting me to speak.

"They are precious," I said, feeling a little silly for repeating what she had said. Honda-san stood and bowed. Hisashi and I did the same.

"This was not elaborate, but I am honored that you joined me," Honda-san said. Hisashi tried to hand her a few bills, but she shook them off. "It is my gift. Nothing should mar the beauty of *matcha* shared with friends." Then she turned to me. "Tosch-san, please accept the apology of my ancestors that you were treated with such disregard."

Hisashi avoided my eyes. Honda-san bowed a final time and left through the secret door in the back. Outside I squinted again. "You told Honda-san about the upskirt incident?"

"I didn't tell her. When I called to make the appointment, she told me she knew about it. Small island. Things get around." He told me that the tradition of the tea ceremony is one of peace and generosity and that any tea host would be mortified to know that a guest had been treated shabbily by a local person. That's part of the graciousness of Japan, he said.

"At heart, the Japanese wish never to offend." The simple eloquence of his statement brought a lump to my throat. He had planned this day for me, to show me something of the culture that I hadn't yet seen because of the chaos since I'd arrived. In the dark sanctity of Honda-san's tearoom, I got a glimpse of the elegant country I'd expected from the start.

We stopped at a curry shop for lunch and shared a plate of chicken and potatoes ladled with spicy yellow sauce, the best meal I'd had since I arrived. I thanked Hisashi for taking me to the tea ceremony. "I had tea with Owen once," I said, feeling more comfortable in confiding in Hisashi. I explained how Owen had performed a makeshift ceremony for me there in his fort with his grandmother's beautiful tea set.

"Owen is sweet like that," Hisashi said, "an old soul. He loves Japanese traditions. He values our culture and history. He knows how to conduct a tea ceremony, he writes *haiku*, he takes time to honor our ancestors." Hisashi's voice rippled with love. It was a revelation. Owen was the traditional one, returning to Tokyo when called by his father. Hisashi, I suddenly understood, was the disobedient son who fled to Okinawa and stayed.

I told him Owen and I wrote a *haiku* together. He gave a little smile and nodded. "But I've never seen the one he published," I added.

"Ah, well, I will show you. It's quite beautiful. Captures the contradiction of Ota family history."

I thought of my sheltered suburban Illinois upbringing. My parents rarely mentioned our Dutch ancestry. What little I knew of it I'd researched myself. In Oakville, I'd grown up unaffected by the type of pressure that Hisashi and Owen had to deal with. I hadn't been raised to be proud of my heritage, but I hadn't been forced to conform to it either. We finished lunch and my curiosity nudged me. With a deeper understanding of Owen now, and an even deeper respect for him, I felt drawn toward information that might provide closure, a final untethering of my heart

After lunch we drove up to Manza Beach Resort, the scene of the alleged rape, another place I'd developed intense curiosity about. Especially since my own assault, I wanted to see the place poor Midori Ishikori had been during the alleged attack, to fully grasp, somehow, that whether walking down a public street or lounging on an upscale tourist beach, women were at risk. We turned into the palm-shrouded driveway and the ocean was on the left, the tall hotel straight ahead. There was no police tape marking a spot, nor any upended chairs or misplaced trash, nothing to indicate a crime had taken place. It was open to the public and we paid a small fee to park and have beach access. The sand was pristine and white, and the shallow water sparkled turquoise. Fit boys monitored the beach, setting up sun umbrellas and sitting atop lifeguard stands. The hotel towered at one end of the beach.

"This is where the Ishikori family stayed?" I asked.

"Looks innocuous, doesn't it?" Hisashi said.

The building was white, a shade lighter than the sand, with a cheerful blue ocean wave logo adorning the side. The lifeguards spread a large blanket for us under an umbrella and offered us plastic cups of wine.

"When I dreamed of coming to Japan, this kind of tropical scene never entered my mind."

"What did you expect, a metropolis like a scene from a Gwen Stefani video?" he said, and I laughed for the first time in weeks, admitted he was right.

"It's embarrassing," I said. And I told him my image of Japan was some combination of busy downtown Tokyo, a music video, and beautiful women like his mother. "She was so kind and lovely."

"That's how she is still, kind and lovely. No idea how she puts up with my father."

In the changing cabanas we put on our suits, then waded into the warm water and stood waist deep. Hisashi was muscular and a little plump, his tummy a rounded mound. I did a mental comparison to Owen who was almost as tall but lean as a street post. Hisashi ran his hand across the water creating a turquoise ripple. "I hated my dad. I blamed him."

"And now?"

"I feel sorry for him."

"Are all Japanese fathers so harsh?" I wasn't sure if that was the right word, but didn't want to say bigoted, which is the word that first came to mind.

"Some are, some aren't. Just like fathers everywhere." Hisashi stared out into the distance, thinking. "Maybe you'll meet him." Standing in the cooling ripples of the East China Sea I could envision a trip to Tokyo with Hisashi. "We'll see," he said, concluding a thought he didn't share.

The soft lapping of the waves was interrupted by loud voices at the hotel. Security guards were pushing a group of people out of a side door. The people held cameras close to their chests and didn't push back. "Reporters," Hisashi said. I was transfixed, watching the commotion between the media and the hotel staff, an argument crescendoed and then stopped as the hotel doors shut. The photographers migrated to a spot by a small pond near the back corner of the hotel, snapping shots of the ground. That had to be the spot where Midori Ishikori said she'd been lured to and attacked. I wrapped a towel around my waist and went for a closer look. Coarse dirt, dry leaves, sticks on the edge of a swampy pool, nothing soft. Her skin must have been bruised and scratched, I realized, her wounds visible and palpable. My own assault had left nothing to see on my body, only a wound to my spirit, and yet I understood that I shared something with this tiny Japanese teenager, something no two women would want to have in common.

Hisashi retrieved his camera from the car, went over, took a few shots, talked with a few photographers. I asked him why the photographers were there today, and he said it was the first day that barriers were gone, a coincidence of timing with our day trip. My stomach churned and I was queasy. I told him we needed to go.

Our next stop was Hiji Falls, a hiking trail another twenty minutes up the road, across from a military campground called Okuma. The parking lot was almost empty, and we parked close to the mouth of the trail. We hiked up a well-maintained path with thick trees that formed a canopy overhead and blocked the sun. I pointed to a black-and-green turtle lounging on a rock and Hisashi told me was a native Ryukyu turtle. A few olive-brown birds skittered around on the ground calling in a high-pitched off-key shout, unlike the melodic robins and sparrows in Illinois. "Yanbaru kuina," he said. "They are endangered and don't fly well. Seeing them is a good omen."

A sudden yearning came over me, to tell my father that I'd seen a rare Japanese bird. That's how my grief had changed over time. Early on, I couldn't think clear thoughts in a mind cratered by loss. Now, my moments of grief came in bolts of wonderment followed by the dull realization that he was gone, the same pattern repeated and repeated. It had been a similar pattern after Owen left me, but with sprinkles of hope that I'd see him again.

At one point in the trail Hisashi and I came to a suspension bridge several stories above a cavernous ravine. As usual he kept his hand on my back to guide me, pushing me at a steady pace over the river swirling far below. "Do you know what the *hiji* means in Hiji Falls?" He was trying to distract me so I wouldn't be scared. "Elbow. So, we are on the way to the Elbow Falls. I don't think it looks at all like an elbow. You'll see."

At the top of the trail we arrived at the falls, an imposing cascade of water running about seventy-five feet down a sheer rock wall, nothing at all like a bent elbow. My skin was slippery from the mist wafting off the falls and I held on to Hisashi's sleeve to steady myself. Signs warned against swimming, but several teenagers floated just in front of the waterfall, weaving toward it and then away before being hit by the crashing water. I had the urge to jump in, swim under the falling torrent and take my chances. Did I hear my father's laughter in the rushing water? A soft feeling of contentment crept over me as we headed back down the trail. The waning afternoon sun shadow danced through the trees and a flightless yanbaru kuina sprinted on a dead run in front of us and then took off. We paused to watch him soar up and take hold of a high branch where he perched like a king.

Hisashi and I were quiet on the drive back and when we got to my apartment, we sat on my little couch downing glasses of cold water and taking sips of beer. He told me that next time we had an outing he would take me to Katsuren Castle, the ruins of it anyway. It was the castle of Lord Amawari, one of Okinawa's most popular rulers before Japan took over, he said. We also talked about Shuri Castle, which I'd read about, how it had been reconstructed after the war by Americans and Okinawans together. "Something good that our two countries did together," he said. My phone rang.

"Upskirt!? Lucy! You should've told me," my mother sounded frantic. "I called Rose and she told me."

"I know, I know. I had to appear in a courtroom where they showed my legs and underwear on a big screen in front of a bunch of people." Mom reacted as I knew she would, sympathetic and also worried about my wellbeing, pleading with me to return to Illinois. She asked again about the rape case and the protests that she'd been seeing in the news. "It's too soon to tell how the case will end up, but my friend at work is reporting on the case. And no, I haven't been scared," I said, figuring it was a white lie to save her some worry. "I have Amista and another friend here who are helping me navigate everything." When I hung up, I again told her I loved her. It felt good to say it and I knew it was what she needed.

I handed Hisashi another beer. His skin was ruddy after our day outside and he had taken the bandages off his cheek to reveal a slender scab and deep black bruising. He said, "Am I your *other* friend?" and we both chuckled. We'd come a long way in a few weeks, from strangers with secrets and misapprehensions, to colleagues working on stories together, to friends who'd shared tough times and warm moments. Seeing his battered face beneath the bandages filled me with sympathy. All day together and he'd never even mentioned the attack. I touched his cheek gently and asked if it hurt.

"My pride more than anything else," he said.

"Are you sure it's best not to tell Ashimine-san?" His eyes went soft and he told me that he understood why it was hard for me to get it, why certain things were best left unsaid at *Okinawa Week*. The police would probably let Ashimine-san know what had happened, he said, but he wasn't going to bring it up if Ashimine-san didn't ask.

"It's the Japanese way, to avoid inflaming conflict, to keep a strong and positive face to the world," he said. As a Midwesterner, I understood the desire to avoid conflict, probably took that concept too far myself. Rose had always told me I'd apologize for falling if a stranger intentionally tripped me.

"But what if they come after someone else at work?"

"This isn't the first time. Both times they called me by name, told me I was a traitor for working with Americans. So, you see...." And I did see. Hisashi was trying to protect all of us from unnecessary stress, from worrying about him on top of worrying about everything else.

Soon he told me he was tired, needed to rest, the lingering effects of the beating and our long day of touring had taken their toll. On the way out, he floated the idea of us taking a weekend trip to Tokyo. A butterfly of hope fluttered in my head. I still wanted to see Tokyo and other parts of Japan; still felt the draw of the exotic country I'd dreamed of. I asked if we'd see his parents and he said maybe. "What about Owen?"

"He won't tell us where he is. He's basically hiding from the family. He calls, but rarely. I don't think we'll be able to find him. Sorry."

"I'm sure he's got bigger worries than a visit from me," I said, sad because it was certainly true.

I imagined meeting Mrs. Ota again. Would she be uncomfortable because I knew Owen's secret? Would sadness have taken a toll on her beauty, etching her beautiful face with lines? And Mr. Ota, I couldn't quite picture what such a harsh, judgmental father might look like. Would his face be sandpaper and his hands calloused, in keeping with his spirit? Would he speak to me kindly or would he judge me, as he'd done to his son?

If and when Hisashi and I made it to the mainland I'd approach him again with the idea of going to Suicide Forest. I couldn't shake the notion that a visit there, the chance to see what it was, would give us both a sense of finality, to pen an end to my story with Owen. I was appalled that such a place could exist, but like a curious reporter, I believed I needed full knowledge, all possible information. It was another conundrum about Japan I longed to understand. A culture so beautiful that taking tea was a memorable occasion and yet so dark it contained a forest devoted to suicide.

Hisashi bear-hugged me without pressing his sore face onto my head. I had the urge to reach up and give him a kiss on the cheek but thought better of it.

When I was alone in my apartment, I kept thinking of Manza Beach and the trauma Midori Ishikori had probably experienced there. Before bed, I wrote a poem for her.

MANZA BEACH

*Below the calm-rolling surface, its blue bluer than the
never-ending sky,
invisible or unseen from the shelter of her shady umbrella where
she digs
her toes into powder-soft sand and sips her soda with a straw,
sharp red plumes jab and flail, slice and slash, precious,
dangerous coral.
She's fearless or maybe stupid, bubble-gum-pink happy, until the
cut comes,
and her broken skin seeps blood and accepts salt,
and she's both empty and knowing.*

CHAPTER TWENTY-THREE

Compared to the quiet comfort of touring with Hisashi, the quiet in the office was somber, uncomfortable. Ashimine-san was out most of the day and we knew he was working with police to help determine the origin of the phone call and graffiti threats. Hisashi hadn't come to work at all, presumably to hide his wounds and avoid further alarming Ashimine-san. Rumiko ignored everyone, kept her nose in her drafting table. My other colleagues were quiet too, even Cece the chatterbox had fallen silent. It was as if we were all waiting for a bomb to go off or the door to burst open to reveal black-masked terrorists.

I slogged through my research about American and Okinawan women's groups, clocking time. I researched the history of cultural sharing efforts between Okinawans and Americans, which turned out to be thin. There were Japanese feminist groups and groups dedicated to helping Japanese women assimilate in the U.S. But I only found one women's group, on Kadena Air Base, with the specific purpose of collaborating with Okinawans. I scheduled interviews with three women, two Americans and one Okinawan. I attempted to ignite my interest in the subject by searching for a unique angle. I wondered if the women became real friends or just polite colleagues. I wondered if they ever discussed politics or the rape allegation or protests or if they focused on their charities and cultural goals and avoided touchy subjects. Discouraged, I went to Ashimine-san and begged for an assignment related to the rape allegation.

"*Chotto matte kudasai*," he said. "Soon you'll have bigger stories."

Jed laughed from his desk. "Soon, to Ashimine-san, is not very soon," he said. Like Kei, Jed didn't say much. But unlike Kei, he had an easy smile and was quick with jokes. I'd seen very little of Kei, which Amista said was just his way, to work and be alone. Rumiko was always present, always watchful. I didn't feel hostility from her, but I still couldn't read her. During my exchange with Ashimine-san, she'd paused, hands over her sketch pad, then turned back to her drawings.

Amista had taken on an even more maternal role with me, especially since my upskirt court appearance. She inquired about my wellbeing. She brought me plastic containers of homemade shrimp and beef.

One afternoon she took me shopping on Kadena Air Base to buy inexpensive toilet paper and other necessities. It was my first time in the base Exchange, and it reminded me of J.C. Penney. It was clean and generic, with inexpensive cosmetic brands and rows of low-end appliances, rubber shoes and children's clothing. The shoppers were mainly youngish American women with kids in tow. The workers were both American and Okinawan. I was glad we didn't run into Takayuki-san, the man who'd told me he hated me during our interview.

Hisashi and I didn't schedule a trip to Tokyo and didn't do another driving tour of the island. We maintained an unspoken time out, when we didn't talk about Owen, or bad news, or anything other than work. When he came back from his time off, his bruises were almost gone and no one said anything about the attack, so I assumed they didn't know.

It rained the day we were to attend the first part of Airman Stone's trial. I was eager to see the Japanese justice system work from the vantage point of a reporter, versus a victim. At the same time, I feared encountering more anti-American hostility. Japan's status as a country "friendly" to the United States meant that Stone's trial would be in an Okinawan court, not in a protected on-base American military court.

Hisashi and I met Amista at the courthouse, the same building where I'd had to confront my upskirt attacker. The nine-a.m. heat created shimmering steam that floated above the entry stairs. The wet air smelled of sulfur and sweat as a throng of reporters and spectators cued to get in. It was first-come, first-served, and luckily for us, Amista had staked out a spot before dawn, so we waited at the front of the line, under the portico.

"Doors should open in a few minutes. They are pretty prompt," Amista said. Hisashi and I nodded. Then, two policemen opened the building doors, checked our IDs and directed us through the metal detector. Amista led us down the hall and toward the courtroom. Like the other professional buildings, I'd been in on Okinawa, this one smelled clean, like lemon and bleach. When we reached the courtroom, we found seats in the front of the section designated for the media. The room was sparse with wooden chairs in the spectating area and no jury box; Japanese criminal courts are presided over by a single judge.

Like the courtroom for my upskirt hearing, this room had the witness stand in the center of the room facing the judge, not angled toward the audience as it would have been in a U.S. courtroom. Japan's judicial system was strict, and this requirement, that witness face the judge, amplified that point. The witnesses were not there so the audience could watch them squirm or assess their appearance or ponder their veracity. Witnesses sat below and up close to a single black-robed decision maker, both judge and jury for the fate of the accused.

The tables for the lawyers of the accused and the accusers were on opposite sides of the room, facing the center, like boxers about to spar. When we took our seats in the gallery, the judge was already sitting behind his bench thumbing through papers, and police officers stood on each side of him and by all the doors. Two women at small desks, a court reporter and a translator, flanked the judge. The room filled with people who held muted conversations so as not to ignite the voltage in the air.

Airman Stone, a hulking man with coal-black skin contrasted against pale blue prison garb, entered the courtroom through a side door. Handcuffs and leg-irons forced him to walk in a heavy shuffle. Guards sat him at the table and took up posts nearby. Colonel Abdir was already seated there and spoke to Stone, touched his arm and patted him on the back. I'd read somewhere that lawyers often touch guilty clients to fool people into thinking the client could be trusted. Another military man and woman, presumably lawyers, came in from the back, commiserated with Abdir and Stone, then took their places at the table. I stole side glances at Stone's face and could see a bulging vein down his temple. He looked powerful and hopeless at the same time, surrounded by guards and suited lawyers. Were they there to protect him or to protect others from him? Stone, already like a convicted felon, separated from other citizens by a blockade of people.

At the other table were two Japanese men in suits, sitting

silently. A side door opened and there she was, the elusive Midori Ishikori, flanked by her parents and two big body-guards. The room went silent, all eyes on the tiny teenager. Her lawyers rose and escorted her to the table, while her parents and the guards took seats at the front of the gallery. Stone didn't look at her, but she glanced at him and then away. She was even prettier in person than in the two photos I'd seen, more mature than her fifteen years, with big eyes and shiny lip gloss. She wore a navy blue and white polka dot dress with a demure lace collar, and a tear bloomed in the corner of her eye.

Hisashi and the other photographers were prohibited from taking photos in court, but he made a little sketch of the scene in his notebook. Amista sat and first looked at Midori, then turned to examine Stone, then back at Midori. Along with everybody else, I quieted my breath, anxious about what would happen.

The next thirty minutes went by in a blur. One of Midori's lawyers made a brief statement, as did Colonel Abdir. Neither Stone nor Midori took the stand, but there was an electric moment where the judge asked Midori a question and she turned toward Stone and pointed a delicate finger at him.

At first, Stone stared into the distance and didn't acknowledge her at all. But then, as the judge began to read the charges against him, "statutory rape, sexual battery," Stone shot up out of his chair. A guard jumped over and grabbed Stone's arm and tried to force him back down, but Stone yanked his arm away. Before police officers could respond, Stone strained toward Midori's table, the chains from his leg irons clanking on the floor. "Whore," he growled.

With one collective intake of air, the spectators and media in the courtroom ossified. "Whore," Stone said again, his voice firm and furious. Before he could speak again or sit back down the two guards grabbed him and dragged him out the side door.

Then the judge yelled something, hit his gavel on the bench and left the room too. Police told the rest of us to stay seated and cleared the way for Midori Ishikori. She ran out of the main doors of the courtroom, her head down, lawyers, guards and parents running alongside her.

"What a headline," Amista said.

Despite the policemen's orders, Hisashi jumped up and ran after Midori, camera in hand. No one stopped him, so other reporters followed. Then the whole courtroom got up and pushed toward the exit. Amista took my hand and we wove out through the crowd. Hisashi was nowhere to be seen and neither was Midori's camp, so we got into Amista's car and drove to the office.

Amista's story, published that Friday, featured a photo of a fleeing Midori, taken by Hisashi. She was running toward a waiting black sedan in the courthouse parking lot. Her face was wet with tears and raindrops and her polka-dot dress was soggy and too big for her tiny body. Her parents were also in the frame, looking back at Hisashi's camera, startled expressions on their wet faces. Hisashi was the only one to get a photo from the day's proceedings and Amista's story had the headline, "Accusation from the Accused," and subhead, "Stone disrupts courtroom with slur." I couldn't help noting the parallel to the slur shouted at me during my day in court. In Okinawa a slur could be hurled at anybody, anytime, it would seem.

Hisashi told me he had to go down south to Naha to take a series of photographs of the new buildings constructed in Okinawa's biggest city. The story had been assigned to Cece, which bothered me, eager as I was to write more important stories. This wasn't a fluff piece because it wasn't only about architecture, it was about a visit to Naha by several high-ranking government officials from Tokyo, there to address the protests and calls for base closures. As happened so many other times since World War II, Japanese officials would attempt to quell Okinawan outrage and maintain the status quo with their American *friends*. Years earlier, the U.S. had promised to shut down one of the many American military bases on Okinawa, the Marine's Camp Futenma, but didn't.

I planned to spend my weekend researching the American Welfare & Works Association and Women Against Military Violence, the two groups I'd interview. The first group was American military women who did local charity, school fundraisers, volunteering at hospitals and the like. The second group was comprised of Okinawan women who fought to reduce American crime against Okinawan citizens. I realized the second group was a bit of a stretch in terms of a fit with my assigned story, how American and Okinawan women work together, but I decided interview them anyway and enjoyed a pang of satisfaction because I knew I was bending the rules about the scope of my story. I didn't want to disappoint Ashimine-san, but I was intrigued by the anti-violence group and thought I could learn about it even if I had to leave it out of my final story. I liked the idea of following my gut instincts instead of someone else's rules.

It was Friday evening, and Amista wanted to take me out on a quick trip up the coast. I agreed, but said I needed to make a stop on the way. I guided her to the shopping center where Hisashi and I had tea, to a little stonework shop next door that sold garden fountains and statues.

"What are you looking for?" she asked.

I scanned the aisles and there it was, a partner for our office *shisa*. It was grey stone embellished with red and gold, a near-perfect male to match the female that guarded *Okinawa Week*. I paid the clerk and put it in the trunk.

As we continued the drive, Amista said, "I should have done that years ago." We're going to Okuma," she said. "It's a military vacation spot. Like a retreat center but with a bar."

It was nighttime, and the street was what I now knew to be a typical Okinawa scene. Brightly lit pachinko parlors and bars, next to small strip malls and mom-and-pop shops, sidewalks crowded with both revelers and protestors. As we neared Okuma the commercial sites disappeared, and the street was lined with lush trees and flowering shrubs. We turned into a long driveway and Amista flashed her military ID at a gate guard. We stopped at a little complex of dark wooden cabins and a larger wooden building, glowing with light and full of people.

Inside was an old-fashioned dining room with rustic tables and a mirrored bar. One side of the building floor-to-ceiling windows faced a little strip of water that reflected the moonlight. Amista greeted several people, including a couple seated for dinner, and we found a table and ordered wine. I asked her what this place was, and she told me it was a place where anyone from any branch of the military could come for a getaway. It reminded me of a country club in a town near Oakville where I'd had dinner once as a teenager, the guest of a more affluent friend. Jocular voices, streamed jazz music, the thick scent of cooked beef and buttery mashed potatoes. We sipped wine while I took it all in.

Here I found myself at another place like nowhere I'd ever conceived. A tiny, fancy camp site in the middle of Japan, just for Americans. "Do the Okinawans have resorts like this?" I asked.

Amista laughed and told me Manza Beach, where the Ishikori family had been staying, was one of many such resorts that cater mainly to Japanese. "The difference," she said, "is that American military can only afford log cabins, while the Japanese stay at five-star hotels."

I thought about the wealthy Ishikori family who'd stayed at Manza Beach, and about the Okinawans I interviewed about English classes they'd taken to get ahead in their careers, to earn a better living. Plenty of Japanese people didn't frequent five-star resorts.

"Lucy," said a voice from behind my chair. I turned to see Nathan, fit and handsome in jeans and a polo shirt, smiling down at me.

I introduced him to Amista, who raised her eyebrows and squelched a smile. I squirmed and mumbled an apology. I hadn't spoken to Nathan since our impromptu date which seemed like a lifetime ago. He said something about following my stories in *Okinawa Week*, and I thanked him. He paused as if to suggest another outing, but didn't, said it was great to see me. I agreed that it was nice to see him too, but he might as well have been a stranger. I was happy when he returned to his table full of friends.

"Ouch," Amista said.

"It's not what you think," I confided in her that we'd shared a meal, but that was it, there had been no hint of romance. "He was like a teacher, he told me about military life. And, it sounded so foreign to me."

"Does this place, Okuma, seem foreign to you, since it's an American military place?"

I pondered the question for a moment, inhaled a noseful of tangy white wine and said, "To be honest, there's nowhere I've been in a month that doesn't seem like another planet."

CHAPTER TWENTY-FOUR

My interviews were set for Monday and Hisashi went with me, to translate, if necessary, and take photos. As we drove toward the base, the protest crowd was as big and vociferous as always. At the gate the guard checked our *Okinawa Week* ID cards and directed us to the Kadena Officers' Club, where we'd meet representatives of the American Welfare & Works Association.

On the way inside Hisashi whispered, "Can you believe they divide themselves up this way? Only officers can go here. Enlisted have a separate club." This didn't come as a surprise; I'd learned from Nathan about the different rules for the two groups.

The Officers' Club had thick burgundy carpet, and the musical clicking of slot machines floated down the hall. Hisashi guided me to a set of doors. I was a bit disoriented and felt like I'd stepped into a secret club, might be asked to leave at any moment.

"I was thinking we could take a quick trip to Tokyo next

weekend," he whispered, and I was caught off guard. "I spoke to my mom," he said. "She says it's okay."

I was surprised by this news but needed to stay focused. We entered a small conference room and I snapped back into the moment. "Hello, you must be Miss Tosch? I'm Susan Warren and this is Barbara Dailey." She had a little airplane charm dangling from a gold necklace and a pleasantly wide face. Barbara was pretty in a mousy way and she shifted her weight from foot to foot as though uncomfortable standing up. Susan didn't say hello to Hisashi, which struck me as strange, but she indicated to both of us that we should sit at the table, which was covered with photos and papers.

"That's pretty," I said, by way of an ice breaker, pointing to her necklace. "Do you like planes?"

"My husband is a pilot," she said. It took a second but then I realized she was wearing a plane charm around her neck to advertise her husband's profession. I pictured my mother wearing an apple or a ruler or some other such elementary school charm around her neck and almost giggled.

"Who's your friend?" Susan asked, not in an unfriendly way, but measured.

I told her that Hisashi was the photographer for *Okinawa Week,* and also served as my translator. "I have an interview later with a Japanese group," I explained. Her eyebrows lifted underneath her hair-sprayed bangs.

She picked up a couple of photographs off the table, shots of smiling women and Japanese children taken at Ishimine Orphanage, Okinawa's largest, she said, from "Spring Break Fun Day." Military wives from the Air Force, Marine Corps and Navy went to the orphanage with a local charity group, Help Oki, to set up a bouncy tent, games and a picnic for the kids. "It's just one of many things we do to help the local community," she said, sounding like a quote from a press release. She showed more photos from that event, all similar, happy kids and women.

I asked to see a schedule of their charitable events. It was a bit of a ruse because I knew from my online research that ninety percent of their activities were social: soba noodle class, street shopping excursions, *karaoke* nights. I wanted to see what she'd say.

"We don't have a printed schedule, but the Spring Break Fun Day was one of many charitable events we do in the outside community."

"You do social events too?" Hisashi shot me a surprised look. Barbara stiffened in her seat and started tapping her feet and Susan smiled the practiced smile of a PR professional.

"It's true, we like to have fun. But since our inception in nineteen-fifty-two, we've donated eight million dollars to local charities. That's nothing to sneeze at. I've personally overseen the dissemination of baby blankets and an ultrasound machine to a local hospital in need."

I didn't want to put her on the defense any more than I already had, so I softened my next question. "What's the best thing about being in this group?"

"Community," she said, without hesitation. "AWWA is a group of like-minded women, supportive of the military community but also of the Okinawan community." She sounded like a PSA. I couldn't help myself.

"Do you feel part of the Okinawan community?" I said. Then, "You live behind a guarded gate." Hisashi bowed his head and muttered under his breath. I pressed on. "Do the protests affect you at all?"

Susan and Barbara stood, apparently finished with my questions. They extended their hands and thanked me for my time. Barbara was shell shocked, and Susan was angry. "Ms. Tosch," she said, "is there some reason you assume that the possible rape of a young girl would be any less horrifying to us than to you?"

"No, but I wondered how much what's going outside the gates affects you here, on this guarded base." She took a step closer to me, anger flashing in her eyes.

"You have no idea how many lives have been lost so that you can traipse around in total freedom and ask rude questions," she hissed. "I don't know if the rape allegation is true or not and you don't either. What I do know is that without the military, Okinawa would be like a third-world country." Susan and Barbara whisked themselves out and left us standing in the empty conference room. I was shaken but proud of myself for asking about difficult topics, like an experienced reporter.

We exited the club, past the blinking, dinging slot machine room, and past the dark bar where couples sat drinking, laughing. "Nice work, Lucy," said Hisashi, sarcasm dripping from his voice. "*Okinawa Week* will be blackballed from Kadena now."

I shot back, "Just like we were called out in the media for my courtroom outburst?"

Thick tension filled the car during on the way to the next interview. Why should he be mad? It's a reporter's job to ask tough questions, to get to the truth. I couldn't stand his angry silence. "Hisashi, why do you get so upset with me?" It was as diplomatic as I could be in that moment.

He inhaled and exhaled, exasperated. "Lucy, I like you. You're smart, a little puerile, but a good reporter. But you don't get it. In Japan you can't be so blunt. It's impolite."

"They were Americans, remember? Americans are used to bluntness." I sensed his irritation but didn't care.

"Why can't you learn? Your 'American' manner is offensive, even on a military base." He'd made little air quotes with his fingers and plopped his hands down hard on his lap. "They're used to being treated respectfully by *Okinawa Week*."

This conversation was more heated than our past disagreements. Was this to be the nature of our relationship? We're friends and then not, in the blink of an eye? Was Hisashi going to continue getting mad at me for things I said? I had finally felt comfortable with him, finally had some relief from all the stress and now in a flash, we were back at square one, squabbling strangers. I had to say what was on my mind.

"You claim to be a rebel, bucking tradition by living on Okinawa. Well, you're not." We stopped in the parking lot of our next interview. "You care more about appearances than you care about the truth."

More silence. Then, "I'm going to forgive you for saying that," Hisashi said, and got out of the car.

I sat there catching my breath and took a look around before I got out. I hadn't noticed anything on our drive and now we were parked in front of a dilapidated building in a slum area of the island. An elderly man slumped over on the curb half asleep, a scrawny grey terrier lounged in the shade of an abandoned food stand. Two kindergarten-aged boys in tattered t-shirts ran around playing street baseball with a broken bat. The sign on the building said, "Women Against Military Violence," in faded red lettering, above a *kanji* sign I assumed said the same thing. Hisashi was already out of the car, walking toward the door.

My heart raced, both because of my disagreement with Hisashi and because I expected disapproval or discrimination here because I was American. I'd emailed my interview request to set up the meeting and a woman named Takazato-san had responded in English, so presumably she already knew. Inside the office was spotless and organized, with three Japanese women behind computers. The one closest to the door spoke. "Miss Tosch? Lucy?"

"Yes. Takazato-san?" She came over and took both of my hands, greeted Hisashi with equal warmth.

"Please call me Akari." She offered us two metal chairs by her desk, and we sat. On the walls were photos of Japanese women and girls, their names and the dates of the crimes against them. "Mika Sakaguchi, May 30, 2015," "Yuka Tomayasu, February 2, 2001," "Chieko Aiko, October 2, 1995," and on and on and on, all the way back to "Etsuko Fumie, December 10, 1972." Akari watched me take it all in. The faces of the women looked out from the wall, smiling, the photos taken at some happy moment before their assaults.

"It's difficult to see these faces, knowing what happened to them," Akari said. She leaned forward thoughtfully and pushed a wisp of hair behind her ear. Her clothes were utilitarian, leggings, sneakers and a plain black t-shirt. "I know you have your questions, but may I first give you some statistics?" I nodded. "These one-hundred-and-twenty photos represent the reported rapes of Japanese women by U.S. men. There are thousands more, unreported," she said. In 1972, the U.S. military occupation of Okinawa ended, she explained, and before that no data was kept. The Battle of Okinawa ended seventy-one years ago, so for almost thirty years, rapes and other crimes were undocumented. She paused while I absorbed this data. "Heartbreaking, isn't it?"

"How do you know there have been thousands of unreported rapes during those years?" I was in reporter mode, far off my script of questions about collaboration between women's groups and determined to get the story she wanted to tell. She maintained a friendly demeanor, smiling and polite but beneath her professional polish, I sensed her passion for this cause

"Lucy, you know women are reluctant to report rape. Even in the most civilized countries and situations, few women come forward." I thought about the humiliation I had felt after my upskirt assault, my empathy with Midori Ishikori. I didn't want to let those situations affect my objectivity.

"Do you have data to back up your claims?" It wasn't so much that I doubted her veracity, but I needed proof for any story that I might eventually write.

"Your own government provides compelling data," she said. "In 2012, the U.S. Department of Defense announced that in one year there were an estimated nineteen thousand sexual assaults *inside* the armed forces. Soldier on soldier, not even counting soldier-civilian instances. Nineteen thousand, in one year. Hard to grasp, isn't it?"

"I don't see how that relates to Okinawa."

"Well, consider that in a press conference in Washington D.C. your government spoke about the rape of a woman soldier by her superior officer. They talked about it as an example of all that was wrong in the U.S. military. That rape took place on a base on Okinawa. If rape can happen on base, can't you see how it can happen even more so off base, where soldiers roam freely?"

This woman was beyond articulate. She provided me with data, quotes and context, not only for a news story, but for the broader story about what was happening on Okinawa. I might not be able to use it but would pass it along to Amista.

"Let me give you an anecdote," Akari said, pointing to a photo on the wall of a young girl, snuggling a creamy brown rabbit on her lap. "In 2005, this ten-year-old girl was victimized." After hearing that news, Akari explained, another woman came forward to report that twenty years earlier, three American soldiers raped her. Because she didn't take the case to court, it wasn't counted among the one-hundred-and-twenty. "I wonder how many more invisible victims there are? From every year and in every era?"

The truth of her statement settled into me. I knew she was right and felt deflated by this sad set of facts. I changed course and asked, "What is the goal of your group, Women Against Military Violence?" I knew she probably had a stock answer, but I wanted to hear how she put it.

"Our goal is to reduce or remove U.S. forces from Okinawa. This as the only way to end the violence that comes to us from the bases."

I wanted to bring the conversation around to my story, although my story seemed silly at this point. "Akari, the subject of my piece is how you work together with American women's groups." I sounded ridiculous, but I went on. "*Do* you work with American women's groups?"

Akari's face went hard. "We work with anyone who will fight to end U.S. violence against Okinawans." She sat back in her chair, serious now. "What about you, Lucy? Will you work with us to end violence against women?"

She'd turned the tables on me, and I didn't have an adequate answer. "I'm here as a reporter," I said, lamely.

"I understand. Think about it. At least consider the possibility, okay?" She was serious. Think about becoming an anti-military activist for a Japanese nonprofit? The idea was farfetched, but her sincerity was piercing. "Lucy, have you ever been victimized?" Completely disarmed, I said I had, but not as bad as rape. "Is any level of assault okay?" she asked.

I told her I needed some air and she nodded sympathetically. "It's difficult," she said.

Hisashi followed me outside. "Don't let her rattle you, Lucy," he said, concerned.

I was relieved he wasn't still angry because of our earlier disagreement. I took deep breaths of florid subtropical air. We went back in and sat down.

"Please let me share just a few more facts," Akari said. She went on to say that eighteen percent of Okinawa's land was in use by military bases, cordoned off by fences, where U.S. soldiers lived and worked. Anyone associated with U.S. forces can go in and out of the gates freely. "Okinawans must stay outside the gates. If you look at it this way, you can see that all of Okinawa has essentially been handed to the U.S. military."

"Handed to them?" I wanted clarification.

She took her time in responding. "Okinawa is an open target for those with evil intent. We are off the radar of many Japanese, who prefer to forget about us. We are off the world radar because we are so small and powerless."

To my surprise, Hisashi spoke up. "She's right, Lucy. Okinawa is exploited and ignored." I was a spectator at this point, a civilian, dropped into a conversation with two veterans, about the proxy war on Okinawa with its longstanding battle zones. Akari Takazato had a few final points and I kept my recorder on and didn't ask anything more.

"Marine Expeditionary Force Commander Lieutenant General Nicholson pledged to 'tighten discipline.' That hasn't happened. After each crime, we stage protests and the U.S. imposes a temporary curfew or lockdown. But only until the uproar dies down. Then another heinous crime is committed and on and on. It's an intolerable circle of pain," she said.

I was at a loss for words. I didn't have the bravery or the energy to say I'd join her cause. But she said it again, "Consider joining us." I thanked her for her time. "I look forward to reading your article, Lucy," she said.

I couldn't bring myself to tell her that I wouldn't be writing the article about what she shared, just giving the information to Amista. For once I was glad that Ashimine-san had me on fluffier stories. She was right, I should join her cause, but I lacked the will, didn't see myself as an activist.

I rolled my window down and turned my face into the

wind. I'd just been schooled by a woman my age, but much wiser. Okinawa itself was turning out to be my biggest *sensei*.

When he dropped me off, Hisashi told me we ought to go to Tokyo sooner and not later. "We both need a break," he said. I was surprised that he still wanted to take me, but too bewildered and tired to question it.

CHAPTER TWENTY-FIVE

I slept the next day away. My spirit had given out and I climbed into bed with no plan to get out. I didn't play music, just stared at my chipped ceiling tiles until my eyes closed. The sounds of car engines, yelling protestors and hawking vendors on Kadena Gate Street woke me up a few times and I fell right back to a dreamless sleep. My cell phone dinged with texts and calls from Rose and Mom and Amista and Hisashi and even Ashimine-san. When I woke up Tuesday night I knew exactly where I was though I was no longer sure who I was. The person I used to be had evaporated or disintegrated. I ate boxed noodles and fell back into bed until the morning. Then I limped into work as if still asleep.

I gave Amista the interview recording and told her it might help with the rape story. Work on the women's group story seemed ridiculous. Rumiko had concern in her eyes. I knocked on Ashimine-san's door and asked if I could take a few days off. "I'm exhausted," I admitted. And like the kind, fatherly man he was, he agreed to give me the time off, but warned that I'd need to finish my story the minute I got back.

. . .

Hisashi guided me through the airport procedures at Naha terminal with the efficiency of a seasoned bodyguard. We made it through baggage and check-in in about ten minutes and onto the plane in another twenty. I came around from my exhausted stupor as it dawned on me, I was leaving the pressure cooker of Okinawa. I hadn't realized how out of it I'd been.

"You sat at your desk Wednesday for three hours without doing anything," Hisashi said. "Even Rumiko was worried." Ashimine-san, he added, recognized the toll that the whirlwind few weeks on island has taken on you and suggested this trip. "He said you'd feel better after seeing more peaceful parts of Japan."

I asked Hisashi if his parents knew we were on the way and he said yes, and we'd stay with them. I could have been intimidated after all Hisashi had told me about his family, but I was more numb than afraid. "I will be glad to see your mother," I said. "She was so gracious to me." I didn't say anything about Mr. Ota.

"Dad knows I'm bringing you," Hisashi said, answering my unasked question. I gave him a skeptical face. "It's best not to mention Owen around my father," he added. More advice to keep my mouth shut. Out of respect, I would do it.

"Can we see Owen?" I asked.

"I'm afraid not. We think he's in Tokyo, but he's asked us not to contact him. Said he needs time to restart his life, outside the reach of his family."

"Ah. Understandable," I murmured. I barely admitted to myself that I felt a touch of relief; it would have been awkward to see him. It seemed better to hold on to our shared memories, as unvarnished as they were by harsh realities.

Hisashi stretched in his airplane seat. First class on Japan

Airlines was like a television commercial, the flight attendant kept filling our little champagne glasses and, though a quick flight, she fed us plates of warm ham and cheese and cups of mint sorbet. The plane ride went by in a flash of clouds and blue ocean.

As quickly as we boarded in Naha, we deplaned in Tokyo. The Tokyo airport was crowded and nondescript as was the start of the cab ride, down a busy grey-walled highway. We exited into the city and wove through traffic, crisscrossed deeper downtown, crept slowly into the city, our vehicle speed impeded by the throngs of walkers at the edge of the lanes. People, people and more people. Crowds waited at each cross-walk, and then moved across it as one tightly sewn piece of living fabric. The streets were lined with all types of busi-nesses, from a matchbox-sized yellow-and-red McDonald's, to steel-and-glass skyscraper Citibank and BNP Paribas offices. It was a crush of bodies and commerce and my impression was serious, serious people in a hurry on their way to important places as they stared at cell phones. I did see some teenagers dressed to the hilt in funky clothes—knee socks, mini-skirts, patent-leather shoes and bright red lipstick—finally, the hipsters I'd expected from music videos. In person they looked like kids playing dress up, which probably is what Owen was too, when I knew him.

We exited the heart of the city into a more suburban area, drove up a long driveway lined with tall trees to arrive at a striking white contemporary house. Before I could open the car door, someone opened it for me. Standing in front of me was Mrs. Ota, exactly as I remembered her. Beautiful, with skin like polished silk. "Lucy!" She seemed delighted to see me. "Wel-come. What a small, small world. You told me you'd come to Japan and here you are."

She ushered us into a front hall with double-tall ceilings

and an enormous bouquet on a huge pedestal, purple morning glories and pink lotus blossoms. "Let me show you your room," Mrs. Ota said. "You must be exhausted." As we headed down the hall, I turned back and took a quick photo of the flowers.

Hisashi headed down another hallway and I found myself alone in a spacious bedroom with sliding doors out to a little patio and garden. The bedroom had fluffy bedding and more vases of fragrant flowers. The bathroom was ivory marble with a spa-sized tub and a television on the wall. I'd never been in such a luxurious room. It seemed impossible that a few hours ago I was in my tiny sparse apartment and now I was here in this posh room, in Tokyo, at Owen Ota's house. We must have been on a hill because when I went outside, I could see all the way to the city and the mountains beyond. And right before me, in the center of a manicured back yard, stood a tall Japanese maple tree with fiery red and orange leaves. I'd seen such trees depicted in photos but had never seen one in person. Its color was splendid against the jade-green lawn. I took a photo and texted it and the flower photo to Rose.

She responded immediately, "Whoa. Where are you?"

"Tokyo. Owen's house."

"Double whoa!"

Hisashi texted me. "Meet us in the garden room?" I brushed my teeth, smoothed out my rumpled dress and patted down my unruly hair. In the mirror my cheeks had a soft rosy glow, not a hot-pink flush and not the skinny timid face I had when I arrived in Okinawa a month ago. Tuning out for a few days, sleeping, and not thinking, had smoothed the stress lines between my eyes.

Down the hall and past the expansive dining room I found a living room with doors flung open to an enclosed patio. Hisashi stood and introduced me to his father, Mr. Ota, who looked so much like Owen my heart jumped. Same deep-set eyes and high cheekbones, tall and lanky. "Miss Tosch, welcome to our home. Hisashi says you've always wanted to visit Tokyo."

"Yes, thank you," I said, swallowing my surprise. Mr. Ota was a three-decades older carbon copy of Owen. I collected myself and said, "Your home is beautiful."

The four of us, Hisashi, Mr. and Mrs. Ota, and I, chatted for a few minutes. They asked how I liked *Okinawa Week* and if I missed my family. They wanted to know if I planned to stay in Japan. "I'm not sure. I'm still deciding," I said, the first time I'd voiced that particular truth to anyone but Rose. Hisashi opened his eyes wide, questioning.

"Once you see Tokyo and the surrounding areas you'll never want to leave," Mr. Ota said. "We can't understand why Hisashi wants to live so far away." His tone was sweet, kind, not the growling ogre I'd expected. He sounded like any parent who missed his child, like my mom, when she asked me to come back to Illinois. "Okinawa is a world away from Tokyo," he added.

I had no idea what if anything they knew about my tumultuous time on Okinawa but didn't think this was the time to mention any of it.

"Lucy and I plan to go south tomorrow, to Mt. Fuji," Hisashi said.

"Lucy knew Owen," Mrs. Ota said, sucking the air out of the room.

"Ah, well," Mr. Ota said, as if waiting for an explanation.

"They knew each other briefly at Northwestern," Hisashi said. "Right, Lucy?"

"Yes. We were friends." I wasn't sure what Mr. Ota would say, maybe spit vitriol or walk out of the room because I knew the son he was ashamed of.

"That's nice," Mr. Ota said. "Nice to know he had a friend

in Illinois." His shoulders slumped and his eyes were weary. "We miss him." His sadness was palpable, and I glanced at Hisashi. I'd been led to expect a fiery judgmental dictator and here, a sad father who missed his son.

We had a casual dinner on the patio and spoke about Okinawa and all its problems. The Otas were thoughtful, well-informed, and of the opinion that the U.S. should reduce its presence there. "Americans have outstayed their welcome," Mr. Ota said. About whether or not Airman Stone was guilty, Mrs. Ota said what most Japanese believed, "He probably did it." Both parents expressed admiration for their son living on Okinawa and working as a journalist to expose difficult truths. I sensed nothing of the scorned father I'd expected.

"You're in the truth business too, right, Lucy?" Mr. Ota said. "Is journalism going to be your lifelong career?"

I'd been thinking about my meeting with Akari Takazato. "I thought so, but now I'm not sure. I'm going to explore my options." Hisashi shot me a look and I shrugged. Saying it out loud made it real. I would contact her when we went back to Okinawa.

Dinner with the Otas was not strange at all. It reminded me of a more elegant version of dinner at my own childhood home, chatting about news of the day. Owen's name did not come up again, but there were family photos on the mantel showing him as an adolescent, same handsome face, same mysterious aura. Sitting with people who had twenty-one years of photos with Owen—birthdays and family gatherings—reinforced how little I really knew about him.

Hisashi walked me back to my room after dinner. "What was that about not being sure you'd keep on doing journalism?"

"I don't know. I might need to get out into the real world more."

"You've had a big dose of the real world in the last month."

"Yes, but Takazato-san made sense to me. I'm thinking."

Hisashi said I was full of surprises and told me to be ready at eight a.m. because we'd have a long day touring. "We're going to Aokigahara," he said, and the hairs on my arms stood up. He hadn't mentioned a trip to Suicide Forest and was resistant to the idea when I'd brought it up before. "It might be good for both of us," he said. He kissed me on the cheek, the way a brother would do. He pointed out my back window across the city. "Look out in the distance. You can't see it yet, but Mt. Fuji is out there, not far. And Aokigahara is near its base."

I stared out across twinkling Tokyo lights and into the dark distance. I was finally in a place I'd longed to be for years, had fantasized about. Not with Owen, but with another man who I liked and felt protected by. Okinawa, its trials and troubles fell away like a layer of dust from freshly washed skin.

CHAPTER TWENTY-SIX

I woke up doused in anticipation about Suicide Forest, both fearful and eager, emotions that typically didn't coexist in me. It was much cooler in Tokyo than it had been on Okinawa and on that day, the sky was pale blue washed in layers of low clouds. Haze floated outside my back window.

Hisashi arranged a private car. Speeding out of busy Tokyo the scenery morphed into greenscapes and wooded areas. We passed small towns with traditional elevated houses, and sloped farmland covered in rice paddies and wheat fields. We wound our way through hills where cows grazed, standing at diagonal angles, and we passed a stunning field of fuchsia flowers, "pink moss," Hisashi said, in bloom for an unseasonably long time this year.

After two hours we came to the edge of a lake and stopped in front of a path lined with a profusion of orange and red maples that led to a giant Buddha statue. Hisashi told me many such monuments dotted this countryside. The statue was imposing, made of stone, seated like a king on a throne of blossoms. We spent a few minutes there among the other tourists, meditative and respectfully quiet. I silently prayed we wouldn't encounter people in Suicide Forest or see remnants of death.

Next, we drove to a little village with an unobstructed view of Mt. Fuji across glassy water. "This is Lake Ashi," Hisashi told me, "Lake of Reeds." He said we wouldn't take a tourist boat ride but that we should grab a bite. The town was called Fujinomiya and it was popular with visitors. We sat in an open-air restaurant and ordered beers. My urge to drink had waned in the past week and one beer hit the spot. Glasses of wine or sake didn't appeal to me the way they had during my first tumultuous month in Japan. The sun was muted, and the air was light and crisp, scented with fried fish and flowers. The day felt like a new beginning, like a do-over of my arrival in Japan.

Tourists on foot followed guides with tall signs. "Holiday Inn." "Viator." "Mr. Carlinski." Hisashi told me the signs were ad hoc or proper names so that tour groups wouldn't lose each other. There was a blonde family with Australian accents, a gang of twenty or so stout elderly folks, and two groups of Japanese.

In the near distance, thicker clouds blanketed Mt. Fuji's peak and its wide, brown sides were not as majestic as I'd expected. Hisashi filled me in on the history of the mountain, its popularity as a place for climbers, artists and spiritual seekers for hundreds of years, and its status as a national symbol of Japan, with its symmetry and gentle slopes. Things I already knew, but I enjoyed Hisashi's confident professorial tone as he spoke. "The mountain is like the spirit of its people," he said. "Gentle and beautiful." I remembered Owen teaching me about *haiku* in a similar tone. They both were natural *sensei*.

After lunch he said, "Are you ready?"

"Ready to go to Suicide Forest?"

"No. Ready to hear my lesson about it." He grinned and I nodded. He told me that in the nineteenth century and other eras when Japan was in famine, poor families deserted sick young children and old people in Aokigahara, those they couldn't afford to care for. Today, some Japanese believe their spirits remain in the forest in the form of ghosts, goblins and even demons. "*Ubasute*. That's what the practice was called. It means abandoning the infirm."

I shuddered and imagined an old woman on a forest floor, wasted away, and Owen, swinging from a dark tree. "It's a quiet, windless forest," he continued. "Such dense growth that it's almost silent inside." Hisashi pointed toward the left base of the mountain, anchored by a blur of shadowy foliage. "The ground is dried magma from a volcanic explosion one thousand years ago."

The rumor, he said, is that the forest is infected with sorrow down to the tree roots and the dirt. Some say the forest itself has taken on the pain of the people left there to die and that it holds their misery captive somehow, so a depressed person finds it easier to kill himself there. "That's what I believe," Hisashi said. "Owen might not have tried to do it if he hadn't gone to Suicide Forest. His depression would have passed, and he could've worked things out with our father." It surprised me to hear that Hisashi believed a haunted forest could have contributed to Owen's suicide attempt. I hadn't known Hisashi had a mystical side, had thought of him as practical, solid, of the here and now. I pointed out that his father hadn't been as harsh as he'd led me to believe he'd be. "That's because you were there," Hisashi said. "He'd never want you to be uncomfortable in his home. That's the Japanese way."

We drove around the lake and soon we arrived at a parking lot near the edge of a thick wall of trees and the dark entrance to a trail. There were a few cars in the lot, several covered in telltale leaves and grime; they'd been there a while.

"Let's go in just a little way," Hisashi said, and gripped my hand. I paused to collect my thoughts. This could very well be the forest opening that Owen had seen. I shuddered and we started to walk. Though it was still summer, the trees at the start of the trail had a mixture of dead leaves and sickly green and yellow leaves hanging by threads, clinging to life.

The path was hard and uneven under my feet, with tree roots that crawled in every direction, twisting around and over each other, in a fight for survival. The dusty lava floor of the forest was penetrable to a few inches only, so trees had a slack hold on the ground. Many tilted at crazy angles or drooped as the weight of their bulk strained to yank them from the earth. Over our heads, black branches clawed at each other and pointed bent fingers in blame. Which tree was the one Owen had approached, which others bore dark witness? Hemlock firs, Japanese cypress and andromeda, and Mongolian oaks had a death-grip on the sky, blocking all but tiny shards of light. I breathed in the sour smell of mold and moldering moss, and some critter, a lone mole or a mouse, careened away from our approaching feet. The silence was broken only by our labored breathing and our feet as they crunched rotted leaves. The dank atmosphere pressed down on me and I had a sense of dread, as if we could somehow lose our minds and meet our doom here as so many others had done.

After a hundred yards or so the charcoal green and grey foliage trail bled into an ochre and slate gauze that muddied our visibility. We reached our hands out in front of us, to avoid colliding with the fallen corpse of a tree. The air grew icy and my skin jolted with goosebumps. It was at least twenty degrees colder inside this frightful forest.

Hisashi squeezed my hand, stopped and pointed to a placard nailed to a tree. "'Think of your family.' That's what it says," he said. "The police post signs to discourage people from going further." His voice was tattered and quiet. Owen could have seen that sign and ignored its plea. Perhaps he felt drawn in by the sorrowful spirits who perished there and sought the company of other sad souls.

We kept moving and came to a small clearing, another placard on a tree, the name and phone number of a suicide prevention hotline. It was horrifying to realize that some one hundred people a year encountered that sign and chose to ignore it. Despite the cold, my hands were clammy as we moved on past several more placards.

"We aren't supposed to go off the path," Hisashi said. "These signs warn hikers to stay on the path."

I had my sights set on a tree trunk just ahead—a giant, bigger than the others. I strained for some sound, another human voice or the rustling of foliage, but the forest was mute. Suddenly, a solitary shrill bird call echoed around us and I jumped, almost fell.

"Slow down," Hisashi said, and tugged my hand. But I kept going toward the massive tree that towered in front of us. It was licorice-black and stark naked. It looked as though it had always been dead.

A flash on the ground caught my eye. I fumbled for my phone and flicked on the light. At our feet was a royal blue ribbon, faded a little from weather or time. It was on the path and wound around the base of the dead giant. "What's this?"

Hisashi frowned as if unsure he should answer, then said, "That's what people use when they aren't sure they really want to go through with it. Someone would track his steps with a ribbon. If he changes his mind, the ribbon helps him find his way back out."

I reached down to touch it but then realized it might be sacred, someone's last memento, a relic leading to the spot where they took their last breath. I drew back my hand. "Can we see where it leads?" I asked Hisashi.

"Okay. But be ready for what might be at the end."

My legs were shaky, but I was determined to know what revelation or misery we might find at the end of the ribbon. It felt imperative that we make our way to its final point, to bear witness to what was there.

"If we go, can you find the way out?" I asked, and he assured me he could. I was aware that my resolve to go on was somewhat careless, but Hisashi didn't try to stop me. He swung his arm over my shoulders and drew me in so that our torsos touched. Strangely, in this gloomy place, Hisashi's presence offered a layer of protection, both physical and emotional. He was my own personal *shisa*, able to guide me and keep bad spirits at bay. He was confident when I was afraid, cautious when I was reckless.

After a few hundred yards, we reached the ribbon's end. It was nailed to a low tree branch. I scanned the ground. I didn't see any sign a person had been here, no empty water bottles, no discarded granola wrappers, no lost sunglasses. Then something caught my attention, sticking up near a knotty bunch of roots. We peered and moved closer—it was the toe guard of a pink and white sneaker. I sprang backward and bumped into Hisashi and he tottered but then regained his balance. Together we brushed away the dirt and discovered that the other shoe was there too, next to the first one. I was alarmed. What if legs were still attached to the shoes? Hisashi swept away more debris until he got to smooth ground below. Nothing else was there. Just this pair of shoes, about a women's size seven, in good shape.

Hisashi tapped my arm and pointed his phone light up the tree. I squinted to bring the jumble of branches into focus. Then I saw it, four pieces of thick rope hanging over a limb, their frayed edges uniformly cut. The remnants of a noose. And here below, her shoes, having fallen off during the suicide or perhaps she'd removed them before. I went hollow inside.

"The authorities probably cut the rope to remove the body, but didn't see the shoes," Hisashi whispered. "Otherwise they would have taken them away. It must be recent, or they'd have taken the rope too."

I stared up at the rope. October. That's when Owen had left Illinois. November, that's when he wanted to die. The article had said there were four suicides on the day Owen was here. This forest would have been even darker and colder, with deadness all around. Dead trees, dead bodies, the ghosts of ancient dead.

As I backed away, my foot caught on a tree root, and I fell hard on my backside. Hisashi bent and hauled me up with both hands. I was disoriented as we headed back toward the path. We trudged along as briskly as we could, taking high steps to avoid another trip and fall. In an hour or so, the sunlight up ahead beckoned us. I'd never wanted to get out of anywhere as much as I wanted to get out of that forest. It's as if the ghosts of the dead tried to wrap their phantom fingers around my arms and legs and drag me back in. Owen must have felt them too, and he found the will to pry them away.

A man in a black uniform came crashing out of the woods and stood in front of us, shouted and gestured toward the parking lot. Hisashi bowed and said, "*Hai, hai, onegaishimasu.*" The ranger's face was a mix of irritation and concern. Clearly, he knew we'd been off the path and wanted to make sure we exited and didn't go back in. We hurried toward the light, toward the way out.

When we emerged into the parking lot there was a group of uniformed men and a tow truck taking away a filthy car. Underneath the grime, the car was the same royal blue color as the ribbon we'd followed, and its license plate was framed in pink crystals, the color of the pretty pink gym shoes we'd found. I felt sick and turned away, walked back to the mouth of the path. Peering into the murky forest, I tried to imagine what Owen had seen and felt when he walked in. Despair must have been so deep in Owen's bones that he couldn't see the light that shone out from within him, so apparent to everyone else. He had been so young, as I had been when I knew him, with emotions so intense they overshadowed the reality of his situation. Maybe with the passage of time, Owen would outgrow his shame, and learn to accept himself whether or not his father did. My heart ached, not only for the loss of Owen from my life, but also for my new awareness about the nature of shame. I'd been ashamed by the upskirt attacker, and by the man who yelled a slur at me in the courtroom, but they were minor indignities compared to what it must have been like for Owen, shamed by his own father.

We stayed a few more moments and looked back through the entangled dark branches. Shadows and fuzzy shapes shifted in and out of focus and from this vantage point, outside looking in, I swear I heard the trees hiss dire warnings. A stiff wind rustled my curls and Hisashi wiped his eyes. I didn't want to intrude on his grief; mine was so small in comparison. I lost an emotional fantasy, but he lost the presence of his brother in his daily life. I'd expected to understand more about Owen from this pilgrimage to Suicide Forest, but instead I learned more about Hisashi, a man who though he suffered because he missed his brother and understood the folly of my feelings for him, still treated me like a little sister, to be safeguarded and guided.

My search for answers had driven me to these haunted, forsaken woods, *Aokigahara*, Suicide Forest, a place so vile that Japanese deny its existence, and so frightening only the most desperate dare to enter. When I began my search, I'd known nothing of this vast wasteland of lost souls or the strange path I'd take to get here. I'd gone from Evanston to Okinawa to Tokyo, and finally to *Aokigahara* and now, it was time to go away from this sad place, and to let Owen go too.

We didn't speak on the way back to Tokyo, both lost in our own thoughts. Back at the Ota's house, Hisashi excused himself to shower. While he was gone, I sat in my bedroom window, watching the Tokyo lights twinkling on the horizon. The city of my dreams was stretched out before me like a star-lighted prairie and tomorrow I'd get to see it up close in the light of a cool new day.

When Hisashi came back he said, "I don't feel better, just sadder." I hugged him, squeezing his broad torso, inhaling the soapy smell of his hair. Of course, his sadness about Owen's absence from the Ota's lives needed more time to subside.

"You know, I bet he'll contact you," I said. He moved close to me and dropped his head on to my shoulder and I felt his tears dampen my sleeve. It was a sweet, sorrowful moment that I have remembered ever since.

Later that night, I asked Hisashi about the *haiku* Owen had published. He left the room and returned with a little paperback book called, *Hotaru*.

"Firefly, that's what *hotaru* means. It's the name of the literary journal." He told me that in Japanese lore, *hotarus* signify love and are a popular image in romantic poetry. He opened the book and handed it to me. There it was. "Lit," by Owen Ota. The *haiku* he'd published as a teenager.

Sky doused and skin moist
    hands like hotarus *in clouds*

My heart, lit at last

I thought back to the *haiku* lesson that Owen and I had shared so long ago. He'd told me a *haiku* uses nature, but with a twist that illuminates the end of the poem and clarifies its meaning. I read his *haiku* again and maybe I understood what Owen was trying to say. I was glad he'd felt lit up, for at least some of his life. I wished I could tell him how much he'd lit up my world, opened my heart.

The next day, Hisashi and I toured Tokyo and it was what I knew it would be. Vibrant, beautiful, exciting, hectic, exotic, but also, anything but exotic, with people bumping about talking on cell phones, not looking at each other.

EPILOGUE

Hisashi and I visited Tokyo many times in the next few years and on one trip, I was astonished to see Owen, standing in the Ota's doorway. He looked precisely as I remembered, tall, dressed in black, and the coolest human I'd ever seen. I didn't have the chance to say anything before Hisashi ran over and smothered him in a hug, lifted his feet off the ground.

"Man. I've missed you," Hisashi said. And Owen smiled his big bright smile at Hisashi and then me. They exchanged a few words in private and then Owen turned to me.

"Lucy!"

I got a chill from the shock of seeing him again, hearing his voice. "Owen!" And we hugged, the hug of old friends.

We went inside and sat in the living room. Mr. and Mrs. Ota were already sitting, sipping cold sake. Mr. Ota was radiant, glowing from happiness at the arrival of his wayward son. "He surprised us! It's been too long, and we are thrilled he's returned."

Owen told us that he lived in downtown Tokyo and had an

editorial job with a nature magazine. He said he'd managed to finish college and got his degree in journalism, just like I had. "Lucy, you work with Hisashi?"

"Yes. How did you know?"

"I keep track of people I care about," he said and shot me his familiar sweet smile. I was elated to be sitting with Owen after being certain I'd never see him again.

"Are you staying for a while?" Mrs. Ota said, her voice edged with hope.

"I'll stay overnight," Owen said. "I have to get back to work tomorrow."

The conversation carried on, with the family getting caught up on all they'd been doing, galas, travel, Hisashi's work at *Okinawa Week*, Owen's love for life in the city. I stayed fairly quiet, not wanting to intrude on the family's reunion. It had been almost two years since anyone had seen Owen and the atmosphere in the room felt celebratory. If Mr. Ota still felt ashamed of his son, it was not evident.

Before we turned in for the night, Owen took me aside. We stood in the long hallway and put both his hands on my shoulders. "I'm sorry, Lu. I really am. For confusing you and for leaving so suddenly. I should have apologized much sooner. I was very insecure back then."

"You did text. You texted, 'Sorry Lu.'"

"Please tell me you don't hate me," he said, his eyes searching mine. He could never know the depth of my heartbreak over him and I wouldn't tell him. I didn't want him to feel worse.

"I don't hate you," I said, and hugged him. "You're the reason I'm in Japan at all, and I'm thankful for that."

"You came here because of me?"

"Yes. Sort of. You ignited my interest in your country and culture." This was a partial truth, of course; I'd never admit to him the childish obsession I'd had for him. "So, thank you for setting me on a course to Japan."

And in that moment, I was thankful, for my brief but impactful time with Owen, and for his influence on my life. Both Hisashi and Owen had the lovely ability to make me feel comfortable and safe, no matter what else happened in the world.

"Oh! Hisashi showed me your *haiku*."

He looked a little sheepish and said, "Did you like it?"

"It's beautiful."

"Lucy, you always treated me with respect and love. I'm not only sorry for how I treated you, I'm thankful for how you treated me."

We hugged again then I realized my heart was fully intact, no longer broken or bruised. Just as I'd gotten through the death of my father, I'd come full circle with Owen. I'd reconciled my memories of him with the reality of who he really was. It was as happy as I'd been in years and I was grateful to Owen and to the universe. As I slept that night, a new sense of peace and purpose seeped into my heart.

Hisashi and I didn't dwell on Owen after that trip, except for an occasional toast of thanks that he'd been the catalyst that brought us together. Owen was off in Tokyo, living in freedom and finding his way, and we focused on our work on Okinawa. The whole time we worked together at *Okinawa Week*, Hisashi fussed and worried about my American bluntness. Likewise, I considered him a prissy fussbudget in a big man costume, always worried what others thought. Of course, that's a cultural difference, American versus Japanese. But they are surface differences, not at our cores, just skin level. Our cores are made up of the same emotional goo. We love our families and try to be true to ourselves. We strive to do well in the world, and despair when others hurt.

I never told anyone at *Okinawa Week* that I'd applied for reporting jobs in Tokyo and Osaka too and had prayed I'd get one of them, had hoped to live in one of the big cities, with their bullet trains, dance-party bars, Harajuku scenes and cherry blossom parks. After that first trip to Tokyo with Hisashi, I knew I'd do it all over time, and would have the chance to reconcile my fantasy Japan with the real one.

My young love for Owen set the course for the rest of my life. He opened my eyes to a distant and beautiful culture. I liked to think he strung a black silk ribbon through the trees and that he used it to come back out of the forest. That he aborted his own suicide attempt, versus failed at it. I never pressed Hisashi for those grim details. It seemed best to let it go.

Even from a distant vantage point, I still can't define precisely why Owen affected me so much. It may have been the confluence of losses, losing my father and Owen in such a short time. But also, the mix of new beginnings at Northwestern, the allure of an exotic lover, the inspiration of writing and poetry we shared, the hormones of my age, and then the mystery of Owen's disappearance from my life. All of these things cemented my short time with Owen into an arrow in my heart and propelled me to Japan. And in the end, I realized that when we were in Illinois, I understood as little about the composition of Owen's heart as I knew about Japan when I first arrived.

Poor Midori Ishikori. Poor Reginald Stone. I think of them sometimes when I walk the Sunabe Seawall or swim at Manza Beach. Their fates were intertwined, and their futures altered, in the same way the fate of the island is intertwined with that of its American occupiers. Stone was acquitted for lack of evidence, Midori retreated into her gated enclave in Tokyo. I believe the verdict was unjust. I believe Midori. History tells me Stone is probably guilty.

I spoke to Nathan only once after our encounter at Okuma, but I've always been grateful for the germs of knowledge he'd shared with me, an interlude that deepened my perspective. For me, a relationship with a military man was too odd, the military, with its airplane-wearing wives, too uncomfortable.

A few months after my first trip to Tokyo, I left *Okinawa Week*, not content with reporting the actions of others. After a lifetime of watching without risking anything, I wanted to be an actor in my own life. Ashimine-san took the news hard but so graciously. "Thank you for your work, Miss Tosch. You are welcome here any time," he said, and bowed.

I took a job with Akari Takazato. I'm a victim too, after all, though I still hate to see myself that way. Akari and I battle to get the bases removed from Okinawa, without success so far. From time to time, I still write and publish journalism, and I'm still close with Amista, my first friend in Japan, and Hisashi, my best friend in Japan. Rose and Mom visit me sometimes, and I'm proud to show them around, to give them a glimpse of the island and the culture. After their first trip to Okinawa, my mom told me she was proud of me. "And your father would be too," she said, hugging me goodbye. She seemed to have recovered from my father's death, finally, and I saw soft contentment behind her eyes.

These days, I spend my days fighting for what's right and my nights communing with my island home. Okinawa, for all the pain and stress it rained down on me, was the place I grew up, the place where I learned that feelings can be fleeting or fixed, fluctuating with the wind or stuck inside our stomachs like cement. I learned to apply logic to my emotional reactions, to temper my feelings with thought, to be an adult.

Sometimes on a moonlit night when the East China Sea is sparkling black glass out my window, I whisper thanks to Owen Ota for shaping my life, being my original *sensei*. I followed him all the way to Japan and am so glad I did. At times, I still hear my father encouraging me in the ocean breeze. "Good for you, Lu," he always says, and I know he's right. Japan is good for me and I will be good to it.

Notes

1. First-hand reporting inspired descriptions of Okinawa protests, as well as a variety of sources, including: Jon Mitchell, "Okinawa: pocket of resistance," *The Japan Times,* July 9, 2014; "Two NASJRB Sailors Arrested in Japan on Suspicion of Sexual Assault," *NBC DFW,* October 17, 2012; Vicky Tuke, "Understanding the complexity of Okinawa," *East Asia Forum,* November 2, 2012; "Outnumbered and aging Okinawa protesters oppose U.S. base," *Reuters/The Asahi Shimbun,* April 3, 2019.

2. The history of *haiku* was synopsized from a variety of sources, including: The Poetry Foundation; *"Haiku,"* Wikipedia; Esther Spurrill Jones, "How to Write Haiku," The Writing Cooperative, September 28, 2018.

3. References to accidents involving Osprey aircraft came from various sources, including: Yuri Kageyama, "Crime, Osprey add to Okinawan anger over US bases," *Associated Press,* December 13, 2012; Mari Yamaguchi, "US military Osprey crash-lands off Okinawa, no fatalities, *Associated Press,* December 13, 2016.

4. Data cited about American crimes against Okinawans and assaults within the U.S. military came from: Takazato Suzuyo, "Okinawan Women Demand U.S. Forces Out After Another Rape and Murder: Suspect an ex-Marine and U.S. Military Employee," *The Asia Pacific Journal,* June 1, 2016.

5. Descriptions of suicide forest were inspired by:

Kristy Puchko, "15 Eerie Things About Japan's Suicide Forest," *Mental Floss*, January 8, 2016: Yamanashi Tourism Organization, "The nature found in the Aokigahara 'sea of trees'"; Shane Berry, "Sea of Blue Foliage: A Night in the Suicide Forest – Part 4;" "Aokigahara," *Wikipedia*.

ACKNOWLEDGMENTS

Many thoughtful people helped me at different stages as I wrote this book, too many to name individually. Both writer and reader friends provided me with invaluable input that shaped the final form of the novel. I am deeply grateful to all of those who shared their time, talents and creativity.

To all my peers and professors in the Fairfield University MFA program, you gave me the confidence to follow my creative dreams. You made it possible for me to switch from journalism and business writing to fiction and poetry. It was my dream come true. You showed me it was never too late to reinvent myself into the writer I always wanted to be. You know who you are. Thank you and I love you.

To my writers groups online, in California, Vermont, Illinois, Ireland and Connecticut, who read story after story and version after version for the past decade, thank you so very much. As I struggled to morph into a creative writer, you bolstered my spirit and improved my work. Without you, I might have given up. You know who you are. Thank you and I love you.

Places are key characters in my life and in my writing. I gathered inspiration at Ender's Island in Mystic, Connecticut, Walloon Lake, Michigan, The Ragdale Foundation in Lake Forest, Illinois, Rancho Santa Fe, California, and Okinawa, Japan.

Finally, to my editors and publisher, thank you for believing in me and my work.

BIO

Sarah Z. Sleeper is an ex-journalist with an MFA in creative writing. This is her first novel. Her short story, "A Few Innocuous Lines," won an award from *Writer's Digest*. Her non-fiction essay, "On Getting Vivian," was published in *The Shanghai Literary Review*. Her poetry was published in *A Year in Ink, San Diego Poetry Annual* and *Painters & Poets,* and exhibited at the Bellarmine Museum. In the recent past she was an editor at New Rivers Press, and editor-in-chief of the literary journal Mason's Road. She completed her MFA at Fairfield University in 2012. Prior to that she had a twenty-five-year career as a business writer and technology reporter and won three journalism awards and a fellowship at the National Press Foundation.

Past Titles

Running Wild Stories Anthology, Volume 1

Running Wild Anthology of Novellas, Volume 1

Jersey Diner by Lisa Diane Kastner

Magic Forgotten by Jack Hillman

The Kidnapped by Dwight L. Wilson

Running Wild Stories Anthology, Volume 2

Running Wild Novella Anthology, Volume 2, Part 1

Running Wild Novella Anthology, Volume 2, Part 2

Running Wild Stories Anthology, Volume 3

Running Wild's Best of 2017, AWP Special Edition

Running Wild's Best of 2018

Build Your Music Career From Scratch, Second Edition by Andrae Alexander

Writers Resist: Anthology 2018 with featured editors Sara Marchant and Kit-Bacon Gressitt

Magic Forbidden by Jack Hillman

Frontal Matter: Glue Gone Wild by Suzanne Samples

Mickey: The Giveaway Boy by Robert M. Shafer

Dark Corners by Reuben "Tihi" Hayslett

The Resistors by Dwight L. Wilson

Open My Eyes by Tommy Hahn

Legendary by Amelia Kibbie

Christine, Released by E. Burke

Tough Love at Mystic Bay by Elizabeth Sowden

The Faith Machine by Tone Milazzo

The Newly Tattooed's Guide to Aftercare by Aliza Dube

Upcoming Titles

Running Wild Stories Anthology, Volume 4

Running Wild Novella Anthology, Volume 4

Magpie's Return by Curtis Smith

Recon: The Trilogy + 1 by Ben White
Sodom & Gomorrah on a Saturday Night by Christa Miller
American Cycle by Larry Beckett
Mickey: Surviving Salvation by Robert Shafer
The Re-remembered by Dwight L. Wilson
Something Is Better than Nothing by Alicia Barksdale
Antlers of Bone by Taylor Sowden
Take Me with You by Vanessa Carlisle
Blue Woman/Burning Woman by Lale Davidson

Running Wild Press publishes stories that cross genres with great stories and writing. Our team consists of:

Lisa Diane Kastner, Founder and Executive Editor
Barbara Lockwood, Editor
Cecile Sarruf, Editor
Peter A. Wright, Editor
Rebecca Dimyan, Editor
Benjamin White, Editor
Andrew DiPrinzio, Editor
Amrita Raman, Operations Manager
Lisa Montagne, Director of Education

Learn more about us and our stories at
www.runningwildpress.com

Loved this story and want more?
Follow us at www.runningwildpress.com,
www.facebook/runningwildpress,
on Twitter @lisadkastner @RunWildBooks